SANDBAR SINISTER

PHOEBE ATWOOD TAYLOR

SANDBAR
SINISTER

An Asey Mayo Mystery

W. W. NORTON & COMPANY, Inc.

NEW YORK

SANDBAR
SINISTER

CHAPTER ONE

THE Sandbar episode last June was a field day for those friends of mine who've prophesied for years that my benign optimism would lead me into trouble.

They even began their I-told-you-soing with my leave of absence from the store. I should have known, they said, that Lucius Upjohn looked too much like a cold boiled salmon to play fairy godmother, that he let me go for four months only to save the expense of my salary. I had thought, in my unsuspecting way, that Lucius really wanted me to have a long summer vacation, and I went around telling people how kind he was. In fact, it was my gloating to Lizzie Richards that led to my Sandbar invitation in the first place.

"Four whole months!" I said to her that Wednesday morning when she wandered into the Tiny Tots department to buy a bonnet for her newest grandchild. "Four whole months of basking in the sun and lying on beaches! You'll never know, Lizzie, what a loathsome sight rompers get to be after you've sold 'em for eight solid months! I'm going to write the Cape Cod 'Item' that East Pochet's hardy perennial is all set for her forty-ninth consecutive summer, and I've got just enough money to hire the Carters' little camp—"

"Why, Penelope Colton!" Lizzie interrupted. "I've just thought—look! I mean, listen! Why don't you come to Sandbar and stay with me? Really, Pen, it's been perfectly wonderful the way you took all—well, all that happened last fall, and went to work without a whimper. Lucius did right to give you a breathing spell. What you need is a nice quiet rest without any cares, and that's just what you'll get at Sandbar."

"But I couldn't possibly foist myself on you—"

"Caleb's turned the whole place over to me," Lizzie continued triumphantly, "because he's sailing for England Friday. We'll have a lovely quiet time, with Gregory and Mathilde to do all the work, and then there are the cars and the boats. Just a nice quiet rest, Pen, and you won't have to spend a single cent!"

Of course I gave in eventually. The person who could turn down a luxurious vacation at Sandbar is probably not yet born. And though it seems incredible to my friends, it never for one moment entered my head that there might be any catch in the invitation. I felt like Aladdin and said so, though I remember thinking that Lizzie more nearly resembled a composite cartoon of all the Boston matrons in existence than she did a tenuous genie.

But even now I can't quite see why I should have anticipated any catches. I'd known Lizzie since we went to Miss Meredith's, and I'd always got along with her very nicely indeed, for all that she's subject to spells of

what she calls "nerves." And when New England's last
bank failure forced me to become a department store
clerk practically overnight, Lizzie was one of those loyal
souls who didn't seem to feel that selling rompers was
a variation of leprosy. The only actual drawback to Lizzie
at any time is her brother Caleb Frost, who owns Sandbar.
I place Caleb in the same category with Laura Bush's pet
leopard: both possess excellence in spots, but I've never
made any pretense of liking either.

With Caleb safely abroad, however, the thought of
four restful carefree months—I'd even believed the carefree part—added a Pollyanna aura to the whole business.
I literally bounced with gladness when on Thursday afternoon we rolled over the little bridge which connects
Sandbar with the mainland of East Pochet.

Sandbar is perhaps three miles long and a mile and
a half wide, and is protected on the ocean side by a row
of high dunes. Caleb Frost bought it from a disgusted
Brooklyn Shylock after the Cape Cod land boom petered
out into a feeble cap pistol report. Disregarding every-
one's advice, he'd caused two Cape houses of different
sizes and shapes to be hitched together in the center of
the bar, and then added on one ell for the kitchen and
servants' quarters and another ell for the garage. The
result was far from being an architectural triumph, but
the place is admittedly charming inside.

Now the whole length of the bar gleamed white
under the sun, and the beach grass swayed gently with
the east wind. Waves crashed on the ocean side and rip-
pled quietly up the beach on the harbor side, and over-

head a flock of white gulls swooped and circled and darted tirelessly against the blue sky.

"Just think," I said to Lizzie as we drove up the log road to the house, "if it hadn't been for you and Lucius, I'd be selling panty-waists this minute! I'm perfectly positive that no luckier woman ever lived!"

I was less sure Friday morning.

Then it had dawned on me that Lizzie, for all her talk about rest and quiet, fully expected me to sing for my summer. I should have known, according to my friends, that Lizzie never gave something for nothing.

"Any woman," as Laura Bush put it, "who'd spend twenty cents going to Boston to save half a cent on six bars of soap, would never make a gesture without good and sufficient reason!"

The reason was subtly driven home when Gregory and Mathilde automatically accepted me as a sort of glorified housekeeper. They gave me grocery lists and laundry lists and calory lists—Lizzie was presumably on a diet; they presented me with five dozen new sheets and pillow cases to be marked; they consulted me endlessly on subjects ranging from New Zealand spinach and what was the matter with the electric pump to Mathilde's fallen arches and the price of pickled walnuts.

"Business women," Lizzie said complacently when I made a decision on who was to supply us with chickens, "always know *so* much!"

With infinite control, I held back my caustic query as to why a romper sales clerk should be expected to have at her fingertips all the lore of the poultry world.

By Friday afternoon I was beginning to have pretty definite qualms about the whole situation. A telegram arrived from Lizzie's young daughter Deal, announcing that she was coming over from New York for a week or two, "and bringing darling Quin."

Deal, who was christened Cordelia, is twenty-four and could step without alterations onto the cover of practically any fashion magazine. She works for a restless aviator who amiably gives her vacations whenever the roving spirit seizes him. Quin, her fiancé, writes detective stories for a living. I've often wondered whether his parents had that in mind when they named him, or whether he felt it was his duty—his whole name is John Quincy Gunner.

With the advent of that telegram, all my visions of restful baskings in the sun vanished completely. I saw that guest rooms were prepared, personally supervised the week-end provisions, and made out a two-week repeating menu purely in self-defense. Then, Saturday morning, the greatest blow of all fell. Caleb Frost telephoned to say that he'd postponed his sailing for a few weeks because he didn't care for the weather reports, and would arrive at Sandbar Saturday night. He might bring a friend.

At that point I would gladly have returned to Upjohn's third floor had there been a train before Monday morning. But there wasn't, and in a zealous mood, I'd sublet my two rooms and folding accessories to Mary Carter until September. Escape was entirely out of the question.

Deal arrived in Quin's big roadster around five o'clock. Quin, plump and bespectacled, was as full of nonsense as ever, and twice as noisy as I remembered him. With them was another young man, very quiet and polite, and nice looking in a tooth paste advertisement way. He was Tom Willing, and that was all I knew about him for several days, since neither Quin nor Deal made any effort to explain him.

"Darling," Deal said accusingly to Lizzie, "you've been eating desserts again, and I thought you'd promised me you'd get down to at least a forty-two by the first of this month! Oh, and Jane Buckland's coming down from Boston to-night. I phoned her. Isn't that nice?"

"Who?" Lizzie asked without enthusiasm. "Who's she?"

"Oh, you know, darling! She was at school with me. That dark girl with the eyes. Tall. Her father was asbestos or nitrate or something. One of the first big companies to flop in twenty-nine, anyway. She's just back from Europe, been doing something fascinating with books. Buying them for some one, I think. You liked her."

Lizzie was still looking dubious when Deal turned to me.

"Pen, I hardly knew you with your hair cut! Awf'ly smart. Most marvelous figure anyway. Are the boats out? That's swell. We're simply dying to go out on a fishing trip to-morrow. Will you—some one—see to lunch and sandwiches and things? I'll phone Zeruah right away that he's to take us out, rain or shine."

"Not Zeruah!" Lizzie said anxiously. "Not—Caleb—really, Deal, you mustn't ask Zeruah!"

Deal kissed her casually and telephoned Zeruah, while I went upstairs and fitted up the last two guest rooms for the strange Tom Willing and the prospective tall dark Miss Buckland. It was no easy job, since all the odds and ends had been hurriedly thrust into them while the other rooms were being fixed. Then I saw to the fishing trip luncheon—Gregory and Mathilde were standing on their ears by then.

I rather enjoy making sandwiches, but after the first six dozen, I began to lose interest. After I'd heaped ten plates full and covered them with damp cloths, I straggled up to my room and retired for the night. No one ever gave a more truthful headache as an excuse for omitting dinner with Caleb Frost. Selling children's underwear, I told myself as I crawled into bed, was a pipe dream compared to the job I seemed to have taken on.

I was wakened just before twelve o'clock by Deal, who wondered where extra blankets were because Jane was an old coldy, and then Lizzie dropped in to ask if I'd made any nut and date sandwiches, because Deal always liked nut and date sandwiches on fishing trips.

"At least," I said to myself after she left, "rompers mercifully cease at five-thirty!"

Somehow the fates must have got that comment mixed up, for it was just five-thirty Sunday morning when Tom Willing banged at my door.

"Oh, I'm sorry!" he said, blankly surveying my dressing gown, mussed hair and general state of anger. "I'm awf"ly sorry. Deal said she'd told you to—oh, please go back to bed! Truly, I thought she'd—that you'd—"

"Just what," I demanded coldly, "did she expect me to do?"

"Why, she said I was to drive you, or you were to drive me, up to town to get that man who's to run the boat. Don't bother, Mrs. Colton. Please. I—I'll find him."

"You couldn't find Zeruah Nims's house," I said wearily, "in a thousand years. Of course it's practically drizzling right this minute, but I don't suppose Deal will let a little drizzle interfere with—oh, run along downstairs and I'll be with you in a few minutes!"

It annoyed me so to think that chauffering and guiding were to be added to my other tasks that I didn't say a word to Tom Willing until we reached Willow Lane. Then habit got the better of me.

"We're coming," I announced, "to Main Street. Prepare to be impressed."

"Why?" Tom asked obediently.

"Because the Main Street of East Pochet," I said, "is the Mona Lisa of Cape Cod. Tourists stare and then rave forever after about the dear-quaint-picturesque Cape. Artists spread its towering elms over miles of canvas. Photographers," I yawned in spite of myself, "break bones in their efforts to take from new angles the colonial houses and old-fashioned stores. Except—"

"How many times, Mrs. Colton," Tom inquired suspiciously, "have you recited this before?"

"I lost count in 1912," I confessed. "Anyway, except for two blind authors and a few laymen unable to wield a pen, I can think of no one who has not, at one time or another," I swung the station wagon off the Lane onto Main Street itself, "scribbled down impressions of its cool dignity and charm—"

Then we hit the crust of broken glass and the front tires blew. I gaped at the street till my jaw all but parted from my face. Tom, after one brief glance, chuckled.

"The Mona Lisa," he observed, "seems to have given way to Ten Nights in a Bar-room!"

It had.

Clumps of sprawled snoring men, and mounds of smashed bottles dotted the length of the street.

Cars were crazily parked at all angles in Railroad Square. A ten-ton truck was carefully secured to the old hitching post by pieces of cod line and a flaming red lobster buoy. A brand new sedan was wedged solidly into the entrance of the moving picture theater.

Cats lapped at melted ice cream which trickled from overturned containers outside the candy shop; flies buzzed above the trodden mess of fruit and vegetables which marked the grocery store sidewalk. The usually conservative windows of the Ladies Exchange were devoted not to gingham house dresses and embroidery silks, but to a display best described as intimate. Every inch of plate glass along the street was plastered with smatterings of dried egg and squashed tomato.

Even the air was alcoholic.

I leaned back heavily against the seat and thought of Russian villages and Bolshevik hordes, Hungary under

Bela Kun—this shambles couldn't be Main Street, East Pochet, at six o'clock of a Sunday June morning!

"Nero," Tom indicated a particularly Bacchic figure, "at Baiae, just like the old print. Just what, Mrs. Colton, caused this—uh—rape of the Mona Lisa?"

"This," I answered, "is entirely outside my forty-nine years of experience with East Pochet. Why, *I* thought the town was bone-dry by conviction—"

"The worm," an amused voice beside us commented, "seems to sort of upped and turned cartwheels, don't it? Mornin', Mrs. Colton."

I turned to find Asey Mayo of Wellfleet, dressed in his usual corduroys and hunting jacket, standing beside the car.

Of course Asey is and has always been my favorite Cape Codder. He is a Cape Codder, he talks like one, and he even looks almost the way tourists expect natives of the Cape to look. Most people nowadays think of him as a successful detective, but to me he's an expert mechanic, a hired man de luxe, and a wholly competent jack of all trades.

"Asey," I said, "what—when did this happen?"

" 'Round ten last night, they say." He grinned and tipped his broad brimmed Stetson on the back of his head. "Guess it'll take East Pochet another three hundred years to crawl back into the pious an' God-fearin' class."

"Did it rain brandy?" Tom asked interestedly.

"Almost. This," Asey announced with a casual wave of his hand, "is the end of a r'gime. You take a good look at it, 'cause the chances is you'll never see the like again.

Regan tried to run in his unsold pre-repeal booze last night in eight boats. Coast guard got him, but not till he'd dumped two hundred cases off the bay shore by Tim Smalley's. You know Tim, Mrs. Colton. He never kept nothin' to himself yet. Coast guard was too busy chasin' a stray boat load of Reganites to bother with the loot right off—an' you're now viewin' the r'mains. Wheeee—see them pink whiskers wavin' to the breeze yonder in the hedge—why, that's—"

"That's Zeruah Nims!" I interrupted disgustedly. "And we were after the wretch to take us out on a fishing party. Well, it looks as though the chances of his remembering about that piloting job were exceedingly slim."

"I sort of think," Asey said, "that the last twenty-four hours is goin' to be pretty well blotted out of most East Pochet minds for some time to come. Say, you know you got two flats on this craft?"

"I'd temporarily forgotten," I told him, "what with all this chaos. Asey, you'll have to summon Jimmy B. for us. This car has no spares."

"I can do better than that," he said. "My own car's parked in the Lane, an' I'll run you back to Sandbar. Kind of damp for a fishin' trip, ain't it?"

"You know Deal Richards," I said. "Weather means nothing to her—Asey, I don't suppose you'd care to rescue this party?"

I had suddenly remembered how Deal could act when her plans were thwarted.

He squinted at the sky. "Um. I wouldn't want to go outside. It's goin' to pour pitchforks an' gun-shovels before long, an' I think there'll be fog. But—sure, I'd just as lief run the boat, if Deal's willin' to stick to the inside harbor. I ain't had no fresh flounders for a long time."

"You're kinder," I said, "than you'll ever know. And —man alive, don't tell me you've another new roadster?"

"Uh-huh," he said as we changed cars. "Bill Porter got out a new model, an' he's tryin' it on the dog. Nice, but kind of costly to run. Say, is it true, Mrs. Colton, that you're spendin' the whole summer over to Frost's place?"

"It's true," I told him, with something resembling a sigh. "It seems—oh, this is Tom Willing, Asey. He's visiting Deal. And Quin Gunner's down, too. Yes, it seems I'm going to spend the whole blessed summer here."

Asey smiled. One of the pleasantest things about the man is that he rarely requires any explanation. I rather felt, too, that his opinion of Caleb Frost coincided with mine.

"My cousin Syl," he remarked innocently, "has some awful nice cottages over Weesit way. Not to toot the fam'ly horn, but—well, you might know some folks that'd like one. Cheap, they are, too. You—"

"It's really raining now," I said hurriedly. "This June weather certainly is the most variable variety the Cape has."

"Seems," Asey agreed blandly, "like it is. Well, I'll run in an' see if Jimmy's s'vived last night's goin's on. An' I'll call Syl an' have him bring over my rub' boots an' oilskins an' some clams. Zeruah would of been goin' to provide them, wouldn't he?"

"He would," I said. "And I'd forgotten. Thanks a lot, Asey."

"Amazing man," Tom remarked as we watched his lean figure swing up the oystershell walk. "Who is he, anyway? He talks like a native, but he can't be, with a sixteen cylindered chariot like this!"

"Why, he's Asey Mayo," I said. "He—"

"Asey Mayo? Oh! But you didn't mention his last name to me at all! Of course—he's the detective Quin was raving about on the way down. Said he was a triple extract of Euclid, Scheherazade and David Harum. Tell me, Mrs. Colton, how old is he?"

"When I was a babe in arms, I thought Asey was a big boy. After seeing him vault that picket fence, I wonder if he's as old as I am. He's over fifty—what's the news, Asey?"

"Jimmy says he'll go right up an' tend to your car soon as he's finished his coffee, so maybe he'll get there by suppertime. I told him to get a wiggle on, but he said in a real hurt voice that it took it out of him to hurry. He couldn't do his best work."

Tom laughed. "Apparently Jimmy's not an active sort?"

"Active?" Asey said. "Thirty years ago he bumped into a wasps' nest an' no one's seen him hurry since. Seems like the effort ruined him for all time."

As we drove over the connecting bridge to the bar, I mentally contrasted the scene and my reactions to it with those of Thursday afternoon.

The fine rain gave the sand a dirty grayish tinge,

and the water was gray and somber. The gulls, instead of swooping in picturesque circles, hovered above one particular dune and just plain squawked their heads off, as though they were trying to compete with the hollow booming of the surf on the outer beach. When I looked at the house, I conjured up no visions of comfortable chairs and other luxurious addenda. I simply stared at the spiral of smoke from the kitchen ell and hoped that Mathilde and Gregory hadn't waked Caleb.

"Yesterday," Tom curiously echoed my thoughts, "I said I'd never seen anything half so beautiful as this place. Now it seems absolutely the last word in bleakness. Almost sinister, sort of."

"Bleak, yes," I said, "but not sinister. There's nothing sinister about East Pochet. Tom, will you get out here at the fork of the road and run up and tell Mathilde to have breakfast ready in about fifteen minutes? I've got the boat house keys and I want to show Asey where the 'Stepanfetchit's' gear is. We'll be up as soon as he's looked things over. Oh—and warn Quin and Deal and the other girl not to make any noise. Caleb's not coming, is he?"

Tom shook his head. "No, but the fellow with him—"

"D'you mean to say he brought—who? Where was he put?"

"Oh, I just moved in with Quin downstairs. I've forgotten his name—fellow, about thirty-odd. Seems to me Mr. Frost said he was a literary agent—"

"Durford Ames," I said, "without doubt. He's a protégé of Cale's. Looks rather like a newly polished floor, if you know what I mean?"

"Exactly," Tom said. "I'd thought of a row of polished glasses, but he's not that brittle—yes, that's who it is. They called him Ford."

"He's a nice appearin' young feller," Asey said as he and I drove on down to the boat house. "I heard you an' Mrs. Richards was here alone, but it seems like you wasn't."

"The Grand Central Station," I told him, "is lonesome by comparison. Deal, Quin, this Tom Willing, Ford Ames, Caleb, and a girl named Buckland I've not met. Thank the Lord, Cale's coming will at least put a stop to Deal's wholesale invitations. At that, she's not as bad as her brother Ned. He used to bring whole track teams home to spend the night when Lizzie lived in a four-room apartment—here are the keys. I'll get out and show you—"

"Padlock's unlocked," Asey said as he went up the steps to the boat house.

"Unlocked? That's impossible! These are the only keys—but I suppose I must have forgotten to lock it when I walked down here yesterday afternoon. Asey, never divulge the fact to a soul! Oh," I followed him inside the dim little building, "oh, and will you pull up the shades? I meant to, but I was too tired yesterday to make the effort. I was—Asey—look! Look there! He—he's dead!"

Sprawled on a pile of shavings next to an overturned dory was a strange bearded man, dressed in dungarees and a fisherman's jersey.

CHAPTER TWO

ASEY knelt down beside the man and I took a fresh
grip on the door jamb as my knees began to wob-
ble.

"I think," Asey said slowly, "that's he's been killed.
It would—"

"Nonsense!" I said in a voice that I tried to keep
steady. "Nonsense, Asey Mayo! You've just got yourself
mixed up in so many old murder cases that you think
every dead man must necessarily have been killed! For
heaven's sakes, give him the benefit of the doubt—wha—
what makes you think so?"

" 'Count of—here, sit on this nail keg, Mrs. Colton,
or maybe you'd better go out an' sit in the car for a
second. This is sort of unnervin'—"

"Unnerving!" I said feebly, as I plopped down on
the keg. "Asey Mayo, every ganglion in my body is
alternately prickling all over and then going limp as a
dish cloth! I know now what people mean when they've
said they felt like a spoonful of jelly! But Asey, who is
this man? Where'd he come from? And look, I'm almost
positive now that I *did* lock that door yesterday after-

noon. And these keys—" I was still gripping the key ring for dear life, "are the only complete set! There aren't any duplicates for this place! How'd he get in? And— and if he was killed—but what makes you think so?"

"I don't know who he is," Asey said, "nor how he got in here, 'cept I'm willin' to b'lieve he was dumped down there, an' I think he was killed, b'cause he was hit over the side of his head with somethin' that cut him, like a bottle. An' there ain't any busted bottles in here. An' if he'd been hit over the head in here, he wouldn't of fallen on his back like that. An' I don't think he could of cracked himself—fact, I'm sure of it. Some one did it."

"But he wasn't here at six-thirty yesterday," I protested. "I came down here to get a breath of air and to make sure the gas tins were filled—"

"Zeruah's been takin' care of the boats, ain't he?" Asey asked.

I nodded. "Yes, but he hasn't any keys. It seems that Caleb had a fight with him over some bill, and dismissed him, but Deal wouldn't listen to Lizzie's explanations and called him anyway when she came. Asey, I—those eyes are driving me crazy!"

"Looky here, Mrs. Colton," Asey stood between me and the figure on the floor, "you think of somethin' else for a second, an' then I'll drive you up to the house. Prob'ly you ain't had no breakfast, nor anythin' at all. You just think of—"

"How in the name of common sense," I demanded hotly, "d'you expect me to think of anything but that man? Those terrible eyes and bushy eyebrows and that

horrible beard—and the blood! It's too ghastly. Lord, no
wonder Tom thought there was something sinister about
this place this morning! But I'm sure I locked this place
here yesterday! I came down while I was making sandwiches for the fishing party, because it'd been so hot in
the kitchen—"

"For Pete's sakes, have you been makin' lunches for
this crowd?" Asey asked indignantly. "Ain't Mrs. Richards got two chief cooks an' bottle washers already?
D'you mean to tell me she's puttin' you to work, you that
could of bought this place up, lock, stock an' barrel, a
dozen times—"

"The dear dead days when I had an income," I interrupted, "are gone for good and all. I'm just number
6948 in department 213—"

"Fiddledeedee," Asey said, "an' rubbish! Mrs. Richards wouldn't have no business makin' you work even if
you was on the dole! I caught a glimpse of you Thursday
aft'noon, an' it seemed to me then that you wasn't lookin'
awful well. This mornin' you're even more peaked an'
you don't look's good as you did then. You're tired,
an'—"

"Selling rompers for eight months," I stated with
some heat, "is liable to leave any one looking slightly pale,
particularly if she's not used to—but Lizzie's asked me
here, Asey, and if she was kind enough to—well, that's
all there is to it. The least I can do is to help—"

I went on in that same tone for several minutes before I realized that Asey had succeeded in making me

forget the dead man and think strenuously of something else.

"Baiting me, are you?" I asked.

"Nope. It's a gen'ral trait," he pulled out his pipe, "to kick if some one finds fault with your friends, even though you—well, you look like you'd got a little color back in your face, anyways."

"I feel better," I said. "Look—shouldn't we get along? Oughtn't you to phone the police and all? Oh, how Caleb Frost will fume! I've heard him say that murders are limited to the extremes of society—the multi-millionaires and the gangsters. It'll set him off like a roman candle to find that the stratum of upper intelligentsia isn't altogether immune—"

Asey smiled. "If I know Mr. Frost, he'll prob'ly think I done all this just to annoy him. No, I'll tell you, Mrs. Colton, I don't like to leave this feller alone, an' that's why I'm not dashin' off to the house. I'm expectin' Syl, an' he can stay here. Now, will you peer earnest at that wall for a couple of minutes while I look at some things?"

"Go ahead with your grisly business," I said, shuddering. "But of course it won't make the slightest degree of difference if I stared at ten walls. I'd just see those eyes."

" 'Magination," Asey said. "Tell me, Mr. Frost's always been high an' mighty, ain't he?"

"Always," I said, understanding this time that Asey was attempting to divert my thoughts from the obvious channels. "Caleb's a brilliant man in many ways, but he's got two major faults. He always expects full credit and then a bonus besides. I think that half the reason

for Lizzie's nervous spells is that he's never let her forget
that he's supported her since Carter died. He's never let
the children forget that he paid for their education, either.
If he offers you a cigarette, even, he expects to be thanked
twice as much as any one else would be. But his greatest
trouble lies in his absolute refusal to make any distinction
between stupidity and lack of information."

Asey chuckled quietly.

"If you don't happen to know," I went on, "all the
ins and outs of early Byzantine art or of the eleventh
century vowel shift, he promptly assumes that you're a
low-grade moron."

"An' bein' a kind of walkin' encyclopedia," Asey
said, "it kind of annoys folks a lot. Yup."

"When he hears about this," I counted the wall boards
for the tenth time, "he'll expect the police to solve the
thing within the hour. If they don't, he'll telephone
the governor and wire the President and start suit against
the state for damages incurred. Asey, aren't you through!"

"I'm through," he said. "Nothin' in his pockets, no
labels, not even trade marks on anythin' he's got on. An'
I don't think there's any doubt at all that he was cracked
over the side of the head with a bottle, an' hard enough
so's the bottle busted. An' so the chances is he wasn't
hit in here. There's not a trace of busted glass."

"A broken bottle—Asey, d'you suppose it had anything to do with all that mess uptown?"

"Couldn't tell. From what I heard, though, they
pretty well c'nfined themselves to Main Street, an' did
you notice that the bank windows an' the post office

windows wasn't touched? Not a speck of egg or anythin' else thrown at 'em. Shows," he grinned, "that they
had some lingerin' r'spect for the lawr, an' maybe they
wasn't so d'praved as they may have seemed. Still—"

"Here's an old truck," I said, "bouncing along—"

"Syl," Asey said. "Bringin' the rub' boots an' clams.
I phoned him from Jimmy's. Watch Syl when he finds
out about this. He buys detective stories by the gross from
the mail order houses, an' a dead stranger'll affect him
like a case of champagne—"

Sylvanus Mayo, a diminutive little man with a scraggly walrus mustache, climbed out of the truck and bustled
importantly up the boat house steps. There is practically
nothing Syl won't do for his famous cousin. He even
begins to swell with pride the minute he comes in sight
of Asey.

"I got here just's soon's I could, though the old
flivver was steamin' some," he said. "Mornin', Mrs. Colton. Say, Asey, the radio man said fog just b'fore I left.
Sure you ought to take a boat out the harbor?"

"Seems," Asey said, "like we wouldn't be goin' out
anyhows, Syl. Mrs. Colton an' I just found—well, look
for yourself."

Syl looked and his eyes widened and then began to
gleam.

"Now," Asey continued, "we'll go back to the house,
an' you hold the fort till I can call Hanson. An' if you'd
like to help, you can figger out who the gent there is."

Syl smiled. "I already know."

"What?" Asey and I yelled in unison.

" 'Member," Syl said, " 'bout my tellin' you of that man that come to the house a couple weeks ago on a bicycle? He wanted us to put him up for the night, but Jennie didn't like the looks of that beard. She don't seem to like beards. Don't you r'member the time last Thanks-givin' when I started to grow one, an' she—"

"She shaved you by force. Yup." Asey and I grinned. Jennie Mayo tops her husband by ten inches and is easily a hundred pounds heavier. "Yup, but get to it, Syl."

"Well, as he was leavin'—say, I never did tell you that part, did I? I was waitin' to see if 'twas so, first, an' then it plum slipped my mind. Well, I asked him his name, just to be pleasant like, b'cause Jennie'd been kind of short with him. He said he was Varney Cheyne."

"Varney Cheyne!" I said in amazement. "Why, he's the man who writes detective stories and—why, he's made a fortune out of 'em in the last year or two! You can't mean *that* Varney Cheyne!"

"That's just who," Syl said. " 'Greater,' " he quoted the jacket blurbs, " 'than Gab-Gaboriau, Wells, Rinehart, Van Dine, Queen, Doyle, an' yet unknown even to his own publishers.' Yup. That's who he said he was, an' this is him."

"Syl, are you sure of that?" Asey asked. "It—did he give you any proof? Sounds like a fish story to me."

"Sure, I'm sure," Syl said cheerfully.

"But it couldn't be Cheyne!" I said. "No one knows who he is, but he—why, he couldn't be a man like this one here! Nobody who's made the vast sums Cheyne has would ever go bicycling about, dressed in dungarees and a fisherman's jersey! The man was pulling your leg, Syl. If Varney Cheyne ever decided to disclose his identity, you can wager it would be smeared all over the headlines of every newspaper in the United States!"

"That's who he said he was, an' he was," Syl repeated stubbornly. "He proved it, too. B'cause I didn't b'lieve him either, at first. He told me the end of the story of his that was runnin' in the 'Post,' an' even *you* guessed wrong about that, Asey! That's half the reason I never said nothin' about this to you, b'cause I was waitin' to see if 'twas so. An' the last part of that story didn't come out for over a week after he was there!"

"Guesswork," I said, "or else he saw advance copies of the book or the magazine. The man couldn't be Cheyne. It's impossible. Don't you agree, Asey? But there's one thing. I certainly endorse Jennie's opinion of that beard! It's so bushy and ragged that it doesn't seem real. I haven't seen a beard like that for years. I didn't know they were even worn any more."

"By gum," Asey said, "I been thinkin' that—I wonder—"

"Oh, that beard's real enough," Syl declared. "Looks just like it did that evenin'. Jennie said it looked like it come off a crayon portrait. Seems sort of queer now b'cause of bein' matted with—take care, Asey! Hook on your jacket belt's caught—why, my—well, my heavens an' earth! Look at that! It's a fake after all!"

For when Asey straightened up after bending over the man, a patch of the matted beard tore off and remained on the curved clamp.

Involuntarily I stepped nearer the figure, and as I did, I noticed for the first time the man's right hand.

"Asey!" I said. "He—he hasn't any little finger on his right hand! Good—no—why, no wonder those eyes seemed to stare at me! And the eyebrows—but with the beard—he never wore a beard! Asey, was there—did you see a tiny tattoo mark on his arm?"

Asey nodded. "Little bit of a thing on his left forearm. Faded out some, but it seemed like an eagle. Mrs. Colton, don't tell me you know this feller, too?"

"I—Asey—it's impossible." I sat down again on the nail keg. "It absolutely can't be, but just the same, I'm sure. Anyway, he's not Varney Cheyne, and he's no fisherman! Asey, that man—why, it's Richard Thorne of Boston! He used to live on our street! There's no doubt about it, but just the same, it's entirely impossible!"

"Richard Thorne. I seem to c'nect somethin' with that name," Asey said thoughtfully. "But I can't—there was some one—"

"Of course you must remember," I said. "It was the beard that—but, he's *got* to be Dick, even though he can't be. Asey, Dick Thorne was a partner in Frost and Richards. Just after the war—that was when his little finger was amputated, by the way. It got smashed with shrapnel. Then he came back, and was suspected of—why, Asey Mayo, I never heard anything like this! It's too incredible."

Syl pulled a crumpled package of cigarettes from his pocket and presented me with one.

"Thanks," I said. "Listen, Asey. Dick was one of

Lizzie and Carter Richards's best friends. Then, after the war, there was some mix-up in the business, and thousands and thousands of dollars' worth of bonds were missing. Caleb suspected Dick Thorne—and Caleb and Carter Richards all but came to blows over it. During the heat of the rumpus, Dick disappeared. His wife, who was a distant cousin of mine, was simply in despair. She didn't know where he'd gone or what had happened. And in the meantime, the papers got hold of the story, and then Thorne was formally and publicly accused of the theft. Rhoda Thorne killed herself the day after all that came out, and not a week later a man was found drowned in Boston Harbor, and identified by the police as Dick Thorne! Asey, that was all the story you're thinking about. It was all over the papers for days and days!"

"Yup," he said. "I r'call some of it. Happened 'round nineteen-nineteen or nineteen-twenty. But if he was identified by the police as this feller Thorne, then this man here couldn't hardly be Thorne. Still, on the other hand, if he was drowned, there might of been some mistake. Are you real sure about him, Mrs. Colton?"

"Positive. And I remember Sam, my husband, saying that when they found the body, the principal thing on which they based their identification was that finger and the lack of any dental work at all. Dick was one of those rare men who had absolutely perfect teeth. That was all they could work on. Of course it's possible there was another man—they simply must have made a mistake! Dick and Rhoda were at our house a lot. I'm—why, I'm simply flabbergasted! But with that finger and that mark and those eyes—"

"Was Thorne an' Caleb Frost great friends?" Asey wanted to know.

I shook my head.

"Never. Dick and Cale bickered constantly from the time they were children. It was Caleb's father who gave Dick his job, much to Cale's annoyance. Sam said Dick Thorne would probably have become a member of the firm before Cale did, if old Rodney Frost hadn't died. And Lizzie once told me that Cale never intended to let Dick come back to Frost and Richards, after the war was over, but he really couldn't help himself. Dick was a great hero. Went in as a buck private and came out with medals and a colonelcy. Caleb couldn't turn out some one like that. But this is simply too fantastic to be true, Asey. Things like this simply do not happen, and that's all there is to it!"

"They don't," Asey agreed, "but they sort of seem to. Take the mess on Main Street. Things like that don't happen either, but they did, an' they have b'fore in other Cape towns. Huh. You know him as Richard Thorne, an' he told Syl he was Varney Cheyne, an'—we'll go phone Hanson, Mrs. Colton. You stay here, Syl."

Asey was very silent as we drove back to the house.

"You're thinking of Caleb Frost, aren't you?" I asked.

"Him," he said, "an' other various an' sundry things. Hard to make any sense out of this. You say you left the door locked, but the padlock's open. I s'pose Mr. Frost's got his own keys, though, ain't he?"

"Probably. But he never would have left a door open if it could have been locked! You don't know him."

"Huh. Varney Cheyne, says Syl.—But that's fishy. But—"

"But no fishier, in one sense," I said, "than his being Dick Thorne to me."

"Just so. An' he was hit over the head with a bottle, but there ain't no bottle. An' if he'd been hit there in the boat house—oh, well. I guess, though, we'd better tell Mr. Frost about this," he drew the car up in front of the house, "b'fore we call the cops. But we won't mention the Thorne part to him."

"If you're thinking Caleb had anything to do with all that," I said earnestly, "you're wrong, Asey. Cale's a supercilious old stuffed shirt, but—well, give the devil his due!"

As we entered the house, Gregory was just coming down the stairs.

"Where's every one?" I demanded. "In the dining room?"

"No, Mrs. Colton. Miss Deal decided that the fog would be coming in, and so she called the whole thing off. She said she wanted to go out the harbor or else she didn't want to go at all. Mr. Willing and Mr. Gunner are up, but the rest are still in bed."

"Mr. Frost awake yet?"

"No, Mrs. Colton!" Gregory's voice was horror-stricken. "He never gets up till ten o'clock when he's down here. Never!"

Asey grinned at me. "That bein' the case, p'raps I'd

better be the one to wake him. He can't blast me too much—want to show me the way to his room?"

"Certainly I will—don't look so glum, Gregory! Mr. Mayo's got good and sufficient reason to wake him, and we'll assure him that it's not your fault he was so rudely disturbed!"

Tom and Quin strolled out to the hall just as Asey and I started upstairs. Quin, as usual, was chattering a mile a minute, but I must say that the first words I caught sent little shivers up and down my spine.

"Positively the best method," he was informing Tom in his most authoritative tones, "the best method of murdering any one is the good old-fashioned bash! Give me a blunt instrument any day in the week! No noise, no need to get chemical experts and ballistics experts on your trail —but the public yelps, or so my publishers think, for poisoned arrows shot out of an autogiro by a Chinaman who's— Morning, Pen. I didn't see you. Hi, Asey. Don't you like bashes?"

"Wa-el," Asey drawled a little, "wa-el, yes. In mod'ration. In stories, maybe, but not in fact. An' say, Quin, you pulled an awful boner in your last book. I'll tell you about it later."

"Bashes, forsooth," I said as we walked along the upper corridor. "That boy looks on murders the way a chef surveys his pastry bags. I've heard him accost perfect strangers and ask them why they'd murder their great-uncle Osbert. Last year he got arrested in Italy for asking a minor government official why he'd kill his mother—

it just happened that the mother had been killed. There's
Cale's door. Go to it!"

He rapped very gently; then, after a few seconds, he
rapped again.

"Bang," I advised. "Just bang."

He pounded so hard that Lizzie poked her head out
into the corridor.

"Pen," she said anxiously, "you're not waking—oh,
but you mustn't wake Caleb! You know he hates—he'll
be very much annoyed! What's Asey Mayo doing here?"

I patted her soothingly on the shoulder.

"You run back and finish dressing," I said. "This is—
er—something about the boat house, and it's really important that Caleb be told."

Asey kept on banging, and at last he turned the knob
and pushed open the door.

I followed him into the room, and then both of us
just stood there and stared at each other like a couple of
jittering idiots.

CHAPTER THREE

CALEB FROST was not in his room.

The bed, furthermore, had not been slept in, but was still neatly turned down. A pair of purple silk pajamas and a robe that matched were still laid out on a chair, and a glass of orange juice was untouched on the bedside table.

"He's gone," I said stupidly. "He's gone!"

Asey crossed over and peered into the empty bath room.

"Huh," he said. "Tub all full of water, tooth brush an' tooth paste all out. Seems like he'd been all set to go to bed, but he didn't. Guess I won't do no more dallyin' about phonin' Hanson up to the state p'lice sub station—"

"But isn't Jim Williams still constable here in East Pochet?" I asked.

"Jim," Asey said briefly, "was about two yards south of Zeruah Nims up in that bar'bry hedge. Phone's downstairs, off the front hall, ain't it? I'll be back in a second."

Just as he returned, Lizzie emerged from the west room and followed him into Caleb's room.

"What's all this fuss?" she demanded querulously.

36

"Where's Caleb? What's happened, Pen? What on earth have you and Asey Mayo been up to?"

"Mrs. Colton an' I," Asey said rather sharply for him, "was unlucky enough to find a dead man down in the boat house, an'—"

"A dead man? Who—where's Caleb? It's not Caleb —Pen—who is it?" Lizzie's voice became suddenly very shaky indeed.

"Oh, Lizzie," I said, "truly, it sounds fantastic, but the man's Dick Thorne! But where Cale is, I don't know. And Lizzie—Asey says that Dick has been killed—"

"Killed?" Lizzie turned whiter than the blouse she wore. "Killed? Caleb—that girl—he—"

It had occurred to me that the news might possibly precipitate a spell of Lizzie's renowned nerves, but I was totally unprepared for the abandoned outburst of hysterics which followed her incoherent babbling.

Asey and I looked at each other helplessly as she threw herself on the floor and began to howl. After all, when a woman of Lizzie's bulk indulges in a thorough emotional house cleaning, there is practically nothing that any innocent bystander can do about it. I found myself thinking irrelevantly of the old jingle about the pig that died in clover—"and when he died, he died all over." Lizzie's hysterics were just as all-inclusive.

At the fifth or sixth prolonged yowl, Deal dashed into the room and then, murmuring something about green pills, dashed out before I had a chance to tell her to phone the doctor. Then, while Lizzie was alternately hitting out at me and kicking Asey, a tall good looking girl in a scarlet sweater suit hurried in. But instead of hurrying out, she walked over to the hearth rug on which Lizzie was writhing and spoke cheerfully to me.

"Mrs. Colton? I'm Jane Buckland. Won't you let me help? I mean, it may be rough, but I wasted some time in a hospital once."

I nodded gratefully. "We need aid. Asey, you run down and call Cummings at Weesit. She's going to be like a dish rag when she snaps out of this. And Cummings knows all the intimate workings of her heart. He's seen her through these outbursts before."

Asey limped out of the room. Lizzie's kicks were not well aimed, but her shoes had high, built-up leather heels.

Jane Buckland shut the door firmly.

"This may not work," she said. "But I have hopes. It's been known to do the trick."

Calmly, while Lizzie rent the air with shrill staccato shrieks, she strode into the bath room and brought out a towel which she'd apparently thrust into the full tub. Then she knelt down beside Lizzie, waited her chance, and soundly slapped her in the face.

Lizzie continued to yelp, but with diminished enthusiasm. Jane slapped her again. At the third slap, Lizzie ceased her kicking and yelling, though great racking sobs still shook her body.

"There," Jane said with relief. "I'll mop her face up with this towel—d'you mind pulling a blanket off the bed? She's as dripping wet as though she'd stood under a shower. Oh, run along out, Deal! Mrs. Colton and I are looking after her."

"But her green pills," Deal said. "They're for her nerves. She always—"

"If she needs green pills," Jane said, "the doctor'll give 'em to her. Beat it. Scram!"

For all that I was beginning to feel about as limp as Lizzie was beginning to look, it gave me a certain amount of satisfaction to hear some one order Deal about, and be obeyed.

Jane tucked the blanket about Lizzie, smoothed out her hair and wiped off her face. Gradually the sobs stopped, and then a stalwart snore startled me out of my senses.

"She's not asleep!" I said.

Jane smiled. "Yes. She's completely exhausted herself. I've seen it happen before. Whew!"

She picked up a box of cigarettes from the table, offered me one and took one herself.

"Suppose," she suggested, "you sit down, Mrs. Colton. We can't possibly lift her, and she's all right now. You know, you don't look any too—I say, what prompted all this in the first place?"

Beginning with my awakening at five-thirty, I briefly sketched in what had happened since. At the conclusion of my story, Jane got up, went to the door and called Deal.

"Two cups of coffee, a couple of eggs, and other fodder. Pronto. No, your mother's all right. My eye," she added as she shut the door, "all *that's* gone on? No wonder you looked mildly exhausted! But where's Mr. Frost?"

"Your guess," I told her, "is as good as mine. I've given up trying to understand much of anything. I—don't tell me that Gregory's already—I'm sure I hear the sound of plates and the tinkle of glass!"

But it was Asey who brought in the tray.

"I was startin' up with your order just as Deal bounced down. Mrs. Richards all right? Good. Fall to, Mrs. Colton. Doc's comin'. Fact, he was on his way here anyways. Cops phoned him. He's goin' to bring Malvina Atkins over, 'cause he says he knows from past experience that Mrs. Richards'll need some one to see to her for a couple of days—"

"But I could have," I said, "just as well as not!"

"You could," he admitted with a twinkle in his eyes, "but you ain't goin' to. Miss—was it Brooks? Buckland? Well, I 'point you a c'mittee of one to see that Mrs. Colton gets the rest she come here for. If Deal or any one else starts in tellin' her things to do, you tell them to go themselves. Little more of this intensive trainin' she's had in the last day or so, an' she'll be needin' doctors. You know what I mean?"

"I know Deal," Jane said succinctly, "and I know her moods. But what about Mr. Frost? Are you sure that he's not in the house anywhere, Mr. Mayo? Oh," she smiled at Asey's look of surprise, "I know you! I read the rotogravure, and occasionally the papers print a picture you actually can recognize. But what about Mr. Frost?"

"He ain't in the house or the g'rage. I told that butler lad to come up here in a couple minutes. He says

he looks after Frost's clothes, an' he can prob'ly tell us if
Frost was dressed for travelin' or just outin' or what.
Meantime, eat your breakfast, Mrs. Colton!"

"Very well," I said with my mouth full. "I'm eating
—but tell me, Miss Buckland—"

"Jane," she interrupted, "to you."

"Jane, I thought Deal said you did things about
books? I didn't know you were a nurse."

"Since dad's business went," she replied, "I've been
a touch of everything, including a nurse for two months.
Lately, though, I've been doing some book buying for a
man in Boston, and I think he's going to keep me for a
few trips more. It's sort of fun. More fun than most of
the depression jobs I've held. Honestly, I had no idea
there were so many ways to keep body and soul together
as I've discovered since I got through school. I've been a
social worker, a dish-washer—I've run a switchboard,
decorated Christmas cards— I put the red on Santa Claus.
I've worked in department stores—"

"Comrade!" I extended my hand. "Comrade worker!
It—it wasn't children's underwear, by any chance?"

Jane threw back her head and chortled. "Rompers
and panty-waists! You too? I knew we had a lot in
common!"

While we gabbled away about department stores,
Gregory came in and methodically went through Caleb's
closet and luggage.

"Well," Asey said at last, "what's gone?"

"I think, sir, he wore what he had on last night at
dinner, a white mess jacket and black dress trousers. But

his pumps are here. The only shoes that seem to be missing are an old pair of white sneakers. I remember seeing them here yesterday."

"Not," Asey commented, "what I'd call a proper travelin' outfit. What's that you just picked up?"

"His wallet." Gregory passed it over for Asey's inspection. "It was on the floor of the closet."

Asey raised his eyebrows. "Carries enough cash, don't he? An' his check book's here too. I guess he didn't set out with the intention of goin' any distance, if he was dressed like that an' left his pocketbook b'hind. I wonder if—but it seems like he left of his own free will an' accord. No signs that any one forced him."

"He keeps most of his money," Gregory suggested, "in that blue jar on the mantel. He put several rolls of bills in it just after he arrived yesterday, Mr. Mayo."

The blue jar was empty.

"Puzzle," Asey said thoughtfully. "Did he leave deliberate or not? Wan't dressed for it, an' here's his wallet. But—was there much money in that jar, d'you know?"

"Yes, sir. He told me there was over a thousand dollars. In cash, that is. There was a folder of traveler's checks besides."

Asey whistled.

"Sneakers," he said, "would seem like he'd just intended to go out for a walk, but—oho. I hear a car comin'. Doc an' Malvina, I guess. Send 'em up, Greg'ry."

Doctor Cummings, one of those amazingly jovial general practitioners who makes you feel better the instant he steps inside a room, looked at Lizzie, frowned and shrugged.

"Hm. Every blessed time Caleb Frost—uh! Malvina, you and Asey help me get her on the bed. Can't help if it's Frost's. We couldn't lift her any farther if we wanted to. Pen, don't you leave this place without—lord, she's heavy! Without some iron and calcium tablets. Thanks, Asey, we'll look after her. Yes, Pen, you look run down like a top. Hop along, all of you. And Asey, Hanson was just behind us, and was going straight down to the boat house. You'd better see him, and I'll be down shortly."

Out in the corridor, Tom and Quin and Deal, and Durford Ames, who'd grown a silly little mustache since I'd last seen him, demanded in a chorus to be told what the trouble was. Asey enlightened them, but he made no mention of who the dead man was.

"An' now," he said, "you—no, Quin! Murders is right up your alley, but first you let the p'lice have their say. Deal, did you know Richard Thorne?"

"Uncle Dick? Why, yes, but that was awfully long ago, Asey! I—"

"I knew him," Quin said. "Deal was only nine when all that Thorne business happened, but I was in college and I—"

"Very well," Asey said. "Come along, then."

"But where's Caleb?" Ford asked. "I—well, I don't personally care a rap about a strange man in the boat house, but where's Cale?"

Asey shook his head. "Don't know. But if you an'

Tom'd like to go out in all the wet an' wander around the dunes, it might be a good idea."

"How about binoculars?" Ford asked.

"In the rain?" Asey smiled. "Nope, you better go out an' look. Now, Quin. Mrs. Colton, what're you puttin' that raincoat on for? You're not—"

"If you think," I said firmly, "that you could keep me away from all this, you're vastly mistaken. I was tired, yes, but I've got second wind."

There was considerable argument about it. If I was going, Deal and Jane wanted to come; if they couldn't, I shouldn't, and had gone through enough anyway. But I won out at last, and drove down to the boat house with Asey and Quin.

I recognized Hanson as the state police sergeant who'd once found a car of mine that had been stolen, but the other men were strangers.

"Sorry to take so much time getting here, Asey," Hanson said, "but that rumpus up town's been keeping us busy, sorting people out. I'd say that the fellow inside was hit by a bottle, and dumped in there. Probably the aftermath of last night."

"Maybe," Asey said, "but on the other hand—Quin, you pop in there an' see if you ever seen that feller b'fore. Hanson, did Syl tell you who he thought the man was?"

"Yes, and about Mrs. Colton's ideas. And Syl found a key ring under the steps, Asey. Take a look. There's a master key that fits the padlock that was open."

"It's Caleb's key ring!" I said. "It's got his name on it— Asey, he must have—"

Quin stumbled out of the boat house; it gave me a certain malicious pleasure to notice that for all his talk about murders and corpses, he looked as wobbly as I'd felt on our earlier trip.

"My God," he said, "that's Dick Thorne! With a beard, but it is! And—why, he was drowned years ago!"

"Sure of him?" Asey asked.

"Positive. Tell you how I know, besides the finger and the mark. He used to go fishing with dad, and he taught me how to cast when I was a kid. First time, I boggled, and caught him on the neck. It left a little scar. But, Asey—d'you know all about that business of Caleb and Thorne? If Caleb's gone—lord, you don't think he had something to do—but he must have!"

Asey dangled the key ring and told him about the padlock.

"And that—why, it's clear, Asey! Caleb met Thorne and—"

"An' bashed him. Seems so, but where's the smashed bottle?"

"Tossed away in the water, of course," Quin said impatiently. "The whole damn Atlantic's right there for him to toss it in! Or he might have hit him on the other side of the bar."

"An' carried him all this way? Not a chance, Quin. Thorne weighs a hundred an' eighty or ninety, an' Frost ain't a whole lot bigger'n Syl. Then there's that dory, out there, anchored off the end of the wharf. You notice that dory, Syl?"

"It's not a Sandbar boat!" I said. "It wasn't there yesterday evening!"

Syl looked at it and his jaw dropped. "Why, I been so busy lookin' in here, I never noticed it b'fore, Asey. That's the dory you'n I picked up off the Weesit inlet last fall an' sold to Bingo Cook!"

Bingo Cook, the East Pochet fish man, lives in a little shack on the mainland just before the Sandbar bridge. As side issues, he rents boats and sells beer to the tourist trade.

"Why," Syl went on, "Bingo, bein' a heavy drinker, was maybe mixed up in that business last night. That'd 'count for a bottle more'n anythin' to do with Frost. An' his boat—"

"And maybe he rowed Thorne over here," Quin interrupted excitedly, "and—but what about the keys? Well, maybe Cale left the place unlocked. Then, maybe—"

"The doc's comin'." Asey put a stop to the stream of "Maybe's." "Hanson, want me to take one of your fellers an' get Bingo, while the doc's busy? Might help some."

Hanson nodded. "If you'd help us, it'd be swell. But you don't need any of my men. Say, you know what Frost had on? I'm going to send Harry up to the house to phone in and have a description of him shot out over the teletype and radio."

Asey went into the boat house and wrote busily on a pad of paper, and then he and I drove over to Bingo's shack.

"Which d'you think?" I asked. "Bingo or Caleb?"

"Dunno. Perfectly pos'ble it ain't either. Somehow, I

sort of feel with Syl, that Bingo's more the bottle smashin' type than Frost. He might just have gone down to the boat house, peeked in an' forgot to lock it up again. Can't tell."

He got out of the car and banged at the door of Bingo's combination store and home. No one answered, and at last he tried the door and went in. I heard his long drawn out "Wheeeee!"

I was out of the car and beside him in a second.

"Wha—don't tell me anything's the matter with Bingo!"

"Just you take a peep inside here!"

If the Main Street of East Pochet had been a shambles, Bingo's house was a shambles plus. I know no word to sum up the mess.

The furniture, what there had been of it, was match wood. The floor was covered with broken bottles and broken dishes, smashed phonograph records and the remains of a radio. The shades and curtains had been pulled down and torn into strips. I thought at first that a bomb had exploded, and then it occurred to me that a bomb would at least mercifully have scattered the débris.

But worse than the sight was the smell. Apparently before whatever had happened *had* happened, Bingo had stocked up with fish. During the mêlée, the fish had been freely used as ammunition. The result was beyond description.

Even a black and white cat who'd brushed at my skirts and followed me into the shack, turned up her nose in disgust and stalked out into the rain. I followed her hastily.

Asey came out a minute later, bearing a can of condensed milk and a can opener.

"Bingo's cat," he said, "has got kind of a lean'n hungry look. Here, puss, crawl under this box an' dive into this!"

"How in the world," I demanded as he got into the car, "d'you explain that chaos?"

"I'd say that brother Bingo was at the grand openin' of the two hundred cases, an' that sometime durin' the festiv'ties, he come back here with his worst enemy. Prob'ly he's still regrettin' it all in a ditch somewheres. Bingo ain't exactly what you'd call a total abstainer, you know, even if he did say he wan't goin' to touch another drop after pro'bition got r'pealed an' he had to quit the bootleggin' business an' become an honest man again."

I knew Bingo's habits only too well. More than once when I lived on the beach road, I'd gone to sleep to the sound of Bingo's joyous homeward carols.

"Here's Googly," I said, "coming up the beach. Maybe he'll know where his uncle is."

Googly Cook's nickname is derived directly from his appearance. He possesses two of the poppest pop eyes I've ever seen. He's not old enough to have the title of town loafer, but when Reuben Ricks, the present incumbent, is no more, without doubt Googly will come into his own.

This morning he was slouchier, dirtier and drawlier than ever.

"Nope," he replied to Asey's question. "Ain't seen Bingo since early last night. Lot still missin'."

"Know if he's been out in that dory he bought from Syl? Know where the dory is?"

Googly yawned and shook his head. "Don't seem to be on the beach. Guess it's stolen. Lots of boats still missin' from last night."

"Seen the inside of this shack?"

Googly looked and allowed himself a toothy grin.

"Great time," he said. "Lots—"

"I know," Asey said. "Lots of places still lookin' worse'n that. Well, you stay here, Googly, till Bingo gets back. N'en you bring him over to Sandbar, see? To me. Here's a dollar to fritter away, an' you'll get another when you collect Bingo. See?"

"You'll see him just's soon's he gets back," Googly promised.

Asey grinned and turned the car back on the Sandbar road.

"Listen to those gulls," I said as we crossed the bridge. "They look like so many buzzards. Wouldn't you think they'd get tired of flying around in the same circle? They seem to have a grudge against that dune. Probably they've nests there, but I can't see that any one's bothering them. I just caught sight of Ford and Tom way at the tip of the bar."

Asey looked at me and then suddenly turned the roadster off the log road.

"What's the—you'll get stuck in the sand!" I said. "Asey, what are you careening off to the outer beach for?

You'll get stuck, man! You'll never get this car out safely!"

"Air wheels," Asey said. "Car goes good on sand. Bill Porter had 'em put on special."

"But Asey, what are you going to that dune for?"

"Hunch," he said. "I hope I'm wrong."

But he wasn't.

Fifteen minutes later, on the side of the dune over which the gulls still circled, Asey found Caleb Frost's body. He had been shot through the eye, and then loose sand from the sloping dune had been piled over him. Only the tip of one soiled canvas shoe had been left uncovered.

CHAPTER FOUR

I GRIPPED Asey's arm tightly as we plowed back through the sand to the roadster.

The wind had shifted to the northeast, and was roaring dully in and out of the hollows, whipping the rain against our faces and grinding the top sand against my legs with all the force of a blasting machine. The gulls still screamed above us, and the surf on the outer beach boomed steadily like a bass drum.

I found that I was crying. I'd never liked Caleb, and never pretended to, but the thought of him buried there under the sand, with the wind moaning and the birds crying and the ocean crashing out a dirge—it was all too horrible.

"It is pretty terrible," Asey said as he helped me into the car, "but it's better that we found him than—"

"I'm not crying because we found him, and saw him like that! It's because I feel so helpless and so small! Asey, I'm scared to death of this place and all its sounds. Sinister! Tom didn't begin to describe it! But as for Cale —he was vain, and he could be unpleasant, but he never deserved anything like this! And if it hadn't been for that shoe, he might never have been found for days and days. And with him gone and with Thorne dead, you know very well what every one would have thought and said! What you actually thought, and what I believed but never would have admitted—that Caleb really did kill Dick."

Asey nodded and swung the car into a wide circle to go back to the boat house.

"As it is, this is sort of a problem," he said. "Thorne was murdered, an' so was Frost. Did Frost have anythin' to do with Thorne's death, or the other way 'round? An' who, or what c'lection of folks killed the survivin' one, if that was the case? Or was they killed by two dif'rent sets—well, we'll see what Hanson's got to say. This is his job, thank goodness, an' not mine!"

Hanson took the news of Caleb with something bordering on annoyance.

"My God!" he said, "and I was—are you sure he was killed?"

"Sure," Asey said. "In the first place, no suicide ever shot himself through the eye yet. An' then—"

"Why not?" Quin demanded, with a pencil poised over a small notebook. "Why not, Asey?"

"Dunno, Sherlock, but it's a fact. Head, yes, but not through the eyeball. Anyways, Hanson, there wasn't no gun. An' finally, a man couldn't kill himself an' then cover himself with sand. No more'n Thorne could of bashed himself an' then thrown the bottle away, an' so forth an' so on. An' still another thing. Thorne's pockets wasn't the only ones gone through. Frost's been, too. His watch is gone, an' so's the money Greg'ry thinks he must

have had with him, but a plat'num cig'rette case is still in
his coat."

Hanson sighed. "Oh, well. Doc, d'you want to go see
to him? I'll have Harry take you over in the truck, an'
we'll take 'em both away together."

The doctor nodded. "Right. By the way, Asey,
Thorne was killed around one-thirty or so, I'd say, if that's
any interest to you. Later, if anything. And Hanson,
hadn't you better call Forman if Frost was shot? The
sooner he gets to work, if the gun's gone, the sooner you'll
get things going."

"I suppose," Hanson said. He seemed very put out
about the whole business of Caleb's being found, and I
judged that he had made up his mind that Caleb was
responsible.

"All right," he said. "I'll leave some men here at
the bar, and get things started, and then I'll come back
and see if anything can be dug up out of the Sandbar
crowd. Tell 'em to stay put, will you, Asey? I'd do it now,
but there's all that mess up town to be settled, and Jim
Williams was still out when I came through. Combination nurse maids and master minds, that's what you've
got to be in this outfit!"

Asey and I drove back to the house, and Quin rode
off with one of the officers and the doctor.

"Quin," Asey commented, "seems like a kid with his
first long pants, but he'll lose a little of this feelin' of joy
at bein' in on a real murder case when they really start
in to work."

"I never thought of that part!" I said. "It'll be in the

papers, won't it? And then there'll be questionings and inquests—my heavens on earth! It never entered my head that we'd all be suspected, but we will, won't we? And the rest don't even know about Caleb. And think of Lizzie, when she hears!"

"I guess we'd better leave that part to the doc," Asey said. "But the rest of it won't be so bad. Hanson's a good man. No bullyin' third degreein' about him. The rest of the bunch knows their business, too. They'll prob'ly send down a couple detectives an' experts of one kind'n another, but they're all decent."

"Decent, maybe," I said, "but Hanson doesn't seem to me to be very much at home in this sort of work. I feel he'd be better at finding a stolen car or unsnarling an auto accident than finding a murderer."

"Maybe so," Asey returned. "Anyways, I'm glad I don't have to unsnarl this p'ticular accident. Want me to break the news to the rest?"

"By all means," I told him as we went into the living room. "I'll call them down here. And Tom and Ford are just coming in the kitchen door."

"By the way," Asey said. "Tell me before you go just how this house—or these houses—work. I know about the kitchen ell an' the g'rage ell, an' I s'pose Greg'ry an' his wife live above the kitchen one. An' I come through the dinin' room on the other side of this, but what about the rest?"

"Downstairs," I said, "there's a sort of extension living room, beyond the hall, you see. And a bedroom. Quin was to have that, and apparently Tom's joined him there.

Upstairs in that house are four more bedrooms. Then in this house, besides Caleb's and Lizzie's bedrooms, there's a study for Caleb. There's a tiny unfinished attic in both houses, but it's not connected. Why d'you ask?"

"Just thinkin'. Like to get placed. You c'lect the others an' I'll tell 'em."

At the conclusion of his brief recital, Deal, Jane, Tom and Ford sat there around the fireplace like so many graven images. Even Jane and Tom, who hadn't really known Caleb, seemed as completely shattered as the others.

"But it's awful!" Deal said. "Poor mother—how she'll —oh, I don't know what to say!"

Ford got up and crossed to the window. "Caleb," his voice broke, "I—oh, Cale helped me through college, and saw me started in business. I—I lost my family when I was ten, you know. It seems almost as though I'd lost them all over again. Asey, if it's the last thing you ever do, I want you to get to the bottom of this for me! You've got to. I'll give you any amount you ask if you'll sift this awful thing out and give me the chance to—you've simply got to!"

"I'll do what I can," Asey said gently. "But you won't pay me nothin' for it. The p'lice ain't no slouches, an' you can take my word they'll do all they can do. 'Course, if—well, if they seem to me to be hittin' on the wrong track, I'll be glad to do what I can. An' if they hit up against a stone wall, I'll take a whack at it."

"You've got to take a whack at it anyway." Ford's eyes were bright. "You've got to! Oh, I can't seem to understand it! Thorne—I didn't know Thorne. None of us did. He didn't mean a thing to me, though I suppose I was sorry about it in a way! But Cale!"

We all sat there uncomfortably while Ford stared out of the window with his shoulders shaking. None of us knew what to say. After all, there wasn't much that we could say which wouldn't sound flat and futile. All of us felt badly. All of us were thinking of Caleb, lying there on the dune, with the gulls screeching above him. But while we were trying to grasp the horror of the thing, something kept asking us "Who did it?"

That question, pounding like a tom-tom in the back of my own brain, began to grow larger and blot out the picture of Caleb. I began to sense then something which I realized more and more clearly in the days that followed —that while we were sorry for Caleb, appalled by the way in which he and Dick Thorne had met death, the fear for ourselves and for the circumstances in which we knew we'd be involved was stronger than anything else.

As I watched the expressions of those four young people change from amazement and sorrow to pity and fear, even if it was more or less controlled fear, I think I understood for the first time just what people meant by saying that man's first, last and strongest impulse is that of self-preservation. For all that we knew, any one of us might be chosen as the murderer of Caleb Frost or of Dick Thorne. And, what was even more horrible—with two men murdered, there was no guarantee that any one of us might not be the next to go.

Gregory chose that uncomfortable moment in which

to announce dinner, and of course since he and Mathilde
had to be told some time, Asey took the bull by the
horns and told them. Both promptly went into a state
bordering closely on Lizzie's earlier in the day, so much
so that Mathilde had to be put to bed, with Gregory to
look after her. Jane and Deal served the rather hectic
repast; I don't believe I've ever entertained more violent
thoughts against the custom of Sunday noon dinners.

After that was over with, Ford went off upstairs and
Deal relieved Malvina at her mother's bedside. I'd had
some optimistic notion of lying down and taking a nap,
but I found that my brain was too full of buzzing questions. With Asey and Jane and Tom, I sat in front of
the driftwood fire and watched the purple and green
flames, and tried to figure things out. But it wasn't any
use.

"Look here," I said at last to Asey, "why'd Dick
Thorne call himself Cheyne? Why was Caleb out on the
dune last night anyway? And why was he carrying all
that money? And where's the bottle that killed Dick?
And the gun that killed Caleb? And did Dick and Caleb
have a fight? D'you suppose it's possible that one killed
the other and then was killed in turn by some one else?
And why didn't we hear the sound of the shot? And
why were both of 'em robbed? Would it mean that the
same person killed 'em both?"

Asey shook his head. "You got me," he said. "Seems
like as if they'd both been killed by the same person, on
the face of it, with both of 'em bein' robbed. But if that
was so, why's one shot an' one bashed? Why not both

shot, an' so on? An' while Thorne's pockets was clean as a whistle, they left Frost's plat'num case an' his studs. As to the sound of the shot, prob'ly the surf drowned that out. Or some one might of used a silencer. It was a small caliber bullet, anyhow. Tell that from the size of the hole. Wouldn't of made much noise. I dunno."

"Sand dunes," Jane suggested, "won't be a very fertile ground for footprints, will they? And with all the bar, finding any sort of clew at all isn't going to be easy, is it?"

"Not only that," Asey said, "but s'pose you should find a smashed bottle. Prob'ly there'll be a hundred, if you start in to look. Never seen a beach yet, even a private one, that didn't have busted bottles on it if you hunted enough. An' as for the gun—s'pose they do find it. Chances is it'll be a stolen gun, or one that won't be traced. An' with all the Atlantic starin' you in the face, it oughtn't to be hard to drop a gun in it. An' if my idea's right that the rob'ry business is a fake, prob'ly the Atlantic'll be the answer to what come out of them fellers's pockets.— Some one knockin' at the door—funny. I didn't hear no car."

He got up and ushered in Googly Cook and Bingo, both of them soaked to the skin.

Bingo tried to duck behind his nephew when he saw us around the fireplace, and I didn't in the least blame him for the gesture. I've never seen a sorrier looking creature in all my life.

His face was practically obliterated by what the newspapers call general abrasions and contusions; one eye was a delicate violet color which didn't begin to blend with the cerise swelling that surrounded it.

He wore something which had once been a pair of blue serge trousers and something else which probably had been a shirt. An average charwoman would undeniably have refused to utilize either remnant even for the purposes of blacking a stove. All in all, Bingo reminded me of an early movie director's conception of some one who had been in what the caption would have called "A Battle Royal."

"Aw, gee," Bingo said sheepishly, edging nearer the hall, "aw, gee, you seen me in bad shape, Mrs. Colton, but—aw, gee, I guess you never seen me as bad as this, huh? I didn't want to come over here, but Googly's stronger'n I am right now. He made me, an' then Asey pushed me in. Say, Asey, that state cop at the bridge said I was wanted. Is that so? If it is, don't you s'pose you could put in a good word? Y'know, I always said, if a feller needed help, from gettin' a quohaug rake welded to gettin' rid of his mother-in-law, you was the feller that could do it, Asey. Honest, what'd I do?"

He was so pathetically earnest that we all laughed. Bingo tried to, but his lip was cut in at least three places. He winced and shook his head.

"Aw, gee, I can't even smile. Honest, Asey, what'd I do?"

"Well," Asey returned, "what do you r'member doin'?"

"That's just it!" Bingo sat down gingerly on the edge of the sea chest by the fire. "That's just the whole thing.

Seems like Sat'day afternoon, I found an ole bottle of
Jamaica rum in my back closet. Don't know how it got
there, but by golly, there it was. Well, sir, I'd been out
fishin', an' it tasted pretty good, an' then I set off for town
after supper, an' they told me about Tim findin' Regan's
likker, an' by golly, I went out to the bay shore, an' then,
somehow, when I come to, it seems like I was in the
woods over to the lower neck, just the way you see me
now—an' it was Sunday aft'noon!"

"Rent any of your boats Sat'day?" Asey asked.

"Not a one. Won't be no one round for another three-
four weeks. I only had three sharpies an' the ole dory out.
Rest was still in the barn."

"What about that dory? Where'd you leave that?"

"Tied up by my wharf. Googly says to me as how
it'd drifted off, but I seen it tied up to Frost's wharf as
we come along. Guess some one must of seen it driftin'
an' brought it back here."

"How come you got so banged up?"

Bingo sighed. "Asey, your guess's as good as mine.
It was an awful squabble, an' I was awful mad at some
one, but I don't know who the hell it was."

"Seen your house?"

"Ain't it awful? Guess we must of had it out in
there, but I don't r'member comin' back home, an' if I
did, who'd I come with an' how'd I get up there to the
lower neck?" He rubbed his chin carefully. "How? But
I'll tell you one thing. If I'm like I am, it oughtn't to be
hard to find the other feller! He'll be worse off'n me.
Say, Asey, what'd I do the cops want me?"

"Caleb Frost's been killed," Asey said, "an' another feller named Thorne was bashed over the head. We found him in the boat house, an' outside we seen your dory parked, so Hanson thought—"

"Frost killed? An' another? My—God—they don't think I—say, Asey, you know me! I may maul some one up once in a while, but I don't go 'round killin' what you might call my next door neighbor!"

The thought of the slightly disreputable Bingo classifying himself as Caleb Frost's next door neighbor was so irresistibly funny that I laughed till I was weak.

"I'll admit," Asey said with a grin, "that your maulin' is all in the spirit of good clean fun, an' you don't usually start off the day wipin' out half a dozen fam'lies, but—"

"But Asey," Bingo said anxiously, "look at me! If I'd fought with Frost, I wouldn't never of been in no condition like this! Why, if I'd touched Frost, he'd of run! He couldn't of marked me up like this! No sireebob! Whoever done this job on me was a sight bigger'n me, an' a sight harder, an' what you might call pretty well up in the fine art of fightin'. Say, was he marked up bad?"

"Frost? Not a bit. The other man'd been bashed with a bottle, but he wasn't marked up otherwise."

Bingo sighed his relief.

"Oh," he said, "I feel better. If they wasn't mussed up none, you can bet I didn't have nothin' to do with it. No one could of punished me like this without gettin' somethin' in return. You tell them cops that, Asey. I got to get home an' get myself fixed up an' begin to get my house in order. Why, it'll take me a month, easy, to get that place back to normal!"

"You better stay an' see Hanson," Asey advised. "He said he wanted to see you; I'll admit I sort of think there's more'n a tinge of truth in what you say, but they want you, an' you better hang around. Tell you what. Tom, you take him out in the kitchen an' fix him up a bit. Greg'ry can find somethin' to drape over his nakedness."

"Thanks," Bingo said. "I—well, I got just a sort of glimpse of myself out of one eye in a piece of busted mirror, an' I tell you, I scared myself somethin' awful. If them cops sees me like this, they'll 'rest me on gen'ral princ'ples. I look like I was cap'ble of doin' most anythin'."

"Yup," Asey said dryly, "you really ought to get a chance to break yourself to 'em more gently like. Tom'll see to you."

"Poor Bingo," I remarked as Tom and the Cook family departed. "If he feels half as badly as he looks, he must be in mortal agony. But what he says seems sane enough, doesn't it?"

"It does. He couldn't look like that without havin' the other feller look worse. Bingo used to be a third mate on a tramp steamer, an' you can tell his victims a mile off. Nope, unless he fought all the town Sat'day night an' then come up here an' biffed Thorne an' shot Frost—or went after them two an' then took on the rest of the pop'lation—no, it don't sound right to me. Oho—here come the cars!"

Jane and I looked at each other and automatically

drew a long breath while Hanson came in, followed by two plainclothesmen, the doctor, Quin, and three uniformed state police.

"Got Bingo for you," Asey said, "if you'd like to see him."

"And if you want the rest," I piped up, "I'll call them."

"Don't bother," Hanson said cheerfully. "Well, Asey, we got it!"

"Want to know!" Asey's pure Cape God ejaculation sounded just as amazed as I felt.

"Yes, sir. Forman found out that the bullet that killed Frost was a .22, shot from a Woodsman Colt. And the doc says Frost was killed around one-thirty, too. I called up Higgins at the hardware store, just on a hunch, and asked him if he'd sold a .22 lately. I remembered seeing two in his windows a while back. He said yes, and I looked the fellow up, and he confessed. You'll never guess in a thousand years who—that tall gangly chap with the red whiskers that used to work for Frost! Zeruah Nims!"

"Zeruah!" I sat down heavily on the chaise longue. "Zeruah Nims! Zeruah! Zeruah—I know I sound like a parrot, but you don't mean Zeruah Nims!"

"That's who," Hanson said happily. "He told us he'd had a fight with Frost and was sore at him. Said he joined the revelers late, but I guess he caught up with 'em double quick. More he caught up, the more annoyed he got about Frost's firing him. And at the same time, he remembered Miss Richards had told him to take a party out this morning. He remembers coming here, in a car, he thinks. And he remembers hitting some one over the head. And he had his gun in his car—a .22 Woodsman Colt. One shot fired. He's confessed. So—well, that would seem to be that!"

"It would," Asey said. "Huh—how 'bout the stuff he stole from Frost's pockets? An' Thorne's?"

"He isn't sure, but he thinks he threw 'em into the harbor. Well, I'll have Harry stay here to keep out any curiosity seekers, and I'll be getting along. You don't know how cheery I feel, Asey. Honest, I thought I was going to get stuck, and have to ask you—well, I like you, but honest, I didn't want to have to get you to help me again—well, you know what I mean! Now, thank God, this is settled, and will I—well, I'll be seeing you!"

"Congratulations," Asey said. "Straighten out your necktie b'fore the r'porters take your picture. Next time I see you, you'll be a leftenant, an' my, won't you get fan mail—"

"Aw, go on! Aw—well, so long, Asey!"

"Can I string along with you?" Quin asked. "To see the end?"

"Sure." Hanson was expansive. "Sure. String along!"

I went to the window and watched the cavalcade set out, with Quin sitting by Hanson's side. Only the doctor remained.

"Well," he said quizzically to Asey, "and what do you think about that, Mister Bones?"

"Just," Asey said, "what you're thinkin'. You see Zeruah?"

"Uh-huh."

"Was he marked up any?"

"Face was battered a bit. Black eye. But no worse than Tim Smalley and Jim Williams were. I just treated them en route down here. That is, I advised bed."

"Smalley and Jim Williams," Asey said thoughtfully, "an' Bingo, they kind of hang together, don't they? Huh. That might sort of explain Bingo. So Zeruah had a black eye? Well, he plays around with Bingo, too. How long since you took off that shoulder brace of Zeruah's, doc?"

The doctor grinned. "Day before yesterday. That is, he took it off himself. Said it didn't do any good."

"Look here," I said, "what is all this? Don't you two think—well, of course, it doesn't seem possible to me that Zeruah's responsible for this, but with all that business of the gun—Asey, don't you believe it?"

His blue eyes twinkled. "I b'lieve it, Mrs. Colton, my goodness me, yes, I b'lieve it. But with res'vations, like the feller said when they told him for the third time it *was* corn beef hash he was eatin'. It's pos'ble that Zeruah did shoot Frost an' bash Thorne. But I'm kind of dubious, like."

"So," said the doctor pleasantly, "am I. Oh, I told them, Asey, but they wouldn't have believed George Washington and all the angels. And besides, I think Zeruah really believes it, even though he must know it's so much hooey."

"Get to it!" Jane said. "Get to it! Why isn't Zaccheus —no, he climbed the tree his Lord to see, didn't he? Zebediah—Zeruah—whoever he is—why didn't he kill Thorne and Mr. Frost?"

"Because," Asey said, "he's the most right-handed man I ever seen. An' a while back, he twisted the tendons of his right arm, an' went right on usin' the right arm, which made it worse. He ain't been able to lift that arm higher'n his waist for—how long, doc?"

"Three weeks," the doctor said placidly. "And he *is* hopelessly right-handed. Besides which, he's got arthritis in his left hand. I don't think he could fire a gun with that left hand, let alone hit some one square in the eye. And besides that, Thorne was hit from behind by some one who hit a right-handed blow. You know, Asey, I think it would be fun if you picked up Hanson's complacency and general smugness and hurled it politely in his face. Pah! After all you've done for that man and his bunch! He 'didn't want to ask you!' Go ahead, Asey. Do it before they get a chance to indict Zeruah. After all, the fellow isn't guilty!"

"I didn't," Asey said, "care for that crack of Hanson's much, either. Nun—no. I thought better of Hanson than that. I guess, yup, I guess I will kind of make a stab at this. Besides, I been doin' a little quiet ponderin'. I kind of think I know who Varney Cheyne really is."

CHAPTER FIVE

"COURSE," Asey went on, "I may be a thousand miles off, but on the other hand, it's kind of a good likely guess. An' this's the sort of business where a good likely guesser's just as good as any prophet."

Jane and the doctor and I just stared at him.

"D'you mean Quin?" I asked finally. "Quin? But that doesn't seem possible!"

"Not Quin." Asey pulled out his pipe and filled it with care. "I did think of him first off, but—say, any of you read the Varney Cheyne books? They's a whole row of 'em up there." He jerked his head toward the built-in book shelves on either side of the fireplace.

Jane and the doctor had read all of them, but I was forced to confess that I'd only a skimming acquaintance with the first.

"And that only because Caleb all but thrust it down my throat a couple of years ago," I said. "I was laid up with a bad foot and people deluged me with books. I didn't care any more about it than I do for most fiction murders, though I've read every word ever printed about Lizzie Borden and her ax. But who is he, Asey? And why d'you ask about the Cheyne books? How could they give you any clew?"

" 'Member," Asey said, "how you mentioned Frost this mornin' an' spoke about the 'leventh century vowel shift an' somethin' about Byzantine art? Was it just chance that you did?"

"Not at all," I told him. "They're two of Caleb's favorite subjects, and he expects every one to know as much about them as he does—did, I mean." I corrected my tense. "He was going to England just to delve further into the eleventh century vowel shift, if you can believe it. But why?"

Asey got up and pulled down two of the Cheyne books.

"This detective of Cheyne's," he said, "is a great boy for showin' off his knowledge. Stops right short in the middle of a man hunt to chat about—well, listen to these two pieces."

To my intense amazement, he read two paragraphs which made me think for a moment that Caleb Frost was actually in the room; one was about Byzantine art, and the other concerned the eleventh century vowel shift.

"It's impossible," I said, "if you think—I mean, it does sound like Caleb, but any one on earth might make some character spout about those two subjects!"

"They might," the doctor said, "but it is rather more than a coincidence. Come to think of it, that detective of Cheyne's is rather like Frost was in some ways. Always lecturing, bullyragging in a refined way, expecting every one to kow-tow and shower thanks on him every time he does anything—by George, Asey! Anything else?"

"Yup," Asey said. "The last Cheyne book that come out serially. It hinged around the story of a man, kind of like Frost, who employed another, kind of like Thorne, who got into a mixup about stolen money—"

"Why, Asey!" I said. "You mean you think—"

"I do. It come into my head while you was tellin' about Thorne this mornin', while I was puzzlin' at the same time as to why Thorne called himself Cheyne to Syl. Anyway, the employer accuses this man of his, an' the man's sent to jail. Then the employer decides he was wrong in accusin' the man. He's got almost certain proof. But he ain't got the courage to do anythin' about it, an' besides, he don't like the man anyhow. So the employer spends the rest of his life waitin' for that feller to get out of jail an' to get back at him. Story begins with the feller gettin' out, an' then the employer's found dead. Now, Thorne guessed the endin' of the story. Kind of a trick endin', too."

"I remember it," Jane said. "It disappointed me. It was some one else the employer'd done wrong to."

"Just so. Thorne, you see, must of been guessin', but it was clear he knew, an' got the likeness to his own story an' that one. Prob'ly somehow Frost give himself away in the writin' of that book so that Thorne was sure Cheyne was Frost. That's my notion."

"Ridiculous!" I said. "Even granting you the lecturing detective and the vowel shift, and the fact that there is some apparent similarity between the actual story of

Dick and Cale and the situation of that story. Why, it's too far-stretched, Asey!"

"Wa-el," Asey drawled slightly, "it's as good an explanation as I can think of as to why Thorne pretended to be Cheyne."

"I don't understand that part at all," I said. "I think Dick was just pulling Syl's leg."

"Maybe. But assumin' that I might be right, look at it from Thorne's angle. There's somethin' in that book—perhaps somethin' we'll never know, perhaps just Frost's admittin' that he knew Thorne was innocent—that sets Thorne off on Frost's trail. Now, he ain't goin' to do it nice an' outright. Not after all the things he had to go through because of Frost's accusin' him. He's goin' to put on the screws. He comes down here, an' remarks off-hand to Syl an' prob'ly to half a dozen others, that he's Cheyne. Frost'll hear about it. An' then, how'll Frost feel? P'raps Thorne never meant to do Frost any harm, but just to let him know about the Cheyne business. If I'd been Frost, I'd of been scared to death."

"But, assuming that the ridiculous story is true," I said, "remember that Cale—all of us, in fact, believed that Dick was dead!"

"Maybe, an' maybe not. Thorne disappeared. P'raps Frost suggested it. P'raps Frost never did b'lieve the yarn about the drowned man. N'en there's another thing. Frost retired from his firm before the market crash, didn't he? Seems sensible to think that his income'd go down with every one else's. But the last two years, he's spent more money down here than in a dozen years before. You realize that?"

"Why, he has always seemed to have a lot of money, but—"

"Four new boats last year," Asey said. "The 'Step-anfetchit' must of cost three thousand, an' the others, p'ticularly the speed boat, maybe more. Cars. Three new expensive cars. Why, the work that the East Pochet carpenters an' plumbers done on this house lately's more'n enough to keep 'em off the town dole for years to come. He's bought up a lot of land around here, Frost has. His taxes is high enough to knock an av'rage income galley-west for Sundays. But he takes it an' spends an' spends."

I had to admit that Asey was right. "He bought a new house last winter," I said, "and Ned Richards told me once that the firm would have gone smash completely if Caleb hadn't risen to the occasion after the Kreuger business. Yes, Caleb's spending seems more like Cheyne's reputed income than Caleb's usual—but even so, I can't believe he was Varney Cheyne."

"Just the same," the doctor said, "fantastic as it may seem, I think Asey's right. Look, Asey, I'm going to interrupt for a second and make a suggestion. Forman had a tussle with the bullet that killed Caleb. It was imbedded in his skull. He said it was a .22 high velocity, fired from a Woodsman Colt. Of course it had to happen that Zeruah's gun had high velocity bullets in it, too. But the bullet was mushroomed, and Forman doubted if he could tell a lot more from it. Now, we don't think Zeruah's guilty, and consequently, the bullet must have come from another gun. I suggested to Hanson that he comb the place for the ejected cartridge case, but he said it would be like hunting a needle in a haystack. Forman and I thought the gun was fired about ten feet away from Frost. So it's just humanly possible that if we set to work before it gets dark, we may find it. And then, if we find the case, we'll be all set about Zeruah."

"Why?" Jane asked.

"Because a cartridge fired from Zeruah's gun," Asey explained, "would mark the case a certain way; now, we're certain Zeruah's innocent, so's the ejected case from that gun that *did* kill Frost would have a dif'rent mark. A c'mparison of the two would prove they come from dif'rent guns. Yup. I'll get Syl. Say, whatever become of Syl, anyways?"

"He was around the boat house," the doctor said, "the last I saw of him. I rather think he must have—ah, me, speak of the devil!"

Syl, leaving little trails of water behind him, burst into the living room without any formality whatsoever, and raced over to Asey.

"Hey!" He held out a dark blue flannel jacket. "Look! Asey—see what I found on one of the dunes! An'—take a look at what was in the pocket!"

He pulled out Cale Frost's platinum watch and chain, the book of traveler's checks, two thick rolls of bills—obviously the ones Gregory had seen Caleb put into the blue jar—and then he pulled out half a dozen papers.

"I went through 'em," he said. "I held my slicker

over so's they didn't get wet an' run any. Say, Asey, look at this one—this letter!"

The paper was a letter written to Varney Cheyne some four days previously, asking to what address Cheyne wished certain royalty checks to be sent. The letter itself had apparently been mailed to a box in the general post office in New York.

But that wasn't the most startling thing. The real shock came when I found that the letter was signed by Durford Ames and bore his rather fancy letterhead.

"Ford!" I said. "He—why, he must have known! Jane, run upstairs and ask him to come down!"

Ford's eyes were red when he came into the living room, and for the first time in the seven or eight years I'd known him, his clothes looked rumpled and disheveled.

Asey explained first about his far-fetched guessing, and Ford laughed.

"Not a chance, Asey! I don't know who Cheyne is, myself, and God knows I've tried hard enough to find out!"

Silently, Asey produced the letter. "This was in a jacket Syl found, along with Frost's watch an' money an' things."

Ford looked at it and then sat down heavily on the couch.

"Incredible!" he said. "But—oh, I should have guessed! Look, let me tell you the whole story, Asey. When I got through college, I went into an agency in New York. After a couple of years, I wanted to start out on my own, and Cale lent me the money.—Incidentally, I've placed two of the books he's written in the last couple of years. One on antiques, and one on clipper ships and ship models. Anyway, one morning I got this first script of Cheyne's—now that I think of it, Caleb came in a few days later and asked me how things were getting along, and I told him I'd got a peach of a detective story from an apparently brand new man. I placed the script, and then the publishers wanted to see Cheyne. I wrote him, but he said that was impossible. He wouldn't come to New York. The first address he gave, by the way, was a general post office box in Boston. I urged and pleaded, but he simply wouldn't come. Then Bob Trimble said, since it seemed the fashion to have detectives who were men of mystery, how about building Cheyne up as one. That was how it started."

"Did Cheyne know about that 'Great Unknown' business?" I asked.

"Yes. He thought it was fine. Approved heartily. Said he'd thought of it. Then I began to get interested. Sent him a letter and took the midnight over to Boston and hung around the post office till they nearly arrested me as a suspicious person. And by all the gods, it seems silly now—but I met Caleb there! I told him about the Cheyne business and why I was there. And the two of us—can you beat this? We watched that box for three days! When I finally went back to New York, utterly disgusted with the whole thing, there was a letter from Cheyne. Been waiting for me, in fact, saying that his next letters should be sent to the American Express in Paris."

"Caleb went abroad—" I began.

"I know, now," Ford said. "Now I begin to—why, I even told him to see if he couldn't find out anything at the American Express while he was over there! The letters were to be sent to Roger Buntling. You see, the name of Cheyne was practically a household word by that time. Well, I made a dozen other efforts to locate Cheyne, when he sent in his infernal general post office box numbers, but I never got anywhere. Caleb must have thought I'd caught on, for after the Boston incident, I never met him around on any of my tours of inspection, though he was always terribly interested in Cheyne and always asked me about him."

"How about the checks?" Asey asked. "Couldn't you have traced him by those? After all, they must have been big checks."

"They were," Ford said. "The first two or three were sent to Varney Cheyne, and were cashed in Boston. Then he wrote me to have his checks made out to bearer. I objected strenuously, but he insisted. Apparently what he did was to endorse them—Roger Buntling was the name he used, and deposit them in any one of half a dozen banks. I tried to trace him that way, but he carried on all his banking by mail. And let me tell you, Mr. Buntling had even stranger addresses than the ones Cheyne gave me. Oh, it was a mess! I can see—why, it's clearer than daylight that Cheyne was Caleb, but honestly, it never occurred to me. No more than I'd expect any of you here to say that you were Charley Ross. But that's how it was."

Deal came downstairs then, and she had to be told

all about the Cheyne business, and everything else that had happened while she had been out of the room.

"Zeruah," she said, "why—that's absurd! He couldn't kill a fly. But d'you know, I thought once last year that Uncle might be Cheyne. I said as much to him after he gave me a Cheyne story to read. That detective *did* hold forth just the way he did. He snorted, but I think it pleased him, even though the snort was all the denial I needed. He was always and forever thrusting Cheyne on people and then giving an oral quiz on their reactions. He said Cheyne's stuff was great literature. Well, that explains where he got all his money, anyway. I've wondered about that, because I'd heard him speak of his investments and I knew what they were, and I knew damn well most of 'em had petered out."

"What about the jacket Syl found?" Jane asked.

"The only way to find its owner that I know of," Asey told her with a grin, "would be to line up all the men an' boys on Cape Cod an' see who it fits the worst. They can't be much less than a thousand of these blue flannel zipper things in East Pochet alone."

"It might be Zeruah's," I suggested, but Syl shook his head.

"Z'ruah's," he said with finality, "is green."

"This whole thing," Ford said, "is beyond me. Absolutely. Where're Tom and Quin?"

"Quin's still joyfully detecting with Hanson," I said. "Tom set out an hour ago to patch up Bingo Cook—why don't you run out and see what's happened to them in the kitchen, Ford?"

Tom came back, beaming from ear to ear.

"It took some time," he said, "to get the gravel out of Bingo's knees. He figured out that at one time he must have slid for home up in the gravel by the station. I wish I'd known you were here, doctor. I'm afraid I wasn't much good as a gravel picker. Oh, and Gregory requests salve, Mrs. Colton. He burned himself."

"Salve? Why, did you use up any of his salve on Bingo?"

"Just a little raw meat and iodine fixed him up. I suggested salve, but he scorned it. Sissy, he said. He added that he had some skunk grease at home—at least, he hoped it was still there, that would fix him up. He's getting into a cast-off suit of Gregory's right now. By the way, was that the police I heard coming and going?"

"I'll tell you all," Jane said, and did, briefly and graphically.

"Then Bingo's out? Will he ever be glad! I've got to like Bingo in the last hour. Oh—the salve, Mrs. Colton? Gregory's scared his forearm."

"It's a marvel to me," I said, "how that forearm has existed as long as it has. I've looked after three burns on it since I've come here, and as for mosquito bites and ant bites and scratches and splinters—those two would be a nightmare to an insurance agent. But I'm not going to give him any more salve. He—"

"Tch, tch." Asey clucked his tongue. "Cruel."

"Not at all. Yesterday I bought him two tubes of salve just for burns, and there's no reason why he should need any more. You send Gregory in to me, Tom. The doctor can look at him."

The doctor pooh-poohed the burn and advised baking soda paste, and Gregory left, looking rather disgruntled.

"I'm convinced," I said, "that he eats salve as though it were anchovy paste. Well, now we've got the Cheyne business fixed; that *is* something, but I still don't feel that we've really got anywhere. What about hunting that cartridge case? How in the world can you find it? Are you going to paw over all the dunes?"

"A fine tooth comb," Asey agreed, "would be our best bet, but—well, we might as well have a try. Who's goin' to come along an' sift?"

Ford and Jane and Tom volunteered, and while they hunted raincoats and rainy weather clothes—for it was still pouring outside, I spoke to the doctor.

"Hadn't you better look after Lizzie? Or aren't you going to hunt?"

"Hunt? Me?" He laughed. "Pen, you don't catch these old bones clattering about sand dunes on any day like this. Yes, I'll go up and see to Lizzie. Of course she doesn't know about Cale, yet, does she? Deal, you didn't tell her?"

"No. She was still sleeping. I didn't even say a word to her."

"Hm. Well, I'm not going to tell her till she's over all this. No need to stir her up any more. Asey, have you any theories yet as to why Frost went out last night? That's been bothering me. D'you suppose he went out to see Thorne? Doesn't any one know if he went out, or when, or anything? Who saw him last?"

"Lizzie would probably know more than the rest," I said, "since her room's so near his. But I went to bed around seven, so I'm vague about everything."

"We all went up to bed around twelve," Deal said. "I didn't get to sleep for ages, and I didn't hear any one go out. Tom, what about you? You and Quin, being downstairs, should have heard any goings or comings, unless some one went out the ell door."

"After that drive and that dinner," Tom said, "with the thought of getting up at five-thirty staring me right square in the face, let me tell you that when I got to bed, I slept. Quin was dead to the world before I closed my eyes, but I'm sure he'd have mentioned it if he'd heard any one."

"Have any of you thought of Gregory and Mathilde?" Jane asked. "I mean, isn't it the thing to worry about the servants, always?"

"I thought of them," Asey said, "when I first found Frost gone, an' the money gone. But I don't think so. D'you, Mrs. Colton? Deal?"

She and I both agreed that they were out of the question.

"Well," Ford said, "we seem to be ready. Me and Byrd. I'm not sure I'd know a cartridge case if I saw one, but I'm ready to try."

"Probably," Jane fastened the strap of a broad brimmed no'theaster hat under her chin, "probably we'll just find lettuce sandwiches and decayed bits of tongue and hot dogs. And old dead fish. Ugh—I wish I hadn't thought about those. All set, Asey?"

"All set. Oh, God A'mighty, Bingo, I didn't recognize you in that outfit. Why, you might be a head waiter, almost. I'll take you an' Googly back to your place, if you want. Right, Syl? Guess you can all hang onto the roadster somehow."

"What'll I do with this blue flannel jacket?" Syl wanted to know.

"Oh, leave it here," Asey said. "I—"

"Leave it here nothin'," Bingo interrupted. "By golly, where'd you find that, Syl? I thought I'd lost it for good an' all durin' the scuffle last night. That's my jacket, that is."

CHAPTER SIX

"SEE here, Bingo," Asey said, "are you sure that coat belongs to you? After all, one of them blue zipper jackets looks pretty much like another, an' think of the number there is in town!"

"This is mine all right," Bingo said, slipping into it happily. "See? Fits like the paper on the wall. Always did. Even got that tear on the elbow where I caught it on a nail over to Smalley's one day. I—"

"Wait up," Asey said as Bingo started for the door. "Hold your hosses, feller. What about what was in the pocket?"

Bingo's face lighted up as though some one had snapped on a switch.

"My pipe!" he said rapturously. "My briar pipe! Say, did you find that too? I thought it was gone for good. Best pipe I ever owned. Traded a couple of old net corks for it last summer with one of the Hammond boys—oh, why, say! was them Frost's?"

His face lengthened appreciably as Asey displayed Caleb's watch and the folder of traveler's checks and the rolls of bills.

"Frost's?" he repeated feebly. "Frost's? They are! Oh, b'Jesus! That ends it, don't it? Washes everythin' up. Might's well go give myself over to the cops right here an' now."

Asey reminded him that the police had already arrested Zeruah.

"Mr. Willing here, he said Zeruah'd confessed to it all," Bingo remarked sadly. "But look here, Asey. They'll change their minds about him after they sat down an' thought a bit. If Zeruah was drunk, he don't know no more about what happened last night than I do. An' he's a great feller for repentin'. You know yourself he's hit the sawdust trail every time an evangelist ever come within a hundred miles of here!"

Asey took off his slicker, tossed it on the floor and sat down in one of the big arm chairs.

"Yup," he admitted, "Zeruah repents ardent an' easy, but let's just kind of get this coat business thrashed out. Syl, which part of which dune'd you find the jacket on?"

"Up in the grass on the top of a dune near the bridge, 'bout two dunes away from where Frost was," Syl replied.

"Okay. Now, Bingo, can't you make a stab at rememberin' what went on last night? Can't you even remember where you left off rememberin'? Maybe some one might of been around you who was sober, an' could maybe tell just where you went an' what you done."

Bingo eased himself by degrees onto the upholstered window seat. I gathered from his pained expression that almost any muscular effort was sheer agony.

He remembered being out by the bay shore, and he recalled wading in the water. There were sharp stones there, and he'd cut the soles of his feet while going after one of the cases of liquor. But that was as far as he could manage to get. He had sampled as he brought in his loot.

"But like I said before," Bingo added earnestly, "the fellers I had my set-to with'll show just as many signs of bein' in a fight as I do. Bottle—huh! No bottle bashin' for mine while I got two good fists! An' as for Frost, why, I ain't shot a gun since they made me take target practice in the merchant m'rine durin' the war. I don't understand how them things got into my pocket any more'n I see how that ole dory of mine got over here. Look, Asey, I'll do anythin' to—say, I ain't got much money, but it's all yours if you'll find some way so's I don't get 'rested for bein' mixed up in all this!"

"Upturn," Asey observed mildly. "That's the second retainin' fee I been offered. Huh. Don't you look so upset, Bingo. I do b'lieve you. Look, before it gets too dark, s'pose you fellers go do your dune combin'. You—"

"Can I help?" Bingo asked eagerly. "Maybe I might find somethin' that'd show who put them things in my pocket. I tell you, there ain't nothin' I'd rather find than somethin' that'd show me who that feller is! An' when I find out, all I ask is to lay my hands on him—hm!"

If he found the man, I felt there wouldn't be enough of him left to shake a stick at.

"Sure," Asey said. "Tom, Mr. Ames, Miss Buckland, an' you an' Googly, you all go with Syl to the dune where Frost was found. Scatter, an' work in circles, then—"

"Ain't you comin'?" Syl demanded.

"Nope, I changed my mind. Besides, you're a heap better finder than I am, Syl. Work in a circle, then narrow it down. Then, if you got time before it's too dark, do the same 'round the boat house. Maybe you could split up into two parties. Bring in anythin' you can find that might seem to mean anythin'. An' if you find busted bottles, come back an' get me, an' treat 'em with a lot of respect."

"D'you really think," Doctor Cummings asked after they had gone, "that they'll be able to find anything?"

"It does seem sort of silly," Asey said, "to try to sift a bar this size, but I don't see any other way we can find any track of anythin' less we do. No footprints, no finger-prints, no gun. Chances is against findin' anythin', but we can hope."

"If you ask me," Deal said bitterly, "this whole business is a mess and a half. I feel terribly about Uncle Cale. But—with two people killed, I'm scared to death. Asey, you don't—don't suppose there's a maniac loose, do you? Don't you remember about that man out west, sometime last fall, who killed eight people in two days? He seemed perfectly rational and was a bank president or something."

"Bank presidents," Asey said, "are like to do anything. Eight killin's is almost normal for 'em. No, I don't think that, Deal. If some one'd wanted to do some wholesale murderin', they could of busted into this house last night an' gone to it. I think you're all safe enough now. But I'll stick around an' keep an eye out, an' I'll have Syl stay here, an' Hanson's left a man at the bridge, so I think there won't be any trouble. I—"

He broke off as a crash sounded upstairs, followed by the unmistakable sound of a shot.

Deal screamed and I sat there chattering and jittering as though some one had poured a bucket of ice cubes down my back.

Simultaneously the doctor and Asey jumped up and started for the stairs, but Deal grabbed at the doctor's sleeve.

"No you don't!" she said shrilly. "You don't leave us here alone!"

As Asey reached the hallway, Malvina Atkins appeared.

"Only Mrs. Richards," she said calmly. "She woke up, and before I knew what was going on, she knocked a vase off onto the floor, and then—"

"But the shot!" I said. "The shot!"

"The lamp bulb'd gone out, and I'd left the old one on the table. She threw that at the mirror, and they both smashed. Doctor, she's out of her head. You'd better come up."

"Can't I do something?" I asked.

"Don't think," Cummings called back. "No—"

"I'll bet," Deal said, "that she's going to have one of her bouts of malaria."

"Where'd she ever get that?" Asey wanted to know.

"Central America," Deal said. "She and father went there the year after they were married. Dad had something to do with a banana business before he went into the firm. She still gets spells of fever every so often. Oh, I'm weak! You can say all you want to about our being safe, Asey, but I knew when I heard that noise that there were half a dozen madmen upstairs!"

Privately, I agreed with her.

"And tell me," Deal continued plaintively, "where's Quin?"

"Still sleuthin', I guess," Asey answered. "He an' Hanson adopted each other, seems like. Y'know, I think some one ought to have heard Frost go out, or heard somethin'. 'Course, with the surf runnin' high, this place ain't never exactly what you'd call plum quiet, but just the samey, there was plenty of moonlight last night. Seems like some one or somethin' should of been seen by some one."

"I thought," Deal said slowly, "that I did. It was around three. My curtain was flapping, and I got out of bed to fix it. It was gorgeous then, the moon on the sand and the water and all. I thought I saw a woman, but after that drive, I could have seen a Greek chorus just as easily. I was too tired and sleepy to think. Just decided it was my imagination. There've never been prowlers around here, ever. At least, not since Caleb peppered a couple of necking parties with buckshot the first year we came here. You know what I mean, though. I thought there was some one, but at the same time, it seemed silly. I went back to bed."

"Seems hard," Asey said, "to connect a woman with this. Women ain't given to bashin' with bottles an' shootin' people through the eyeball. 'Course I s'pose there's always an exception. How far away was this lady?"

"Oh, way off. In the shadow of the outer beach dunes. But it was some one with a white dress—oh, I suppose it was my imagination. Maybe it was some man in white flannels. Perhaps I shouldn't have mentioned it at all."

"Don't see why not," Asey said, "I—oho. More cars. Prob'ly Quin comin' home. I'll go see."

But it was Malvina Atkins's sister, Nellie Carstairs, whom he let in the door. Her tall thin figure was fairly quivering with indignation.

"That policeman at the bridge," she said with a sniff, "tried to stop me! Tried to tell me I couldn't come! Wanted to know my business! It's a wonder to me they don't teach policemen how to be courteous. Asey Mayo, you've got to help me. That's what I come here for. I'll pay you anything you want, but you got to get me out of this!"

"Offer three," Asey said with a grin. "Why, Nellie? What you been doin'? How come you're mixed up in this business an' where'd you hear about it?"

"News flash over the radio," Nellie said. "Pete was listenin' to the police calls on the short wave, first, and then I heard it on the news. They said Caleb Frost'd been shot to death and a man identified as Richard Thorne of Boston was dead of a fractured skull. Then they described him on both—tall, big man, with a beard. Asey, he was my boarder!"

Asey pushed up a chair, relieved Nellie of her raincoat and tossed a log on the fire.

"Your boarder, huh?" he said. "Tell us the whole story."

"That's what I come here for. The minute I heard about all that, I said to my husband, Pete, I said, I'm going straight for Asey Mayo.—That reminds me, Mrs. Colton, Pete's got some real nice ship models he made last winter. He said you'd asked him about 'em last summer. Anyways, I said to Pete that I wasn't going to get mixed up in this! I told him I was coming straight to you, Asey, and tell you everything so's you could get us both out of all this mess!"

"Why not to the police?" Asey asked. "After all, Nellie, I ain't nothin'—"

"Fiddlesticks," said Nellie briefly. "Fiddlesticks. Mrs. Colton, last fall my chickens begun to go. Just seemed like they melted into thin air, three or four a night. I went to Jim Williams, and he didn't do anything, and then I went to the state police. They begun to fuss around, asking all the neighbors questions and getting them mad with me! Why, Lucy Hopkins hasn't spoken two words to me since! And did they find out what was making those chickens go? They did not! And then I called Asey in."

"And did Habakkuk solve it?" I asked interestedly.

"Who? You mean Asey? Solve it? He came up and shot four skunks, and I haven't had a bit of trouble since! Police—bah! But about this bearded man, Asey? Did he have on blue dungarees and a blue sweater—and no little finger on his right hand? Then there's no doubt about it. He went off last night around eight, and he hasn't been home since. I thought he'd probably got mixed up in that disgraceful brawl, but then when the radio said—"

"What did he call himself?" Asey asked.

"You let me begin at the beginning," Nellie said firmly, "and tell you the whole story. I often thought I might pick up a few dollars renting rooms, but it didn't seem like we'd ever get many folks, being so far off the main road. Just the same, when the good weather came, I had Pete paint a sign, 'Rooms and Bath,' and put it in the front yard. We had three or four nice parties of folks stop in, and one night about a week ago, this man came on a bicycle. I didn't like his looks to begin with, Asey. That beard was against him. But he talked well enough, and he seemed nice enough otherwise. So we gave him the front bedroom—he paid in advance. Next morning, he said he'd like to stay awhile, so Pete and I thought it over and told him yes. He used to go off on his bike a lot, and he walked around a lot, but he hardly ever went to town. He told *us* his name was Richard Smith."

"Did he tell you what he did, or anythin' like that?" Asey asked.

"I asked him, after he'd been there a couple of days," Nellie said. "He told *me* he wrote. Was an author. Of course, I told him all about Quin Gunner and his mystery stories, having known Quin—why, since he was born! He said *he* wrote mystery stories, too, and that he wrote under the name of Varney Cheyne. Well, Pete isn't what you'd call such a hand for reading, and neither am I, though I do read Quin's books when they come to the library. I always say—"

"Told you he was Varney Cheyne, did he?"

"He did. Next time I went to the library, I asked Sarah if she'd ever heard of Varney Cheyne. Well, she showed me all the Cheyne books and told me all about him, how he was a millionaire, but unknown and all that, and—why, I was surprised as I could be. Then," Nellie smiled knowingly, "then, I began to think. It come to me that this Smith was perfectly safe in saying he was Cheyne, because nobody knew who Cheyne was. But *I* knew this Smith wasn't any millionaire, for he wouldn't be riding around on bicycles, dressed the way *he* was, if he was. He was just trying to be funny. Probably thought he'd get Pete and me all excited. So I just never said a word about it, to Pete or Sarah or any one else."

Asey smiled. "Sort of hoist with his own p'tard, he was—go on, Nellie."

"Well, he'd told Pete, but Pete doesn't know one writer from another, except Quin. And he always said, he never quite felt the same towards Quin after he started writing books—a good husky boy like him, who could have been an engineer or—or anything. Not," she added hurriedly, catching the brief smile which flickered over Deal's face, "not that he's not just as nice as he ever was, of course, but you know!"

"Did this feller have any baggage?" Asey asked while Nellie paused for breath.

"Not what you'd call baggage. Just a sort of knapsack, that he strapped on his wheel. But—well, maybe this wasn't the right thing to do, but when I heard that over the radio, I went right straight upstairs and looked

through that pack, to see if I couldn't see something. Why
—there he was, killed, and we'd harbored him for a
week! What would people say?"

"I see," Asey said gravely. "An' was there anythin'
in the pack?"

"Just a few dirty clothes and some clean ones, and
some money—about a hundred dollars. And two letters."

Asey got up and reached for his overcoat. "I guess,"
he said, "we'll run over to your place and get 'em."

"No need," Nellie said casually, "I brought 'em with
me. Here. Funny things, both of 'em. One's a copy of a
typewritten letter, and the other's—well, you just look
at them for yourself."

Deal and I rudely stared over Asey's shoulder as he
read through the two papers. The carbon obviously was
a copy of a letter Dick Thorne had written Caleb Frost.
There was no heading, but it began, "Dear Cale." It
wasn't more than three or four lines, suggesting that the
writer thought that if Cale had always believed him innocent, a monetary settlement was in order.

"Perhaps some division of the most recent Cheyne
mystery royalties. Otherwise, I can almost faithfully promise to be of considerable annoyance."

It was blackmail, of course. But I couldn't feel, as I
read those lines, that Dick Thorne was asking for any
more than was rightfully due him. Apparently, as Asey
had suggested, Caleb Frost had succeeded in persuading
Dick to run away, probably had even promised him that
the whole matter would be ironed out. And in the light
of what had actually happened, it occurred to me that I

should not, in Dick's place, write polite letters. I think I should have set out with a machine gun, several bombs and possibly a large quantity of nitroglycerin.

"He spotted Caleb," Asey said, "from the book and, by gum, I don't blame him for this. I'd have wrung Frost's neck. Let's see the other. Pity he didn't date this."

The other paper was a note from Caleb Frost, in his small precise handwriting, stating that he would meet Dick on Sandbar "since you are down on the Cape," on Saturday night, around one. Under the circumstances, Caleb thought it would be better if they were to meet outside the house, near the Sandbar bridge.

"That's why he changed his sailing at the last minute!" I said. "He pretended it was the weather because he knew we all knew he was a bad sailor! He intended to meet Dick—and that accounts for the roll of bills, though I don't see that the traveler's checks would have done him any good."

"P'raps," Asey suggested, "he mistook them for his ord'nary check book. No envelope on that note, Nellie?"

"No," she said. "There weren't any envelopes at all. I wish you'd tell me about this, Asey! I certainly think that I deserve to know all there is—"

"Just you hang on for a couple minutes more," Asey promised her, "an' you'll know all. Well, chances is that Thorne got the letter while he was down here on the Cape. Frost didn't date his, but Saturday night bein' last night, seems like it must of been sent this week. Thorne could of had it sent to any post office within reasn'ble distance, since he had his bike, or even to East Pochet.

Anyway, we're gettin' a little warmer. We know for certain who Cheyne was, how Thorne found him out, why Frost went out, an' why he took all that cash with him, what Thorne was doin' here, an' that he *was* Thorne. Clears it up a little. Tell you now, Nellie, all about it."

Nellie's eyes bulged as Asey related the Frost-Cheyne-Thorne story for her benefit.

"I always knew," she said triumphantly when he concluded, "that Caleb Frost was a man with a Secret—and a Past. He was always darting little looks about, just like he expected some one to pop up behind him and holler 'Boo!' "

As a matter of fact, Caleb did have a nervous habit of looking around, but somehow I'd never thought it was anything more than a habit. Perhaps it had been.

"Just think," Nellie went on, "ever since he sent that poor Thorne man away, he's gone around wondering—my goodness gracious! Why, it's like a movie, isn't it? Won't Quin Gunner have a time, writing this up? As I said to Pete, here's one time Quin'll have a story all told for him, with nothing to do but write it!"

"Quin," Asey said, "has already solved the whole business with Hanson. You knew about their takin' Zeruah Nims, an' his confessin' to everythin'?"

Nellie expressed herself forcibly on the thought of Zeruah Nims, a perfectly good man even if he wasn't what you'd call solid as a pillar, being arrested for anything like murder.

"He hasn't the gumption," she wound up conclusively. "Just hasn't the gumption. And if you ask me, it was all done by that man that come to see Cheyne—Thorne—or Smith, or whoever he was—on Tuesday. He was a nice—"

"What man?" Deal and Asey and I yelled as one. "What man? Who?"

"Why," Nellie said in some surprise, "didn't I tell you about that young man? He came Tuesday, in a car with a New York license. He knocked at the front door first, so I knew he wasn't a salesman, and then he came around and knocked at the kitchen door. I hadn't intended to go, but I did. He took off his hat and wished me a good morning, and asked if Mr. Smith was in. Well, he was down to the shore with Pete, but I got my whistle out and blew, and Pete came up, and I sent him back for Smith. I asked the young man if he was a friend of Mr. Smith's, and he said, he wasn't exactly, but he was there to see him about some business matters. Then he said how good the kitchen smelled, like his aunt's in Maine, and I gave him a piece of sugar gingerbread, and—"

"Look," Asey said, "look—you make awful good sugar gingerbread, but—what'd the feller look like? Would you know him again?"

"Why, I guess I certainly would," Nellie said. "He was young, around thirty, I guess, and he was just as nice and polite a man as you'd want to see. Brown hair—"

"How tall was he?" Asey demanded. "How much'd he weigh? What color eyes did he have? Did he tell you his name?"

"Why, he didn't tell me his name, though I kind of

hinted around. As for his height and weight—why, Asey Mayo, I don't take yardsticks and scales to every man that comes to my house! He was taller than—well, Quin. And he had broad shoulders and a nice face. As I said to Pete later, he was just as good looking as that man in the new tooth paste ads, every bit."

I leaned back in my chair. That had been my first impression of Tom Willing.

"Oh," Nellie added as an afterthought. "Pete looked at the car. There were initials on the door. T. W., he said."

CHAPTER SEVEN

"TOM!" Deal and I said it together. "Tom Willing!"
Asey lighted his pipe. "What," he asked Deal,
"what about Tom, anyways?"

"Yes," I said, "what about Tom? Who is he? What
does he do? I've never heard him mentioned before he
turned up here yesterday afternoon. And you never said
a word about him in your telegram."

Deal sighed. "Oh, I wish that wretch Quin were
here! This is all his fault. I told him it was—well, it still
is pretty silly, for that matter. You see, a week ago, Quin's
college class had some sort of reunion dinner in New
York, and—"

"Information," Asey suggested. "Not social notes."

"Information's just what you're getting. That was
how this happened. He saw Tom for the first time in
years and years—"

"Wait a minute," Nellie interrupted eagerly. "You
mean, you know that nice young man?"

"We do," Asey said, "an' I'd like you to stay here a
while an' make sure it's the same feller. I'll catch you up
on him an' what he's got to do with it all later on—come

to think of it, I guess you're as caught up on him now as the rest of us are. Go on, Deal."

"Well, Quin saw Tom at this dinner for the first time in years. Quin wasn't and isn't very rah-rah, and I think it's the first of those folksy gatherings he'd gone to for a long while. He mentioned to me a day or so later that he'd seen old Tom Willing, and that was the end of it. I'd known Tom slightly, you see, when Quin was in school. Then, yesterday morning, when Quin and I were setting out from the curb in front of my apartment, up dashed Tom, all dressed for traveling, and gripping an enormous bag. 'Just in time,' says he, and Quin and I stared and said, 'Just in time for what?'"

"Int'restin'," Asey said.

"We thought so. Well, he was so serious that Quin went very tactfully about the business of finding out just what was going on. Tom said cheerily that Quin certainly hadn't forgotten inviting him up to his shack in Connecticut for the weekend of the fourth, had he? Because he said that Quin had done just that at this dinner. Tom'd gone to Quin's club and found out that he was coming over after me, taken a cab and dashed after us. And that, so to speak, was that."

"But had Quin asked him?"

"Well," Deal said grimly, "you know what college dinners are likely to be. Quin looked dazed and then said for Tom to stick his baggage in the rumble and crawl in. And that's every bit I know about it. I have an idea that if Quin asked him, he'd forgotten all about it. And I also am inclined to think that Quin didn't ask him at all, but wasn't quite sure enough about what went on that night to up and say so. After all, Tom's such a darn nice sort. You wouldn't suspect him of dribbling about and cadging invitations like that. So we explained a little lamely that we were bound for the Cape, and he said he liked the Cape better than Connecticut anyway, and well —there you are. That's the story of how Tom came to Cape Cod, or Forging Ahead in the World."

"What'd Quin have to say on the matter?" I demanded. "Didn't he tell you all about it?"

"He didn't have the chance then, with Tom there. And just as he broached the subject after we got here, Caleb came with Ford, and Tom had to shunt himself in with Quin. Then there was dinner. Then we all sat around together and gabbled and played bridge and listened to Caleb and the radio, and then we went to bed. Oh, Quin and I did make one final, spasmodic effort to get together on the subject of Tom, but then Janey came. And I've hardly set eyes on Quin to-day."

"What's Tom do?" Asey asked.

"I haven't the remotest idea. Quin jabbers so that no one ever has a chance to unburden any life history while he's around. They talked about books. Maybe Tom writes, but I don't think so. I don't know what he does do. Why don't you call him in and give him the third degree, Asey? I'd really enjoy having that business of yesterday morning straightened out."

"Maybe," Asey agreed, "we better had."

"You better had," I said, "but first of all, I'm going to get something to eat. I'm starved, and I should think those clew-seekers out on the dune would not only be wet as fishes but ravenous as so many rampling lions."

Asey got up and peered through the window.

"Flashlights hiccuping down by the boat house," he reported. "You don't know Syl. He's a first cousin to fly-paper, that man. An' Bingo's bound an' d'termined to find out who got hold of his coat. Offhand, I'd say them three didn't have a chance of gettin' out of their siftin' process, with Syl an' Bingo wieldin' the whips. Come to think of it, I could do with a little sust'nance. Let's see what Greg'ry keeps in his ice box."

"I can tell you for a fact," I said, "that it's full. I had the supervising of the provisions thrust on me and I provided lavishly."

It almost shocked me to find Deal blushing.

"You know, Pen," she said, "I—I'm awf'ly sorry I was so fresh yesterday. When we came. I mean, ordering you about, and all. And when I saw mother do it—make you work, and housekeep—oh, hell! You know! If it does any good now, I'm sorry."

"That's quite all right," I told her, faintly puzzled by what was, for her, a handsome apology. "But what's caused this change of heart? Ever since—since lunch, you seem to have undergone a softening process, if you don't mind my saying so."

Deal became a little redder. "Oh, seeing Janey step in, and you—both of you looking after mother. And Cale —I suppose I'm ashamed of myself. Honest, Pen, I promise to be a better girl. Let's go eat. Gregory's probably still holding Mathilde's hand. Come on, Nellie, help us grub."

Nellie accepted the invitation with alacrity.

"I always," she confided, "wanted to see the kitchen of this house. My, just like something out of the women's magazines, isn't it? All aluminum and shiny. Pete helped put in the sink, and the set tubs, and he told me all about 'em. I'm saving my egg money for a new sink, because Pete thinks he can get it wholesale and put it in himself."

I started to get out the sandwiches left over from the ill-fated fishing luncheon, but Deal waved me to a seat.

"Let me do the work for a change," she said. "Just repentant all the way through, that's what. How about some scrambled eggs? I am probably one of the best egg scramblers of my generation!"

"While you're scrambling," I said, "see if you can't locate those two tubes of salve I bought Gregory. I can't understand how they could have disappeared. Why a bit of ointment should rankle so, I can't understand, but it does bother me. Asey, isn't it possible the murderer stole the salve?"

"Judgin' from what you folks in this house don't know about what happened around you last night," he answered, "I'd say he or them might of come in an' moved out the grand piano without disturbin' you."

After I'd had something to eat, I found that I was too tired to keep my eyes open.

"Much as it hurts me," I said with a yawn, "to miss one syllable of what goes on, I'm going to bed. If I don't, Sandbar will produce another corpse. How's Lizzie, doctor?"

Doctor Cummings sat down on one of the living room easy chairs.

"Not so good. I'm going to stay here to-night. Are you bound for bed? Best place in the world for you. No, Lizzie's in bad shape. Can't understand it. Must have been the shock—still, she doesn't know any more than that Caleb's not here. Going out, Asey?"

"Goin' to c'lect my searchin' party an' tear 'em away from Syl b'fore they drop in their tracks. An' I want Tom. 'Night, Mrs. Colton. Nellie, d'you mind stayin' a spell? You an' Deal can improve the shinin' hours by tellin' the doc everythin'."

If I had been tired Saturday night after working like a pack horse, I was utterly exhausted Sunday night.

"Just," I reminded myself of Lizzie's words, "just a nice quiet rest, you and me—"

Monday morning was bright and clear, though the east wind was still blowing a gale. I went down to breakfast around eight o'clock and found Asey at the table, alone.

"I'll tell you," he said with a grin, stopping my question about Tom in mid air. "You tackle your grape-fruit—I'm happy to say Greg'ry an' Mathilde's back to normal. Well, Nellie recognized him, all right. Tom sort of hemmed an' hawed, an' finally he told me the whole story. It's true, too, because I called three men in New York out of bed early this mornin' an' checked up on it. Seems he's the scout for Cheyne-alias-Frost's publishers."

"Whaaat?"

"Just so. A lot of folks realized how simple it would

be to say that they was Cheyne, an' the publishers decided it wasn't so hot all around; they was thinkin' of
the money. Cheyne couldn't expose any impostors or
make any fuss without exposin' himself. But it occurred
to the publishers that it might be a nice thing if they
found out who Cheyne was, in a nice quiet way, an'
then they'd know where they stood. Seems Tom was
picked for the job, 'cause he'd once done some special
agentin' for the d'partment of justice. He begun a year
ago by lookin' up ev'ry tip an' clew an' crank letter, an'
exposin' letter an' all that the publishers got. N'en he
tried Ford's stunt of perchin' 'round one of them gen'ral
deliv'ry boxes. He bribed some one in Ford's office to get
the addresses for him."

"Why didn't he just ask Ford?"

"Because they wasn't at all sure that Ford didn't
know all. An' besides, they could get what they wanted
without lettin' him in on it. Well, seems he seen Frost
get some letters, but Frost got onto the fact that he was
trailin' him, an' doubled back an' forth on his trail so
much that he shook Tom off. Just like a movie. But Tom
knew what Cheyne looked like, anyways. An'—now,
this is kind of funny. At that dinner Deal was talkin'
about, Quin showed Tom a snapshot of Deal, taken
down here at the bar. In fact, he showed half a dozen
snapshots of the place, taken last fall. Frost was in one
of 'em. Tom says he nearly jumped out of his shoes when
he recognized the man, but he managed to carry it off
without Quin knowin'. Next mornin' at his office, was a
letter to the publishers from one R. Smith of Province-

town, suggestin' that if they wanted to know who Cheyne was, they might consult him."

"Thorne!" I said. "But—in Provincetown?"

"Just so. Tom thought 'Sandbar-Provincetown-Cape Cod,' jumped into his car, an' drove over from New York at top speed, an' made for the place R. Smith named. But R. Smith was gone. One of the boarders there said he'd rec'mended Nellie's place as bein' nice an' out of the way an' cheap, so Tom ambled up to East Pochet, drove all over Robin Hood's barn on back roads till it come night, huntin' for Nellie's, then come back Tuesday an' hunted some more. You know what went on at Nellie's. He met Thorne, but Thorne denied havin' written the letter, an' said there was any number of Richard Smiths rovin' 'round. Said it was all a mistake. He didn't quite convince Tom, but there you are."

"I think I see," I said. "Between the time Dick wrote the publishers, he'd got that answer from Caleb, and decided to see what could be done about getting money from Caleb first. Besides, he had the wedge of having written to the publishers about Caleb, and could follow it up if Cale didn't crash through."

"Seems likely. Anyway, Tom went back to New York, after findin' out in East Pochet that Frost was spendin' the summer abroad. Then, Friday, he had lunch with a friend who's a crony of Quin's, an' he found out that Quin was goin' down to Sandbar for the week-end, an' he decided he'd like to horn in. It would give him a chance for another crack at the bearded Mr. Smith, an' he could maybe check up on Frost a bit. Y'see, he'd tried to locate Frost in New York, but he couldn't. An' he couldn't find his name in any of the sailin' lists. Quin was out of town somewheres, turned out he was in Jersey, but none of his friends at the club was very clear about it. Tom'd come to the c'nclusion that he'd better make sure about Frost bein' Cheyne before grabbin' a steamer an' hikin' to England after him. Like he said, after you'd thought twenty or thirty fellers *was* Cheyne, you went slow. So he horned in on Quin an' Deal, just as she said. Seemed ashamed of it, but I kind of gathered that findin' Cheyne'd got to be a part of him, like a third leg or a stomach ache."

"Did Frost recognize him?"

"He's not sure. Doesn't think so. Didn't show it when he was introduced to him Sat'day night, anyway."

"But why didn't Tom speak up when you told about the bearded stranger in the boat house? Why didn't he tell us all this? It seems queer."

"Does." Asey nodded. "I can't see why he didn't take Ford or Quin into his confidence long ago. He said the publishers thought all that business of the checks bein' sent around was childish an' silly, but it 'pears to me that for an ex-department of justice man, Tom did a lot of childish an' sillier things himself."

Deal and Jane came in to breakfast together.

"Mother's better," Deal reported. "At least, her fever's down, and she's sleeping. Glorious day, isn't it? Any news from my attentive and devoted swain, the old skunk?"

"D'you mean to say Quin's not back?" I asked.

"He phoned last night," Deal deftly speared her grapefruit cherry, "to tell me in his best manner that he'd be back some time. He added, sotto voce, that it was all fine work on the part of the police, but that it never would have happened in any book of his—having Zeruah guilty. He said," she waited until Gregory left the room, "he said it was like having the butler guilty, or some entirely unconnected person dragged in at the last minute. Didn't seem to think it was fair one bit. But he was having a grand time with some ballistics expert. Some day I'm going to take time off and find out just exactly what ballistics is, or are."

"It sounds," Jane said, "like a girdle. 'Our new featherweight ballistics, which take you in where you need to be took.' My, I feel bright and cheery this morning. Seeing the sun again, I guess, has been too much, because God knows I found two hundred and ninety-one new muscles while duning. When my book man gives me the gate, I'm going to start a reducing school down here. Just take and let the victims hunt clews all day in the sand. Treasure hunt theory. End of a month, you could push 'em through a keyhole."

I asked if they had found anything of importance the night before.

"Just a miscellany. Syl thinks he's found the place where Thorne was killed—lots of smashed bottles at the foot of a little rise near the boat house, but Deal says it's the remains of an old rubbish heap. We picked up tin cans and lots of bones—birds and fish. Perfectly horrid! And that pop-eyed relative of Bingo's just escaped meeting a skunk. Asey hasn't seen all the collection yet—part of it we left near the dune, and the rest is in the boat house. We were worn out."

Tom wandered in, looking very pale. In contrast to the girls, who all but babbled, he said not a word during breakfast, but Ford seemed to have been imbued with some of their high spirits.

"I feel," Ford remarked, "rather the way I used to when they gave me boys-in-a-motor-boat-going-upstream-at - four - miles - an - hour - against - a - current - of - one - and-three-eighths—remember those old tortures they called arithmetic? And was I ever stiff! Asey, what's to be done about all this?"

Almost as if in answer to his question, Quin came bursting in with Hanson. Both of them looked very downcast.

"I," Quin announced, "am speaking for old Honest John here. He's too sunk to speak for himself. We're groveling, we're cringing, and our heads are trailing on the ground in sheer shame. If you wore a dress, we'd kiss the hem, wouldn't we, Jack?"

"We would," Hanson said. "Asey, I was all wrong and you were right. I should have known you were trying to tell me, but I was too puffed up—it wasn't Zeruah Nims, no matter what he says."

"Did you find out about his arm?" Asey asked.

"Partly. But Forman's been playing around with that .22 Colt of Zeruah's, the one that had one shot fired. Forman says that, sometime, Zeruah cleaned the barrel with something that left a deep scratch. All the bullets he fired out of that gun had a mark on 'em you couldn't miss. And there wasn't any such mark on the bullet that killed Frost. No question of a doubt about it. Asey, will you help? They're going to hold Zeruah a bit longer till they see if they can check up on him; besides, the papers have his confession, and they don't want to take a beating right off. They're going to keep quiet about Forman's discovery for a day, longer if they can. They told me to come and ask you if you wouldn't help."

Asey considered. "You got plenty of experts, Hanson, an' you got a couple of detectives that's whizzes. They know everythin', an' they work the way they ought to, an'—well, it's all right for you to ask me, an' I 'preciate the honor an' all, but this is a job for them fellers."

"Malloy," Hanson said, "is sick. Jackson's busy in the western part of the state, Graham's after some bomb-throwers bothering the mills—look, the boss said he'd send you all the men you want, and the whole works is ready for you to call on. He said this seemed to him one of the places where common sense was needed, and there wasn't any one he could think of that had as much common sense as you. He says for you to pull out your old badge and shine it up, and for God's sake to help us, at least till he can get hold of some one else. He's busy testifying in some mess—look, how about it?"

"Huh," Asey said. "Well, I'll do what I can, Hanson, but it's a problem. We tried combin' that dune, but we didn't get nowheres. Somewhere, prob'ly, there's that cartridge case. An' there must be a smashed bottle. An'—well, there must be somethin' somewhere. Set your fellers to work huntin'. That's all I can think of right now. An' after you've told them what to do, come back an' I'll tell you what I scraped out of this so far. Whole thing r'minds me of a hungry pup an' a plate of scraps. We're lickin' grease spots now."

"Where's the doctor?" I asked after Hanson left.

"He lit out early. Comin' back later on. He an' Malvina had a night, I guess. I r'lieved 'em once. Sent up Miss Atkins's breakfast, Greg'ry?"

"An hour ago, sir. And, Mrs. Colton," Gregory added, "we haven't been able to find those tubes of salve, either, though we've hunted through all the—er—refuse, to see if they were thrown away by accident. Mathilde thinks some one stole them."

"That's all right," I said. "Forget about it. Oh—good morning, Malvina."

"I'm worried again about Mrs. Richards," she said. "She's waked up and she seems all right, but I sort of feel she must know about Mr. Frost. She keeps saying 'Poor Caleb, poor Caleb' over and over, and she wants to see you, Asey. She asked if you were here, and I said yes, and she said she had to see you right away."

Asey got up and pushed back his chair.

"I'll go right up," he said. "Can Mrs. Colton come along, or would that be too much?"

"She wanted to see her, too."

On the way upstairs, Asey stopped and frowned.

"You know what's been stickin' in my mind? 'Member yest'day just before Mrs. Richards went hay-wire, she said somethin' about 'Caleb—that girl'?"

I remembered it, even though I'd tried to forget.

"An' Deal," he went on. "She ain't been actin' natural. Not even if she did 'pologize to you. She's actin' to me like some one with an awful guilty conscience, in kind of the way a child might. Bright an' nervous, an' chattin' a blue streak, like she was tryin' to keep off somethin' in p'ticular."

I knew just exactly what he meant. "Jane was looking at her curiously, too, this morning," I said. "But don't you suppose it's just the reaction? Deal and Lizzie and Ford, after all—and Quin—probably feel more about this than the rest of us. Deal's young, and she's never had anything quite so horrible to face before. I don't think it's any more than that. Besides, Lizzie wasn't really what you could call normal when she spoke those few incoherent words; perhaps she was thinking about Deal, and hoping that she wouldn't be involved in any trouble."

Asey pointed out that Lizzie only knew that Caleb was not in his room and had not spent the night there. "For all she knew, he might of been in his study, workin'. Fallen asleep there. Deal an' her uncle didn't get along, did they?"

"N—yes," I said.

"I didn't think they did," Asey said blandly, and knocked on Lizzie's door.

Lizzie looked better than I expected her to, except that her color was unusually high and she was breathing heavily.

"I want you to tell me the truth," she said without

any preamble. "Caleb's dead, isn't he? Was he—did some one kill him?"

"Well," Asey said, "well, yes. But—"

"That's all I wanted to know," Lizzie said resignedly. "All. Asey, I sent for you because I want to know your fee."

"My—my what?"

"Your fee," she repeated, drumming impatiently on the pillow with her fingers. "How much you charge for —for acting as a detective."

"I'm 'fraid," Asey said, "you got me all wrong. I— but why d'you want to hire me, Mrs. Richards? What is there that's troublin' you?"

"I—I want," Lizzie's voice choked, "I want you to save my darling girl. Deal. She's only a baby, really, for all that she tries to be so sophis—"

"Save her from what?" I asked.

"Why, from being arrested for killing Caleb, of—of course! She said she was going to."

CHAPTER EIGHT

"BUT Lizzie!" I said, "why—when did Deal ever threaten him? You can't—it's preposterous to think that she might have been in earnest!"

"She was," Lizzie said. "I know. I'll tell you all about it."

It began, apparently, shortly after Caleb Frost arrived at Sandbar Saturday evening. He was enraged to find so many guests, and I understood, though Lizzie did not say so directly, that my presence had irritated him as much as the presence of Deal's friends. He went to Lizzie and complained in full.

"He said," Lizzie went on nervously, "that all of you would have to leave at once. And then he noticed that I had a new dress on, and that made him angry, too. He said that the minute his back was turned, I began to spend money like a drunken sailor! I said I couldn't turn people out in any careless genteel fashion such as he suggested, and that Deal and her friends were here and had to stay, and that there was another coming—oh, Caleb was—he was really very angry indeed!"

I needed no blueprints to grasp just exactly how unpleasant Caleb had been.

"Did he see the light of reason?" Asey inquired dryly.

"He said that every one would have to leave Sunday morning at the latest. And I—well, I just told him that he could turn our guests out himself, if he wanted to, but I wouldn't say a word. He said he'd make it so—so unpleasant for them that it would be a relief for them to think up excuses for leaving. Then, after Jane came, Caleb called Deal up to his study and went through the whole thing again. I didn't mean to listen, but I couldn't help hearing every word they said, at first."

"Was he always like that to all your comp'ny?" Asey wanted to know, "or was this somethin' unusual?"

"He'd made comments before, but he'd never absolutely ordered my guests out of the house!"

It occurred to me that possibly Caleb must have recognized Tom, and of course he knew that I knew Dick Thorne. Those were probably the answers to his highhandedness.

"Deal told him," Lizzie continued, dabbing at her eyes with a damp handkerchief, "that he'd given this place over to me, and there was no earthly reason why she and I shouldn't have whom we chose to stay with us. If Caleb wanted peace and quiet, she said, he could just have stayed away and got it somewhere else."

"Good for her," Asey said approvingly. "On the face of it, I'd say Mr. Frost's notion was kind of like the feller that used to send his girl expensive boxes of choc'lates an' then follow the gift up by eatin' all the bonbons off the top."

Deal, according to Lizzie, had made a similar suggestion. She added that she was damned if she'd tell her guests they had to leave, although if he wanted to make a scene and throw them out on their ears, he was welcome to do just that. Caleb had retorted by announcing that he would make her and Lizzie sorry for their ungrateful behavior, and that the guests would be even sorrier.

"It was then," Lizzie said, "that Deal threatened him. She said, 'If it's any consolation to you, uncle, let me say that I'd start a fund with the sole purpose of killing you, if I thought I could get away with it. And I've no doubts that it would be a unanimous subscription.'"

That had frightened Lizzie, for she knew by the sound of Deal's voice that the girl was angry, through and through. Like her father, Deal gets calm and frigid when she's really enraged. She started to go into the study to see if she couldn't pour oil on the troubled waters, but she lacked the courage to face Caleb again. So, characteristically, Lizzie covered her ears and buried her head in the pillows.

"And it was just the way I felt, too," Lizzie wound up, "the way Deal sounded. I—I've often wanted to tell Caleb that I understood what made people on the dole so very bitter!"

"I don't hardly blame you a bit," Asey said soothingly. "Now, don't you worry about this, Mrs. Richards. I'll go have a talk with Deal an' see if I can't get this thing settled up. Just you trust me. I don't think Deal was serious about it one bit. Don't you worry any more."

Lizzie sighed. "All right. I—oh, it's probably wicked to say so, but I've prayed for years that something would happen so that all of us wouldn't be under Caleb's thumb. I—I feel responsible—but I never prayed for anything as horrible as this!"

I thought of the woman who'd prayed for a Chinaman to die because her laundryman had spoiled a tablecloth, and then felt herself personally responsible when the Dowager Empress died the next day. And it was also on the tip of my tongue to say that Caleb Frost was just the type to make people just as unhappy and wretched by his death as he'd succeeded in doing while he was alive, but I managed to hold back both comments until Asey and I got downstairs.

"'If our own kin an' kith,'" he quoted, "'was more fun to be with.' Huh. Prob'ly all that fuss was on account of you knowin' Thorne, an' Tom bein' familiar as the one that trailed him. If Frost'd taken so many pains to hide his bein' Cheyne, I bet he knew Tom. Y'know, I been wonderin' why Tom didn't carry a cam'ra, just in case; I bet a nickel Frost did. But it does seem like Frost was kind of masterful 'bout his d'pendents, don't it? Say, where's Mrs. Richards' sons?"

"Ned's in France," I said. "Paris, I think. Bud's in the Maine woods. Miles away from everything with a guide and some friends. They should be told, shouldn't they? I'll get their addresses from Lizzie—will you send the wires? The boys know you, and it will probably reassure them to think you're helping out."

While Asey sent the telegrams, I went out on the east terrace where Deal and Tom were tossing little feathered darts at one of those boards on which playing cards have been pasted.

"Dart poker," Deal said, stabbing viciously. "Want to play? No? Jane's gone. Insisted on going to join the dune combers with Quin. Says it's the liveliest exercise. And Ford threw one dart and almost capsized. He took all the rubbing alcohol he could find and retired to his room. He aches, he says. Oh—Asey. Bet you I can beat you at this. And d'you suppose it would be too indelicate to set up the targets?"

"What targets?" Asey said, deftly spearing three kings and two aces with his handful of darts.

"Oh—expert, are you? I mean the targets we used to float out in the harbor till Tim Smalley and the other lobstermen kicked up a row. Said they'd be shot. Though as a matter of record, we never potted at them while they were around, or any boats, at all."

"You mean, shootin'?" Asey asked. "Come to think of it, you used to go duck huntin' with your father when you was a little tyke, didn't you?"

Deal laughed. "My gun was bigger than I was. Yes. We've a couple of old .22's that the boys and I shoot with —oh, I'd forgotten that it was a .22 that shot Caleb! Oh—that—I shouldn't have said that! Asey, forget about it!"

"No," Asey returned, "I was just on the point of doin' a little fancy third degreein' on you, anyways. We'll take a walk to the outside beach an' back. Tom, you hold the fort an' listen for the phone. They may call up from the station."

We strolled along to the dunes in silence.

"I know what you want, of course," Deal remarked at last. "Mother heard what Caleb and I had to say to each other, didn't she? Well, it's all true. Did she hear every bit?"

"Up to where," Asey brushed off a weatherbeaten bench and motioned for me to sit down, "where you decided the Frost Murder Fund would have a lot of subscribers."

Deal shivered as she curled up on the sand.

"Sounds awful now, doesn't it? That's really what made me so repentant yesterday, Pen. Usually Cale and I managed to smooth over all our differences of opinion eventually, but it dawned on me yesterday that—well, that this one would never be settled. You know. Anyway, after I made that crack about the murder fund, Caleb said I'd find it was rather serious business to make threats like that. I agreed, but I added that if he bullied mother or me any more, I'd have Quin spank him soundly, all eight ounces of him. It always infuriated him to have his size referred to. You may never have noticed it, Pen, but he always wore specially made shoes with awf'ly high heels for a man, just to make himself seem a bit taller. He whaled Ned for wise-cracking about them years ago, and he cut off Bud's allowance for six months his last year in school for just insinuating about them. Anyway, I left while the honor was mine—didn't give him time to think up any answer."

"And did you tell Quin?"

Deal shook her head and pulled a cigarette out of her case.

"I've hardly laid eyes on that lad since we got here. I really started to go weep on his shoulder Saturday night—I was crying mad by that time, but then I remembered Tom was with him, so I didn't. That's the whole story. Except, of course, that I'm an awf'ly good shot. Gives you a peach of a motive for me, Asey. In fact, it's a swell and sterling general family motive. Dad taught mother how to shoot years ago. She's better than I am. And we've all cussed Caleb for years. That is, the boys and I have. I think mother must have too, though I've never heard her say a word against him, and she's had the roughest time, too. She got the aftermath of all our spells of trouble, and she had to be around Cale more than we did. We chose schools just as far from home as we could. And afterwards, we all just cut and beat it."

She picked out a handful of tiny pebbles from the coarse sand and shied them expertly at the points of her white suède pumps.

"Look," she said after a few minutes, "how far have you got this doped out, Asey? I mean, how did it all happen? It's all so muddled in my mind."

"It ain't exactly what you'd call crystal clear in mine," Asey told her with a grin. "Near as I can make out, your uncle was the great Varney Cheyne. Thorne found it out, recognized the story of himself, decided to do a little blackmailin', an' Frost agreed to see him Sat'day night here on the bar, at one. In the meantime, Tom'd been workin' on the Cheyne business an' had a pretty good idea who Cheyne was. Well, far's we know, Frost went out to meet Thorne Sat'day night. Somehow I don't think he ever did meet him, 'cause whoever found the watch an' bills that was taken from Frost's pockets, prob'ly found 'em together. If Frost'd met Thorne an' give him the money, chances is the money an' watch wouldn't of been together. But that's a moot question. Anyways, Bingo was wanderin' around the dune. There's his boat an' his coat, though some one else might of brought over the dory, an' he might of lost his coat durin' the evenin' scuffle, an' some one else might of brought it here. 'Parently Zeruah was here. Prob'ly there was others, includin' the person in white you thought you seen. But the bullet that killed Frost wasn't fired from Zeruah's gun. Which r'minds me, when we go back to the house, you'd better roust out them .22's of yours an' give 'em over to Hanson for Forman to play with."

Deal nodded. "I will, though I don't even know where they are, Asey. Most likely up in the attic. It is sort of a muddle, isn't it? All our family has such lovely motives, and Tom isn't exactly out of it. His story seems awf'ly silly to me, but it's no sillier than Ford's side. And Bingo—oh, it just seems to go round in circles. Thank God, Quin's out of it. He never had any quarrel with Cale in all his life, and Jane never met Cale till Saturday night, and saw him then only for a few minutes. At least, they're out of it. And you, Pen, and Ford."

"Thank you," I said, "for the afterthought. I can

assure you that I never fired a gun in all my life, and it's not my habit to go around bashing men I've thought dead for fifteen years over the head with bottles. But what about Ford? Asey, if he was Frost's agent, he should have known all about the Cheyne business. Particularly when he knew Caleb so well! Probably both he and the publishers were coining money from Cheyne and so were willing to put up with such utterly foolish methods—but I still think they were all silly idiots."

"Janey and I were talking about Ford this morning," Deal said. "Her room's next to his, you know, and mine's across the hall. Both of us were thinking about him and wondering if he didn't have something to do with this—but we're sure he couldn't have. Jane couldn't sleep very well Saturday night. Like me, she has a terrible time when she hits the quiet country, because country noises are so loud at first. You know, you hear the wind hit each shingle, and the screens sing, and the shutters squeak, and every gull that screeches. Anyway, neither of us slept at all well, and we heard Ford snoring like a trooper half the night."

"Are you sure," I asked sadly, "that I wasn't the one you heard? I've been known to snore."

Deal chuckled. "I'm sure. Because I went out into the hall—you know how desperate you can get about noises when you're tired? And I stood outside your door. If it had been you, I was going to go in and be very nasty. But it was Ford. I didn't dare wake him, though I'd have thrown things and made a scene if it had been Tom or Quin. Far from me be it to make any cracks about Ford Ames, but I know the gent well enough to know that he might—just a possibility, you understand— might have misinterpreted my barging into his room. He has been—well, anyway, that lets Ford out, because he began before one, and kept it up for hours and hours. I went in to see Jane finally, and—I say, turn around, Asey! Quick! What are they galloping like that for?"

Jane and Quin and Hanson were racing from the far dunes toward the house, and in their wake were four of the police, stumbling through the sand.

Asey cupped his hand to his mouth and yelled, and at the third yell, Quin stopped long enough to point toward the west terrace.

Very faintly we heard his answering cry.

"Smoke! Fire!"

Deal kicked off her pumps and started only a second or two behind Asey.

"Take 'em, will you, Pen?" she called as she dashed away.

I'd thought that my running days were over, but I found myself jogging breathlessly toward the house, with the shoes gripped under my arm. I remember thinking as I plodded on that running in sand was probably harder than running in a tank of lemon jelly—not that I'd ever tried the latter, but it was the only thing I could think of which would begin to approximate the difficulties I encountered as I panted and slipped along.

As I neared the house, I could see the billowing clouds of smoke float out over the west terrace, and I could hear Asey's voice calling sharp quarter deck orders to the rest.

By the time I reached the house and circled around to the west side, I was too exhausted to do anything more than flop down and stare.

The French doors to the living room were wide open, and from them the smoke still poured out.

Jane, wiping tears from her reddened eyes with a smudgy hand, came over and sat beside me.

"My God!" she said. "Two of those extinguishers wouldn't work at all. Luckily Mathilde'd just filled the washing machine. Asey and Tom wheeled it in and used it as a base while we got buckets of sand and put on the hose. It's all out now. That smoke's just aftermath. Lord, I thought the whole place was going! If you could have seen those flames!"

"But what happened? How did it start?"

Jane shrugged. "When we stumbled in, the rugs and the carpet and the couch in front of the fireplace were all in flames." She stopped and choked. "Damn that smoke! And little trickles of flame were running up the draperies by the window. Wind apparently blew them or forced them—or something—over this way. That room's ruined, what with the chemical extinguisher that did work, and the water and the sand. Pen, what wouldn't have happened if we hadn't seen the smoke!"

I didn't tell her, but I knew very well. The East Pochet fire department is superbly equipped, but it couldn't have functioned if the Sandbar water supply had failed—and it would have failed the instant the electricity or the wiring went.

"And with Lizzie in bed!" I added. "But how did this start?"

That was a question which no one could answer.

Ford had been upstairs in his room, had known nothing until he heard the wild attempts to make the extinguishers work. The wind had carried the smoke away from his side of the house.

As for Gregory and Mathilde, they had their tiny radio going in the kitchen, and that had drowned out all other sounds. The doors into the dining room and the living room, moreover, were both closed.

And Tom, who was out on the east terrace, not twenty feet from where the fire must have started, knew nothing till he saw Asey and Deal dashing into the house from the beach. He'd been asleep and had only wakened at the sound of Asey and Quin yelling to each other.

Upstairs in the north wing, Lizzie had fallen asleep, and Malvina admitted that she had been taking forty winks herself.

"Well," I said, viewing the charred remains of the room, "at least we. can—thanks to the impromptu brigade—rejoice that it was no worse. We can use the other living room till some of this mess gets cleaned up. Everything will have to be repainted and repapered, and that wicker furniture's a total loss. I suppose the insurance will take care of it, won't it, Deal?"

"Yes," she wound a clumsy bandage on Quin's hand, "yes, Cale knew the fire hazards out here and had everything insured up to the hilt. Quin's paw seems the only real injury, and I'm forced to state that it doesn't seem fatal. Everything else can be replaced."

Asey stroked his chin. "Luck," he said. "Tom, you stick around this room for a spell an' keep a couple buckets of water here, so's we'll be sure nothin' starts up again. Mrs. Colton, I'm goin' down to the boat house. Want to come?"

I wondered that he should leave without delving further into the origins of the fire and said as much. He didn't answer until he'd stopped the roadster down by the landing.

"I guess," he said, pulling out his pipe, "about all the delvin's been done that can be done. B'sides, I want to get away from that house for a few minutes. Too many folks around an' too much happenin', an' I'm tired of askin' questions. Like Frost, I want peace an' quiet. An' time to think. They's two pos'ble reasons for that fire, Mrs. Colton. One is that a spark cracked out of them pine logs in the fireplace. Deal tossed on some wood just after breakfast. It could of landed on the carpet, smoldered, an' then caught. There ain't no spark guard, which is plum silly."

"That must have been it," I said. "The same thing happened once at Arthur Brent's place over in Orleans. Don't you remember the excitement? The whole house was a cinder inside half an hour."

"Uh-huh. But there's the other reason. Y'know that Cape Cod firelighter gadget? That porous thing you stick in the little pitcher-like of kerosene, an' then light to start the fire without kindlin'? Well, that copper pitcher, when I got into the room, was lyin' on its side. Seems liks somethin'd knocked it over. An' it was the kerosene runnin' from that that made the fire spread so quick an' so sort of thorough."

"But you don't—you can't think that some one set that fire? What earthly use would—why, Asey, why should any one set a fire in there? There wasn't anything to be gained by one. There wasn't anything to be harmed. Nothing *was* harmed—"

"Only my coat."

"Your coat? But that's not—I mean—" I broke off, feeling a little puzzled as to why Asey should consider the burning of his coat to be of any mammoth importance. "I mean, it's too bad, but—"

"But what of it? Well, you see, them two letters Nellie Carstairs brought over last night was in the pockets. An' aside from Tom's seein' Frost once get the letters to Cheyne out of a box where a letter to Cheyne was supposedly bein' sent—an' all that ain't awful easy to prove, when you stop an' consider it. Anyways, aside from that, them letters was about the only real proof we had that Frost was Cheyne. Oh, *we* can be sure, but them letters, they was proof."

CHAPTER NINE

"BUT why," I demanded, "should any one want to burn those letters?"

"Dunno." Asey returned. "Can't really see just where it'd get any one, but the fact r'mains, if some one wanted them letters destroyed, they did a nice thorough job of it. 'Course, it may be I'm just a mite over-suspicious. Prob'ly I am."

"But who could have wanted to?"

"Only person I could think of that'd really be involved in the Cheyne business is Tom. He was out on the east terrace all the while. 'Course, the wind was blowin' away from him, an' he said he was asleep, but there you are. Chances is that the firelighter might of got knocked over accidental by Deal, or by any of 'em. Maybe it just was a spark that set off the whole thing. Longer I live, the more it seems like the simplest answers is like to be the right ones. All the samey, more strange—my, my. Syl's goin' to get him a sunstroke or a heart stroke or some kind of stroke if he don't stop dashin'. He always kind of r'minds me of a steam engine in corsets. S'matter, cousin?"

"Thought you'd want to see some of the junk we left in the boat house last night. The stuff from the dune. Say, lucky about that fire, wasn't it? You know, if I hadn't seen Tom right out there on the terrace the whole time, I'd of thought he set it."

"You seen him all the time?"

"Yup. I'd kind of wandered off from the rest. I was headin' to you, but I was feelin' tuckered out, so I sat down an' rested. I could see him out there on the terrace —you'n Mrs. Colton 'n Deal, too, before you walked to the beach."

Asey grinned. "Just an ole spark," he said, "that's what it was. How you feel about Ford startin' it, Syl?"

"Don't think. Greg'ry, he told me that that Ford feller was takin' a bath. That was why they was so late fillin' their washer that time. You know. He turned the faucet on full tilt, an' it cut off the water downstairs to a trickle."

Being thoroughly familiar with country self-supplied and self-supported water systems, I understood what Syl meant. Many a time when I've taken pains to arrange for plenty of hot water, when I had my house on the beach road, I've found that my bath had to be postponed because some one had chosen the same moment to water the garden or to hose down the tennis court. Apparently in this situation Ford's bath had curtailed the kitchen supply.

"Just," Asey repeated, "an ole stray spark, that's what. I'm gettin' old. Now, Syl, what about this mess of busted glass an' bottles you found down here?"

Syl led us to a little rise in the sand about a hundred yards beyond the boat house, where there was a quantity of broken glass and half-burned tin cans.

"Ole garbage hole," he said. "Burned over. But it seems likely that the bottle might of come from here, 'less of course it *was* some feller from the town that had his own bottle with him. Asey, you think the same feller killed 'em both?"

"I do," Asey said, "but I can't understand why. That boat house was unlocked with Frost's own keys, but I don't think Frost killed Thorne. He wasn't big enough to kill him this far away an' drag him in the boat house. Stands to reason, I think, that some one killed Frost before he met Thorne, took everythin' out of his pockets so's when the body was found, 'twould seem that Frost'd been killed in a rob'bry. Then, most likely, he dumped, or was plannin' to dump, Frost's things like the money an' the watch an' the keys, somewhere on the dune, an' bury 'em. Or drop 'em in the water. That'd seem a good reason why he'd come down this way."

"But why wouldn't he have thrown them into the water on the ocean side?" I asked.

"Now, Mrs. Colton," Asey said chidingly, "you lived here long enough not to ask things like that. Ain't you never tried to throw picnic rubbish in the surf?"

I had, and I knew what happened, with the undertow and the surf. Usually the things came floating back to shore—not in the same place, but they came back.

"I'm squelched," I said. "Go on."

"Well, I think he started down this way to throw

them things in the water by the wharf. They's stones so's he could weigh the things down. N'en, if he tossed 'em off the end of the wharf, they'd land in the channel mud, an' that'd be an end to 'em. N'en—I may be all wrong, but this is the way it seems to me. N'en, on the way, I think that Thorne landed on the scene. Maybe Thorne'd heard the shot, or maybe seen the thing. I think that's why he got killed."

"By gum," Syl said admiringly, "that's what I call thinkin'. Now, I most busted my brains, tryin' to see what c'nection there'd be between them two killin's, an' I couldn't get nowheres. An' you make it sound just as simple as pie."

Asey smiled. "I was makin' that fire seem just as simple an' on purpose," he said, "a few minutes back. They's a lot of flaws in that thinkin'."

"Now," Syl said, "who d'you suspect, Asey? Some one up to the house?"

"You got me there," Asey said. "I known Mrs. Colton since she wore pinafores, an' I know she's out. B'sides, she's got too much sense of humor to kill folks wholesale. Sense of humor kind of gives you a sense of proportion, an' when you got a sense of proportion, you don't go in for erasin' your fellow men like they was ink spots. Deal an' Jane's alibied Ford out of it. I don't think Deal's mixed up, for all she's a good shot. I don't think Mrs. Richards is, either. If they can shoot, why'd they bash? An' I can't see either of 'em bashin'. Jane didn't know Frost. Tom, I dunno. He may be a victim of circumstance, like the feller said about his eighteen children, an' then again, maybe not. Quin—I hardly don't think—"

"But Asey," Syl broke in, "Quin's the feller that's been here in town long enough to know about throwin' Frost's stuff in the harbor. An' then this mornin'—"

"True," Asey said. "He's known this town since he was a baby. An' I ain't forgettin' what he was sayin' about bashes, either, Mrs. Colton, when we overheard him talkin' to Tom. Just the samey, Quin's got no fight with Frost. Never had."

"But this mornin'," Syl went on stoutly, "he found somethin' on the dune where he was huntin', an' he put it in his pocket. An' b'fore he did, he looked around every which way to see if any one was lookin' at him. Kind of stealthy, he was. I thought it must be the cartridge case, but it was a sight bigger'n that. An' b'sides, I found the cartridge case myself a few minutes later."

"You never told me—where, Syl?"

"Seems to me it'd been tossed up in the dune, 'cause the doc said Frost was shot on a level, almost, an' if the gun'd been fired from the top of the dune, he could of told. Anyways, 'twas in a bunch of dusty miller, an' I just kind of found it by ac'dent. I was pickin' up a gull's feather for Jennie; she likes 'em. An' then I walked on a bit, intendin' to tell you, an' then I sat down to rest, an' then there was the fire, an' I sort of forgot all about the case."

"Well, we'll send some one up to Forman with it, along with the .22's Deal talked of."

"But what about Quin?" Syl persisted.

"D'you really think he picked up anythin' important?"

"Well," Syl replied, "if it'd been a chunk of ambergris, he couldn't of been any more sneakin' about it. An' say, you ain't quite right about Quin an' Frost. When I called up Jennie early this mornin' to tell her I wouldn't be home, she said to be sure an' tell you about that time in the store last year when she seen Quin an' Frost fightin', an' then again they was havin' a fight one day outside the g'rage when she happened to be there. The first time, she said, Frost hit Quin a slap across the face, an' that time at the g'rage, Quin slatted out of the car an' started walkin' away, leavin' Frost sittin' there. Don't seem to me that shows much of what you'd call a friendly spirit."

"Not," Asey agreed, "very clubby an' Rotarian. Huh. Deal seemed to think them two was pals. But, under the circumstances, I s'pose she'd do her best to make me think so."

"An' he's a detective," Syl went on, "even if he is one only on paper. Seems to me that shootin' an' bashin' when he might of shot twice is just the sort of thing some writer'd put in a book, just to throw folks off. 'Course, where Frost was killed was far enough off from the house so's the chances 'd be against a small caliber gunshot bein' heard. But it might be, down this way. It's all fishy to me. I like Quin's well as anybody, but it seemed to me from the first, right off the bat, as you might say, that he had somethin' to do with it. Asey, ain't you goin' down town an' ask questions?"

Asey laughed. "Questions are sort of out, Syl. With all that hullabaloo Sat'day night, no one really knows anythin', an' the surmisin' would be kind of wild an' racy. But there's one thing I am goin' to do. I'm goin' to take a look through the rooms an' folks's b'longin's up to the house. That gun's somewhere. If the feller didn't throw away the cartridge case an' the things that b'longed to Frost, I don't think he threw the gun away either. An' if it ain't been found, I'd say he still had it. May not get us far, but it might be fun to prowl around."

"What about the things that were in Thorne's pockets?" I asked. "And the labels from his clothes?"

"I think he took the labels off himself. They were snipped out careful like, not ripped off. An' I think whatever was in his pockets was prob'ly tossed off the dock. I got a feelin' that the feller got rid of the things from Frost's pockets, except the keys, before he met Thorne. Only way I can 'count for 'em croppin' up in Bingo's coat."

"How *do* you account for that, anyway?" I demanded. "It's not sensible, any of it."

"I think some one else, maybe Zeruah, maybe ten or fifteen others, found Frost's things, an' later found Bingo's coat. An' c'nected the two. That's all the sense I can make out of it. Well, let's go back to the house an' see what we can see, Mrs. Colton. You too, Syl. You're the eagle eye of this fam'ly."

Before we went back, Asey glanced over the collection of articles picked up on the dune the night before. Odd buttons, corkscrews, can openers, a child's shoe, a small tin cup—they reminded me of the foolish objects people used to put on tables at children's parties, make you look at them for several minutes, and then try to make you remember them, in order, hours later. As Asey said, they were amusing if not instructive.

"What about them servants?" Syl asked as we got into the roadster.

"Don't think anythin' about 'em," Asey said. "Like Quin remarked so disgusted, it ain't fair. An' from what I seen of them two, I'd say it wouldn't. They ain't got enough 'magination. They ain't doers. They're the kind you tell twice an' advise three times an' then stand over to see the thing's done. Am I right, Mrs. Colton?"

"Right?" I said. "Any couple who can seriously debate for fifteen minutes on the virtues of two obscure brands of pickled walnuts—without cracking a smile! And helpless—don't get me started. Besides, if they'd wanted to kill Cale, they'd probably have done so before this. They've been with him for years."

Back at the house we found Doctor Cummings alighting from his wheezing and practically paintless vehicle. You really have to call it a vehicle, because it's lost most of its resemblance to a sedan.

"Believe it or not," he said cheerfully, "East Pochet's got another inhabitant since I left here, thanks to me. Matt Eldredge's wife. My God, what happened to this room?"

We told him about the fire, and he sighed.

"All my life I've just missed fires," he said mournfully. "D'you know I've never seen one in all my life?

Even when I was an interne, I always seemed to get called out to bar-room fights and train wrecks, but never a fire!"

"Next time," Asey promised, "we'll keep it under control till you get a chance to view it."

"Do," the doctor said, "do—Pen, you're squinting. Didn't I, at one time or another last fall, delicately suggest that you needed glasses?"

"You did," I said, "and I have a lovely pair—which reminds me that I still owe for 'em. I don't suppose any of you young bloods would care to go upstairs and get them for me?"

Deal, Jane, Tom and Ford promptly started for the stairs.

"Let me," Ford said. "I'm going to get my sun glasses anyway. And let me tell you, Mrs. Colton, that while lifting these aching bones up a flight of stairs is devotion, bringing them down is nothing short of reverence. It would seem that the dune combing proves I'm a softy."

"I can sympathize with him," Jane said. "Only time I was ever more stiff was when we had that substitute gym teacher—remember, Deal? That lusty soul who took such a personal interest in your stomach?"

Deal shuddered. "Used to come into exercise room A three times a week and poke my tum and say in a loud strident voice, 'Miss Richards, I *don't* like your abdominal muscles! You'd better just lie on your back and bicycle till I tell you to stop!' Remember her? Why, she's got a circle all her own in my private inferno. What *was* her name—Buttock?"

"Buttrick," Jane said. "She tortured me about my calves. Didn't like 'em a whit better than she liked your tum. The most poignant moment of my life came the day I sat on the top rung of Carnegie Hall, listening to Toscanini and wondering how I'd ever walk down those millions of steps—wah! It took two ushers and a helpful man with a monocle, and I lurched so people thought I was tight—look out, Ford! That golf club on the steps—"

Ford, coming down the steps one by one, was looking in our direction. As Jane called to him, his foot landed on the head of a mashie-niblick that some one— Deal, probably—had left about half way down the flight. He started to clutch at the banisters, but then he must have remembered that my glasses were in his left hand. He made a convulsive attempt to grip the wall, but he couldn't.

Half fascinated, we watched him tumble headlong.

It pains me to say that my first thought was for my glasses—strangely enough, they escaped unscathed. But Ford's left foot was twisted under him, and I could tell from the twitching muscles around his mouth that he was struggling not to scream.

"Damned ankle," he said, trying to lift himself up. "Oh—guess I'll have to have help. Sprained it twice in college—twisted a ligament last year. The damn thing never loses a chance to get itself hurt!"

Asey and Tom helped him onto the couch, and the doctor bustled out and returned with his inevitable black bag.

I could see, as he removed Ford's shoe and sock, that

the ankle was slightly swelled. Tears rolled down Ford's cheeks as the doctor prodded expertly.

"I don't really intend," he swished a handkerchief about his eyes, "to bawl—but I can't seem to help it. You know how it is when a dentist drills on a tooth that may not hurt, but you find yourself crying like fury—"

"No need to apologize," the doctor said. "Looks to me as though you'd just twisted it, but I'll take you home and take an X-ray, if you'd like."

"I can wiggle my toes nicely," Ford assured him. "Just strap it up, or something. Don't look so serious, all of you! And just who left that club there? I didn't notice it when I went upstairs."

"I did," Deal said. "All my fault. I was going to take some balls out and play sand trap. Look, Tom, I've got a sterling notion. While the doctor's fixing up Ford, why don't we rustle your stuff and Quin's out of the downstairs room so that Ford can have it? We'll shift you upstairs, and he can stay down here, and then there won't be the stair problem. And—why, somewhere in the attic there's a wheel chair we had the year Ned smashed his foot in that auto accident. D'you mind the moving, Ford? And would you use the chair?"

"Swell ideas, all of 'em," he said. "I'll have to keep off this foot for a week—I know from sad experience. And it would be pretty dull up there alone."

I led Syl and Asey up to the attic, and after much poking around, we found the chair. It was slightly mildewed, and no amount of oil would stop its squeaking, but otherwise it seemed entirely adequate.

After the doctor had seen to his foot, Ford was transferred to the chair amid much hilarity. Jane draped her head with a bath towel on which a red cross had been hastily stenciled with lipstick and then proceeded to push Ford sedately around the room. I can't remember all of her running comment—I was laughing too hard, but most of it concerned "dear Mr. Rockefeller" at Ormond; Ford rose to the occasion and bestowed dimes recklessly.

"Oh, dear," Jane said at last, yanking off her head dress, "this isn't the time or the place to carry on such fooling. I'm sorry. It seems so darn heartless, but I didn't mean to be. Come on, Deal, let's help Tom with all that stuff. Poor lad's working like a pack horse!"

"First, Deal," Asey said, "I wish you'd find them guns. I didn't see 'em in the attic, but lord, you couldn't find much of anythin' up there if you didn't know the ins an' outs. I ain't seen such an attic since the days when Bill Porter cleaned out his grandfather's house. 'Member that, Syl? You an' I helped."

Syl rolled his eyes toward heaven. "That man," he said gravely, "a millionaire if ever there was one, he had three hundred candy boxes all full of string up in that place, not to speak of cigar boxes full of ole nails an' screws! My, what a time that was!"

"It was even funnier," Asey observed, "when your wife found us takin' everythin' to the dump, an' made you bring half the candy boxes an' all the string right straight back home."

Syl sighed. "Jennie still makes me piece that string up for bundles," he said sadly. "Can't seem to convince her it'd be cheaper to buy a whole new ball of twine, b'sides savin' I don't know how much time. Say, Deal, want me to help you hunt them guns?"

"Come along," Deal said. "The boys had them last. That means they're practically anywhere. They left their fishing tackle in the chimney, one year, to keep it from being seen and stolen if thieves broke in. Jane—?"

"If you mean that as an invitation for me to climb attic stairs and do a little attic grubbing, no thank you! In fact, now that I'm settled down, I'm retracting my offer to help Tom. He looks sort of cute, staggering around under those heavy piles of clothes. Amazing how many clothes men have, and yet they always insist women do all the fussing about 'em. Never forget the time I went with my father while he had a suit fitted. They discussed the number of sleeve buttons for one solid hour, and pored over blueprints for another—"

"Those clothes," Ford said, "are mine, that he's bringing down. And I do have a lot, I admit. I was going to spend a few weeks with the Paulsons at Newport when Cale inveigled me into coming down here with him for a couple of days first. That little case you've got there, Tom, doesn't contain bricks, in case you're wondering. It's a victrola for little Linda Paulson's birthday. She's my god-daughter, and she politely requested a small vic with lots of Mickey Mouses running around it. It took four days to find an electric one—she's a lazy little brat. Anyway, Linda and Newport explain all the bulk."

"Newport," Tom said, stopping long enough to light a cigarette. "Man, I thought you were thinking of Buck-

ingham or Sandringham at the least! Whew. I'm going
to sit a while before I take up Quin's things. He's not
stayed put enough to do any unpacking, so I can just
cart up his suitcases. It seems to have slipped your mind,
Jane, but I—me—I also dune hunted in the rain yesterday. And my muscles are human, too. Tell me, Asey,
how far've you got?"

Asey lighted his pipe. "Lot of surmisin', mostly.
Syl's found the cartridge case, an' soon's Deal gets them
guns that b'long here, I'm goin' to take 'em up to Forman, or have Hanson do it. I sh'd think Hanson an'
Quin'd know every grain of sand on this spot by its first
name, by now. Tom, you look tired. I'll take pity on you
an' cart them cases of Quin's up. Are they closed?"

"Poor Tomsy-womsey!" Jane said in mock pity.
"Woozums all charley-horsed? Oh, Asey, they're stu-
pendous cases—and you—my word, we can't let you fall
and crack yourself up. Give me one. I can so manage it!
And what ducky—you know, I've always wanted luggage with those trick letter locks! Wonder if his initials
open 'em?"

She set the canvas covered case down on the floor
and began to fiddle with the letters.

"They don't work!" She surveyed the "J.Q.G." and
turned up her nose. "Oh, dear, that's shattered an il-
lusion. I always thought people had their initials open
their cases. Father did. All over the world he found other
people opening 'em, too. They'd read his initials on the
side, and then try 'em on the locks, just for fun. He finally
had them changed after all his clean shirts had been

spilled out in a million stations and hotel lobbies—not to speak of all his dirty linen that got aired in public. Asey, what's the secret?"

"I know," Tom said, "because I asked Quin. Give you three guesses, master mind."

"Mean me?" Asey said. "Well, knowin' Quin, I'd say there was only one answer. I read some of his books while they was still a lot of messy typewritten sheets, an' I know his fav'rite three letter comb'nation. You try 'Q.E.D.,' Jane."

Jane twirled the letters rapidly and pressed the locks. The case popped open, and a miscellaneous assortment of neckties, and shirts, and underwear, all cascaded over the floor.

"That," Tom said approvingly, "is brainwork, Asey. What a burglar was lost to the world in you! Don't bother to fold things up, Jane. Quin hates things folded up. Untidy chap. He always stuffs—"

"Look," Jane said. "L-look—look what was rolled up in those pajamas—Asey, I'm weak!"

Asey took the short, ugly looking pistol from her hand and glanced at it thoughtfully.

".22 Woodsman Colt," he said slowly, and then examined the clip. "An' one cartridge gone—"

"But what's that gadget on it?" Jane interrupted. "What's that?"

"That gadget," Asey said, "is a silencer."

CHAPTER TEN

I T was several minutes before any of us were able to utter a single word.

"Well," Jane remarked nervously at last, "well, that —that would seem to be the reason that no one heard the shot, wouldn't it?"

"Seems's if." Asey slipped the gun and the silencer into the pockets of the soft chamois jacket he'd taken out of his car. "Seems's if. Oh, you got the guns already, Deal? I'm startin' out to see Forman right now."

"They've melted into thin air or something," Deal answered. "We absolutely can't find a trace of 'em. Bud or Ned must have taken them away last fall. What— what's the matter? You all look as though you'd been playing statues, and some one'd just yelled 'Still pond— no more moving!' What's wrong?"

"I was playing with the lock on Quin's case," Jane said. "It popped open. The gun—it was in there—rolled up in a pair of Quin's pajamas!"

"*The* gun? What gun?" Deal demanded. "You mean, you found Quin's old .45? He always carries that with him wherever he goes, hoping to find a burglar he can shoot some day. But that's nothing to make you all look so solemn; if you're thinking about Caleb, that's utterly absurd. That was a .22, Asey said."

"This is a .22," Asey told her. "Woodsman Colt. Here, look. Here 'tis. C'mplete with a silencer. An' one cartridge gone."

Deal looked at the gun and then she looked at us and her eyes began to blaze.

"That's not Quin's!" she said. "He never had any gun like that. It—some one of you is trying to get him into trouble, or else it's some one's idea of a very funny joke! Which one of you played this ridiculous trick?"

Ford and Jane and Tom looked at her blankly.

"Oh, come, Deal!" Jane said. "After all, perhaps some one *did* plant that gun in there, and of course Quin's the light of your life, but that doesn't excuse a crack like that! You can't mean that you think any of us—"

"That's exactly what I do mean," Deal said stonily. "Exactly. Perhaps you didn't, yourself, Jane—after all, you didn't know Caleb, and that lets you out of this. But Ford and Tom—which one of you planted that gun in Quin's things?"

Their fervent denials didn't begin to convince her in the least. Finally Asey stepped in and took charge. If he hadn't, I think Deal would have started a knockdown dragout fight on the spot.

"This isn't the time or the place, Deal," he said quietly, "to go into all that. It's entirely pos'ble that this ain't the gun we're after. P'raps it was planted on Quin.

But there's no reason for you to take it on yourself to get everybody worked up about it. I don't want to pin this on Quin, nor does anybody else. My job is to try to unpin him, if I can. So, just sort of 'vast heavin', will you?"

Deal's answer was a brief but expressive sentence which she never learned in the bosom of the Richards family.

One by one all the traces of cheery amiability which had characterized her since the previous noon were disappearing. Once again her lips had that sullen, cynical twist, and her eyes were acquiring their usual glint of hardness. Her entire manner, in short, was rapidly approaching its acid best.

"Yup," Asey said dryly, "to save any more arg'ment, I'll admit I'm all of what you say. But I wouldn't go into it much farther, if I was you. An' I wouldn't go out on the dune after Quin, either. I'll see him myself when I'm good an' ready. Mrs. Colton, you want to drive up to see Forman with me? Tom, fetch her coat, will you?"

"D'you mean," Deal snapped, "that you're forbidding me to leave the house or to see Quin? By what authority do you—"

"I mean just that," Asey said. "When people behave like kids, they got to be ordered about like kids. You can promise me you'll r'strain these liv'ry stable pers'nalities, an' hold your tongue an' stay put, or I'll see you don't get no chance to. Your mother told me to look after you, an' her orders beat your tantrums any day in the week. I'd hate to have to turn you over my knee an' spank you, but I might say, offhand, that I was ready an' willin'. Do I make myself clear?"

Deal shrugged. "Good old brute force!"

"I take it," Asey said, "that you'll obey orders. Tom, you an' Jane see she does, please. Okay, Mrs. Colton? Oh—an' will you come outside a second, doc?"

"What a hellion," the doctor commented as he helped me into the car, "that girl can be when she makes up her mind to it! Comes of having Frost around, I suppose, displaying his cussed manners—not to speak of a semi-neurotic mother. Deal learned at an early age that Ned and Bud would give in to her rather than have to listen to one of her scenes. Asey, you don't really expect me to curtail her, do you?"

Asey smiled.

"I do. Go ahead an' spank her if you have to, doc. Do her good. Look, will you stick around till we get back? You got to look after Mrs. Richards, anyway. An' don't let any of them fellers get off the bar, an' don't you let Quin come into the house, or see any of 'em. It'd take him an' Deal less'n thirty seconds by the clock to make up a nice plaus'ble yarn about that gun. I'm goin' to see Forman an' make sure about it, an' then I'll see to Master Quin. But—don't you let him chatter with any of those fellers inside, see?"

"Quin," the doctor observed, "is plumpish and soft, but the fact remains that he's five inches taller and sixty pounds heavier than I am."

"Then sic Tom onto him," Asey suggested, "an' give him a hypodermic. It's your duty an' you got to. Don't think you'll have to be strenuous, but I want to make sure about this."

He started the roadster off like a streak of greased lightning.

"I can see, Cannonball Baker," I said, "that you've got your dander up. When you begin to drive cars like this, something's happening."

He smiled and slowed down.

"This's the first solid thing we've hit on so far," he said. "At least, it's the first thing solid enough to chew reflective on. I'm goin' to cut over an' see Hanson—hold on while I slew her off the logs—hi, Hanson! Yup— c'mere."

Hanson loped over to the car.

"Gee," he said, mopping his forehead, "this comes nearer to work—found anything?"

"Yup," Asey said briskly, "an' I want you to take Quin Gunner off this bar an' keep him till I get back from seein' Forman. Found the right gun, I think." He showed it to Hanson and told all the details about Jane and the suitcase.

Hanson whistled.

"I thought I saw him pick something up this morning," he said. "I asked him, but he said no. It was just before that fire broke out. What d'you make of it, Asey? D'you suppose he picked the gun up then, or had it all the time?"

Asey shook his head. "Dunno. But you take him— huh—take him down to Provincetown. Say I had a tip— oh, about Thorne. That'll do it. Find Nellie Carstairs and see if she knows where Thorne stayed—Tom would know, but you might as well kill time an' do it round about. Go to P-town an' ask a lot of silly questions. Let Quin jabber, too. Just so's you keep him away from here for a few hours. An' don't let him speak with any of them youngsters up to the house till I get back. An' don't let him suspect about that gun. Be seein' you!"

Again the roadster shot off.

On the mainland side of the Sandbar bridge two state police were playing Horatius to a miscellaneous crowd of staring men, women and children. It didn't take much more than half a look to tell me that they weren't natives.

"Early for so many tourists," I remarked as we sped along. "And those *are* tourists. The hog-the-road and throw-papers-on-the-nice-white-beach kind, too."

Asey nodded. "They're the kind of folks that don't have nothin' else to do but worry about other folks's business. Thank God, they stayed out of Sat'day night's blow out. Take just about three tourists to of made that little orgy you seen yest'day look like a pre-War Sunday school picnic. Well, I s'pose tourists is retribution, as you might say."

"Why?" I asked.

"Way I figger it out, when the Cape begun braggin' it was God's country 'cause it was so quaint an' all, an' 'cause it'd killed off the m'skeeters that blotted the landscape, why God just substituted tourists. An' you can't kill them off, worse luck, by sprayin' a lot of oil."

We reached Main Street in less time than I'd ever

made the trip before. As we stopped for the red light at the four corners by the state road, Jim Williams, the constable, and Tim Smalley, who'd discovered the dumped liquor, jumped breathlessly on the running board of the car. The faces of both men, although they couldn't begin to stand comparison with Bingo Cook's, nevertheless bore evidence that their owners had enjoyed and participated in Saturday night's revels.

"Asey!" Jim said. "My God, man, we was just startin' out to get hold of you. Look, we all went home an' went to bed yest'day, an' didn't know what'd happened really till a little while ago. Say, Zeruah's not the feller that killed Frost and that stranger! You got to help us get him off. The lodge's raisin' a fund for it. How much'll you want to straighten things out? We can prove all about Sat'day night. We was out on the bar an'—"

"Fifth offer," Asey said to me. "Maybe I should go into the detectin' business. Zeruah's all off, boys, or he will be in a day or two. But—d'you really know what went on at Sandbar Sat'day night?"

"Both of us was at the bar, with Bingo an' Zeruah," Smalley said. "Honest, Jim remembers everything. He hadn't had but a couple drinks—"

"I hadn't *any*—" Jim protested. "I—"

"Then," Asey said, "you go down on the bar an' get Bingo. Here—I'll write a pass for you. Get him, bring him up to the station. I'm in a hurry. Follow up in your car. An' say, hop over to the Greek's an' grab a handful of sandwiches an' some tonic, will you? I forgot Mrs. Colton an' I hadn't had no lunch."

Just as we were leaving, after wolfing down some dubious sandwiches, Lorena Baxter, Jimmy B's cousin, called at us and waved wildly.

"She says," I reported to Asey, "that she's got something to tell you. Hadn't you better stop?"

"Now Mrs. Colton," Asey said, "you know her rep'-tation as well's I do. What she's got to say'll keep. I ain't got time to listen to her now. Funny how folks who got nothin' to say always takes twice as long to say it as anybody else, ain't it? Nope, right now I want to find out about this gun."

With a hamburg in one hand, Asey drove up the King's Highway as though it were Fifth Avenue, and a squadron of police were clearing the way.

"First chance," he said cheerfully, "I had to try this car out, really. Seems like Bill was turnin' out better cars than the Porters used to when I worked for 'em. An' to think it took ole Cap'n Porter an' me five days to bring the first Porter auto from Boston to Wellfleet. We carried it bod'ly most of the way. Hm. Things is lookin' up. Once we get settled as to what was really goin' on with them fellers out on Sandbar—you know, it comes hard to me, callin' that place Sandbar, just like—well, like you'd put BATH MAT on bath mats. To me, it's just Lobster Island."

I chuckled. "Thoph Hawes at the P.O.," I said, "wrote 'Try Lobster I.' on all the mail that came addressed to Sandbar, in spite of all Caleb's letters to the postmaster general, until the new administration."

"End," Asey murmured, "of rugged ind'vidualism.

Huh. But to me, Lobster Island sounds a lot friendlier than just Sandbar."

"What about Tom?" I asked, recalling his comment about the bar being sinister and unfriendly.

"I been thinkin' about him. He knew the comb'nation of Quin's cases. For all we know, he might of found the gun Sunday night an' stuck it in there. Can't tell. They's a lot to this. But I got hopes, an' that's more'n I been havin'."

Up at the police sub-station, I was introduced to Forman, the ballistics expert. He proved to be an engaging young man with blue eyes and a pleasant grin. Outwardly there was nothing to distinguish him from a bond salesman.

"Sand in the barrel," he said, looking at the gun. "I'd say offhand it'd been lying out on that dune in all Sunday's rain. Can I tell if that's the gun? Sure. Sit down and wait a while till I find out."

In less than half an hour he was back.

"That's it," he announced. "That's it all right. Come back here and look—no, guess you won't even have to look at 'em under power. You can see this mark with your naked eye. That's from the scratch in the barrel. That's the important thing, but there are a lot of other similarities. Oh, yes—and that cartridge case's the one, too. No doubt at all. Bullet that killed Frost was fired from this gun."

"An' now," Asey said, "what could you do about tracing the gun for me?"

"Wouldn't be too optimistic about that, Asey. I can

trace it if it was bought in this state. Not if the fellow got it in, say, Rhode Island or New Hampshire, for example. We keep full records here. But maybe it's a stolen gun. You know, this sort of savors of the gangster—leaving the gun behind."

"I'd thought of that," Asey agreed. "If it was left out there on the dune, and if Quin picked it up, chances is that the one who left it knew it couldn't be traced—or he'd have dumped it into the ocean. What about the silencer?"

Forman shook his head. "Can't buy those legally in this state. When they're bought, usually they come by mail order from Brown or Maxim's or one of a couple of others out in the mid-west. Person can send a money order and have the silencer sent to John Jones—that's what they usually do. We might trace the silencer back, but I can practically promise you that we couldn't trace the buyer. I know that from past experience. All the John Joneses who've bought silencers, if laid end to end, would reach to Mars and back. But I'll phone Boston and see about the gun."

He left us alone again in the tiny hall.

"It's a wonder to me," I said, "that murderers flourish, if people can trace bullets with a flip of the hand like that. What chance do murderers have?"

"On a percentage basis," Asey said, "they don't. Lord, some of these experts they got can take a single hair an' a piece of toe nail an' wheee—there you are! An' as time goes on, an' people get onto the fact that p'lice d'partments need a little modernizin', they's goin' to be less chance for murderers. But even when you got your bullet traced an' know what gun it was shot from, you still ain't got no snap job. Take the Sacco-Vanzetti case. The head of the shell picked up at the scene of that murder had twenty-seven identifyin' marks in common with a test shell fired from the .32 Colt automatic taken from one or the other of them fellers at the time of their arrest. There was the scientific proof, but look at all the wah-hoo that followed."

"But suppose," I said, "that this gun should prove really to be Quin's. And suppose Mr. Forman says a bullet from it killed Frost. There's the scientific proof, but how could you make sure?"

Asey smiled. "If this lands like that on Quin, under them circumstances, he'd be indicted an' prob'ly convicted. Wouldn't be no ballyhoo about Quin. He's a blinkin' cap'tlist. His father was a banker. He wouldn't have a chance. Tabloids'd call him 'Wealthy Mystery Scribe and Decayed Heir of Millionaire,' an' like as not, he'd get the chair. 'F he was a ditch digger, or supported a widowed mother an' fourteen brothers an' sisters, they'd sob-story him off, an' make a hero out of him. Shows it don't pay for what middle class there is left to c'mit murders. Anyway, that's the sort of thing the p'lice got to cope with. Oh—here they be—"

Jim Williams, Tim Smalley and Bingo filed into the hall.

"Welcome," Asey said. "I'm—what's the matter with you, Bingo? You look like you'd bit on a tack an' two persimmons."

"I," Bingo was breathing heavily, "I found out who put them things into my blue jacket pocket, Asey, an' let me tell you right here an' now, that I ain't goin' to take—"

"Now, Bingo," Jim said soothingly, "we got all that thrashed out. You promised us you wouldn't lose your temper till you'd heard the whole story. An' r'member this, we're gettin' you out of a bad business. If it wasn't for us, they might be choosin' you to fill Zeruah's shoes!"

Bingo clenched one brawny fist and surveyed it lovingly.

"You promised!" Smalley said nervously. "You promised—"

"I'm keepin' my word," Bingo said, "till Asey hears the whole shootin' match. But when we get back to East Pochet—"

He left it at that, but every word was pregnant with foreboding.

"Okay," Asey said. "Now, Jim, you was the sober one? Tell us what went on."

"I was on my way down to the bay shore," Jim began, "when all this rumpus started. I was takin' down some gas for my boat. Anyway, Tim was goin' strong when I got there, an' when Bingo come, *he* started goin' stronger. I decided I'd better stick around an' stay sober an' see that too much didn't happen. You know how Bingo can get the boys started—"

"I resent that!" Bingo said. "I resent that, Jim Williams!"

"You just let Jim tell it," Asey said, "an' then you

can give your additions an' c'rections. Only as I r'call, you didn't think you was a one to do much in that line, was you?"

Bingo subsided and took to considering his fist again.

"Anyway," Jim went on hurriedly, "I didn't have but one drink. After a while, Zeruah come, an' he got worse than the others, he tried so hard to get caught up. Besides, he found a case of champagne. Then Bingo an' Zeruah an' Tim all decided they wanted to go to Bingo's to see if his Jamaica rum was as good as French brandy. I decided I'd better go along. Most of the other men, by that time, was just tryin' to get as much stuff as they could, an' I sort of felt they'd stay sober till I could get those three packed away somewheres. I—"

"But how was it," Asey asked, "you was sleepin' in that hedge Sunday mornin' if you was so sober?"

"That came later," Jim said with a sigh. "Anyway, I drove the three of 'em out to Bingo's. That was around twelve. They played the radio an' started a poker game, an' got quieted down so much that I thought I'd better leave 'em there an' go back to look after the others. But Tim was gettin' awful sad. He was thinkin' of the days when he used to help run a river boat from Rangoon to Mandalay, an' he got to broodin' about the ole Iriwadi River so much that he lit out an' took a dory of Bingo's. An' before I knew what he was goin' to do, almost, the crazy fool set out, rowin' that ole dory! Way he was, I guess the channel looked more like the Iriwadi—well, anyway, I figgered from the way he was headin' that he'd come ashore by Sandbar, so I set out on foot to get him, knowin' how much Frost hated cars on his property. N'en Bingo an' Zeruah must have followed me, because after I got Tim ashore an' got the dory anchored off Frost's wharf, I met 'em about two hundred yards on the Sandbar side of the dune."

"What time was that?" Asey asked.

"Oh, long after two, Asey. I tell you, herdin' them three was one of the hardest things I ever done in all my life. First Bingo got hot, an' took off his coat, an' wanted to go to sleep right there, with the coat for a pillow, an' then Tim tried to get back to the boat, 'cause the temple bells was callin'!"

"Temple bells—oh, I get it," I said. "Luring him back to Mandalay?"

"He seemed to think so," Jim said. "An'—well, it took me a solid hour to round that gang up an' get 'em together as far as the bridge, Asey. Then—"

"Wait up," Asey said weakly. "Who picked up Bingo's jacket an' put the watch an' things in it?"

"I did." Smalley looked warily at Bingo. "He wanted to leave his jacket there, an' I thought he ought to take it. I remember that much. I remember pickin' somethin' up when I went back to get the coat, too. That was one of the times Zeruah'd broke loose, an' Jim an' Bingo was after him. You see, Zeruah wanted to go see Frost an' tell him how much he hated him. I think I just found the things lyin' there in the beach grass an' took 'em for Bingo's. Didn't look at 'em, p'ticularly. I was—well, I just stuffed 'em into Bingo's pockets, an' then Jim come after me an' made me come back, an' I guess I left the jacket there. Jim had quite a time."

"Time!" Jim said. "Time! You crazy loons! Bingo wanted to sing, an' you wanted to go to Mandalay, an' Zeruah wanted to go paste Frost's front teeth out—an' me—me the law! All I could think of was what would happen if Frost heard the noise an' found me there with you three!"

"I would of given money," Asey said appreciatively, "to seen that, Jim. You—oh, my goodness!"

"I'd of given money," Jim retorted, "to of had you there to help! Well, I finally got 'em all back, Asey, an' then Tim here, he wanted to go home. Wasn't any place like home by then. I was willin' enough to take him if I could only think that Bingo an' Zeruah'd stay put. Tim went out to the car, an' finally he went asleep there. Then Zeruah passed out, an' I carted him out to the car. An' then," Jim sighed, "then I tried to put Bingo to bed. That was a pretty good fight, because I was sober, an' Bingo was kind of off his form. N'en Zeruah trailed back to see what was goin' on, an' he an' I had a little rumpus. He tripped me an' got me down on the floor, an' did a little fancy wrestlin'—"

"Did he hit you?" Asey asked.

Jim smiled. "While we was rollin' around the floor, he bashed me with a sofa pillow, but that's all the hittin' he did."

"Good," Asey said. "That clears up his idea that he hit some one over the head. But how'd Bingo come to get so marked up?"

"Well, after Zeruah quieted down, I tried again to get Bingo to bed. That trip, he went crazy. He showed me just now, before we come up here, how his place looked—Asey, he done all that himself. Every single bit of that smashin' was his own work. You see, he'd got the idea that he was fightin' a whole crew what was mutinyin'. I tried to stop him, but lord, you might as well of tried to stop the tides. At last he stopped an' seemed to be asleep, so I took Zeruah an' got him out to the car, an' left, with him an' Tim. Near as I can make out—this was after four, by the way—Bingo must of come to again an' finished the job on his place, an' then started out on shank's mares. Only way he could have acted to land up on the lower neck. Anyway, I took the other two up town, but before we left—"

He broke off as Forman came in.

"Asey," the latter said, "you're lucky. The chief's always said so, and Hanson says so, and now I know it."

"Did you trace the gun?"

Forman smiled. "They did. Listen." He read from a paper he held in his hand. " 'The gun number—so and so and so and so—was sold by R. L. Johnson of Boston on September 6, 1932, to John Quincy Gunner.' "

CHAPTER ELEVEN

ASEY took the memorandum from Forman and read it through very carefully.

"Don't s'pose," he said at last, "that there's any doubt about that at all? No chance of any slip up?"

"Not a chance," Forman was very positive. "I made them check twice because it seemed almost too simple. Well, want us to have him brought up here?"

"Not just yet," Asey said. "They's a lot of little odds 'n ends I want to get fitted in first. 'Course, it may be that Quin give this gun to—but we'll see about that. What time is it? Well, b'fore I go, I want to finish up with you three fellers here. First of all, Jim, can you 'count for the shot fired out of Zeruah's gun?"

"I was just gettin' to that when he come in," Jim answered, jerking his head toward Forman. "You see, after Bingo seemed to be through fightin' his crew, I took Zeruah to the car. I got him in the back seat, an' it was then that he yanked out this gun. He was goin' to set out an' kill Frost, he said. While I was tryin' to get the gun away from him, I fired that single shot by accident, myself. So that's why they's a bullet gone from his gun."

"Well," Asey said, "this is almost progress, this is. The shot was fired from Zeruah's gun by you—that settles that. He remembers bashin' some one, an' it was you with a pillow while you was on the floor."

"He'd tripped me, see," Jim said, "an' then he knelt down an'—"

"I get it. An' Zeruah *was* mad with Frost. That jibes with all he says or thinks he remembers. An' it straightens him out. Clears up the mess at your house, Bingo, an' how your jacket got on the dune—"

"I still don't think," Bingo said stoutly, "that I—but by gum, I guess I *must* of fought myself! There ain't a soul in town that looks bad enough to of been at the other end, an' it'd take a good husky man to smash my place up that way!"

"You done a thorough husky job," Asey said. "Figgered out who give you the eye? Did you, Jim?"

Jim glanced at Bingo's fist. "Certainly not," he said in righteous tones. "He must have walked into the door!"

I caught the flicker of Asey's eyelid. "Um," he said. "Prob'ly tried to swallow the pump handle. An' Tim, you're the one responsible for the dory an' the stuff in Bingo's coat pocket. Well, it's nice to get them bits sorted out. None of you come near the house at Sandbar, did you?"

"Not within half a mile," Jim said. "Lord knows Zeruah tried hard enough, an' Bingo had some idea, one time, of serenadin' the place, but they didn't get there, thanks to me."

"None of you had on anythin' white, did you, like white pants?"

Jim looked disgustedly at Asey.

"You gone crazy? Did you ever see me in white pants? Or Bingo Cook? Or Tim? Or Zeruah? Nope, we didn't none of us have on white pants, nor stove pipe hats, nor ooze leather boots! An'—"

"No offense," Asey said. "No offense meant. Just wondered. Say, Jim, if you was so sober all this time, how come about that bar'bry hedge?"

"Well, after I got that gun away from Zeruah, an' got him an' Smalley packed away in the car, I drove up to the four corners. An' let me tell you, I was just about as dog-tired as I've ever been in all my life! There was a couple bottles of champagne lyin' there on the curb, an' I was thirsty, an' the street was all full of broken glass, an' I had on sneakers, an' I didn't want to take a chance cuttin' myself, walkin' clear over to the pump—"

"I grasp it," Asey said. "I grasp it now."

"An' then," Jim said, "I—well, I woke up next mornin' next to Zeruah in that hedge. And the dressing down I've got from every one because I was there! You think of me, savin' Tim from drownin', an' Bingo from gettin' pneumonia out on that dune when he wanted to lie down an' go to sleep, an' Zeruah from shootin' up Frost an' himself—an' all the thanks I got for all that is a lot of criticism from the people who only seen me there in that hedge! Look, couldn't you put in a good word for me,

Asey? I done my duty as I saw fit, an' maybe it wasn't spectacular, but—"

"But you saved four lives," Asey said, "an' no one could do any more. Sure, I'll do what I can. Now, you can all run along. I'll want you later, an' I'll see that they let Zeruah off soon's pos'ble."

Smalley whispered in Jim's ear.

"Oh, yes," Jim said hurriedly. "How about—I mean, I got a couple errands to do on the way home. D'you suppose you could take Bingo back to the bar in the rumble of your roadster? Then he'd—"

"Tryin' to get out of it, hey?" Bingo asked. "Tryin' to get—"

"You come along with us, Bingo," Asey ordered. "After all, there's been enough trouble in East Pochet since Sat'day night. If you turn yourself loose on Jim an' Smalley, people'll think the town's a branch of a slaughter house. Okay."

"There's just one more thing," Tim Smalley said as he started to follow Jim out. "Look, Asey, I know I can't remember a lot about that night, an' what went on, but— did any one say anythin' to you about a woman wanderin' around the bar, dressed in white? Honest, it sounds kind of silly, but there was one time there when I thought I seen a woman. 'Course, it might just been my 'magination, but I thought so. I even chased her."

"Tch-tch." Asey clucked his tongue. "Catch up with her?"

"I wasn't in no condition to catch anythin'," Tim said with a grin. "But it was just after I come back towards where the rest was, from chasin' her, that I found them things of Frost's. Then Jim, he come an' dragged me away the next time I started after her. That was when we was almost up to the bridge. I thought first, Sunday mornin', that I'd been seein' things, like—"

"Yup," Asey said. "Like you heard the temple bells an' the paddles thunkin'—"

"Uh-huh. But the more I think of it, Asey, the more sure I am that there *was* a woman!"

Asey asked Jim if he had seen her.

"Say, Asey," Jim answered with infinite patience, "don't you think I had my hands full enough as it was, with three crazy men, without seein' any stray white ladies? But—say, there was one time there, the second time Zeruah started back for the house to kill Frost, that I lost him. I thought I seen him lie down in a dune, an' then he come runnin' from the other direction. Maybe— say, maybe there might of been some one else there!"

"Almost seems so," Asey said. "Thank ye kindly, the lot of you. No, Bingo! You ride with us!"

After a brief conversation with Forman and some of the other officers, Asey and Bingo and I set out for the bar. According to my calculations, we covered the distance in something under a mile a minute—and that road is as full of curves as an old-fashioned wire hairpin.

Bingo's face was white when he climbed out of the rumble seat.

"I thought," he said, "I'd seen—some day, Asey, they're goin' to sweep you up in a dustpan. Look, I won't touch Smalley or Jim. I was just foolin' 'em. An' any time you need any fish, you let me know. An',", he whispered industriously in Asey's ear.

"What was that last?" I inquired as the bridge guards let down the rope barrier for us to go through.

"He said," Asey announced with a grin, "that if I ever had a cold, or any aches and pains, he still thought he maybe might have a little Jamaica rum left over from the old days that he'd like right well to donate to the cause. Huh. Hanson's car isn't here, but—"

"But they're coming right behind us," I said, twisting around as a horn sounded.

Asey waved Hanson to come up to the house, and he and Quin drew up just as we were getting out of the car.

"Whoever gave that tip to you, Asey," Quin said, "was batty as a hedgehog. Those people in P-town don't know a thing; didn't know as much about Thorne as Nellie did. Find out anything?"

"A lot," Asey told him. "We're goin' to have a little council of war out here on the terrace soon's I c'lect the others. No, you stay here, Quin. Come with me, Hanson."

Ten minutes later all of us, including Ford in his wheel chair, were gathered out in the sun.

Deal was the last to arrive, but Asey gave her no chance to talk with Quin. He motioned for her to take a seat and began.

"This business," he said, "is workin' into a first-class mess for you folks, b'cause it's turnin' back home to you. First off, it didn't seem like any of you was c'nected.

Now—well, to cut a long story short, I want the truth out of you. I don't want any hemmin' an' hawin' an' lyin.' It won't do no one any good, b'cause I know where I stand, now. Quin, how'd this gun get into your suitcase?"

He pulled the .22 from his pocket and laid it on his knee.

Quin looked at it and then he looked at Asey.

"It didn't, Asey. I never saw that gun before in all my life."

"You picked it up this mornin' on the dune," Asey said, "just b'fore the fire in the livin' room, didn't you?"

"I did not."

"I told you," Asey said, "that there was no use lyin'. An' what I meant by that was, you was to tell the truth. You say you didn't pick up this gun, an' you never seen it b'fore?"

"That's it," Quin said.

"Very well." Asey got up. "I'm sorry you choose to be this way, Quin. Forman's traced the gun. You bought it. An' the bullet that killed Frost was shot out of it. Hanson, you just better take Quin along with you an' call it a day. All right, everybody. That's all."

He put on his Stetson, buttoned up his chamois jacket and strode to the roadster.

"Okay," Hanson said briskly. "Going to behave yourself, Quin, or shall I have to put on bracelets?"

Quin was biting his underlip so hard that a tiny prickle of blood appeared.

Asey started his car.

"'Bye, Mrs. Colton," he said cheerfully. "So long, the rest of you. I'll—"

"Wait!" Deal said. "Wait, Asey! Come back! You've *got* to—"

Asey leaned back against the seat. "I ain't *got*," he said crisply, "to do anythin'. I told you, an' Quin, an' the rest, just what I wanted. Quin's chose his own bed, an' he can have all the nightmares he wants. I got better things to do with my time than to listen to him tryin' to bluff. He thinks he's got a great brain. He thinks he can bluff himself out of this. Maybe he can. He's goin' to have a lot of time to bluff in. An' it's goin' to take a better set of wits than his to get him out of this, the way things is now. That's that. So long!"

Deal ran down the steps to the car. "Asey, please! You know he—come back! He'll tell you the whole story! Truly, he—"

"I'm sorry," Quin said. "I—I can't get out of this by myself, Asey. I know it. Come back. I'll tell you the works. I—"

"Prob'ly," Asey drawled, "prob'ly you would. You got a right nice 'magination. Let's see—how'll the works go? You bought the gun from Johnson, an' you had it— um. A year's a good time. Then three men, one of 'em with cross-eyes, broke into your apartment an' stole it. That's the last you seen of it till you found it on the dune. Or—was it a big black man with a big black mustache an' a wooden leg that pinched it out of your pocket at the bike races? Or did a magician yank it out of your coat in a theater an' turn it into a rabbit an' forget how to change it back? My, yes. I just bet you can tell me everythin'. Well, you tell it to Hanson an' his fellers. They might believe you. I shouldn't."

Quin's eyes were flashing.

With the quickest motion I've ever seen, he picked up the gun from where Asey had left it on the table, in front of Hanson, and swung himself over the terrace balustrade.

"Stick up your hands, Hanson!" he ordered. "You too, Asey. Get out of that car. Deal, get in and take the wheel. I'll—"

Asey continued to lean against the seat with his arms folded.

"Come, come, Edgar Wallace," he said gently. "Put the big gun down. It ain't loaded. Hanson, take it away from the little boy. That's right."

He got out of the car, took the gun from Hanson and proceeded cheerfully to remove the clip.

"There," he said, "I feel better. I didn't think, Quin, that you'd be fool enough to try a stunt like that. Honest, the longer I live, the more I wonder at the plum dum-foolishness of—"

"It *was* loaded!" Deal said. "It—it was!"

"It was," Asey said, "but it ain't. Now, Quin, stop gaspin' an' gettin' purple in the face, an' thank your lucky stars you didn't try to get away. Hanson'd of picked you off before you got to the bridge. Or else Deal'd of been picked off if she was chump enough to of gone with you. Just forget your detective stories for a few minutes, an' do a little hard figurin'. You're in a spot. An' 'less you give up this crazy notion of tryin' to shield Deal, you're goin' to find yourself labeled the murderer of Caleb Frost an' Richard Thorne. An' it won't take long for that to cover the papers an' get sent out over the radio. You'll never live it down. Your fam'ly's too big. How about it?"

"How did you know," Quin demanded, "that I was trying to shield Deal?"

"When any reas'nbly sane man," Asey said, "begins actin' like somethin' out of 'The Ole Homestead,' it ain't hard. Now, how'd you lose the gun?"

"It was stolen from my car last fall," Quin said glibly. "Thieves slashed at the top while it was in a parking space, and took it from the compartment back of the seat. Took my fur coat at the same time. I—"

"Stop it!" Deal interrupted. "Asey knows that's not true! He knows your car and the top—remember you were down here every weekend till Christmas last year! You'd have told him if anything like that had actually happened. Don't—"

"Will you let me tell this my way?" Quin demanded, "or shall—"

"I will not let you get yourself in this any deeper than you already are! Asey, one weekend last fall he forgot to pack that gun, and I put it in my suitcase for him. Forgot to give it to him later, and took it all the way back to New York with me. When I got back, Major Bird—he's my boss, tripped off and forgot to give me the check I had due. And I'd forgotten to pay the rent the month before, and I had about ten cents, and the landlord started a riot. He said I could pay up the last month and the current month and the next month, or I could pack up and leave. There wasn't anything to do but to take everything hockable around the corner—some rings and a diamond bracelet and some pins. And—"

"Why didn't you call on Quin?'" Asey asked.

"I should have, but he'd left for Chicago. Anyway, I took that junk, and the gun—I felt nervous carrying that stuff around. But the lad at the hock shop saw the gun in my bag and said he'd take that, too. I practically had to give it to him, because I was still short. He saw I needed the money and gypped me to the bone. I got my check from the major in a day or two, and got everything back, except the gun. That was gone. And that's the story of how Quin really lost his revolver."

"You can't carry or own a gun in New York state," Asey said, "without a permit. An' as for hockin' one, that's out of the question."

"Asey, don't you—"

"Of course he doesn't believe you, Deal," Quin said. "I knew he wouldn't. I told you then that the joint was crooked, but you wouldn't let me make a fuss about it because you thought Cale might hear of it—"

"What was the name of the place?" Asey asked.

"Why, it was just around the corner—the something or other loan association, or something. Quin, I told you!"

"I know you did, but all I can think of is Humpernickel, or Katzenjammer—"

"Reinbecker!" Deal said. "That was it. That—"

"Sure of that?" Asey asked as he got up. "Or are

you goin' to change your mind? No? Then be so good
as to p'sess your souls with patience while I do a tall lot
of phonin'. I—"

"You don't really think you can trace all that, do
you?" Quin asked.

"I can make a stab at it. At least, we can see if there
is a Reinbecker, an' what sort of place it is, an' how come
they got fellers around that offer to buy guns."

We were very silent during the twenty minutes he
was away.

Jane sat and smoked one cigarette after another, and
Tom puffed nervously at his pipe. Ford, his eyes closed,
leaned back in his chair as though he were asleep, but
his fingers beat a steady tattoo against the padded chair
arm. Deal stared out over the harbor, and Quin stared
miserably at her. Hanson made one or two unsuccessful
attempts to whistle, and finally played a game with the
buttons on his blue coat.

"Amazin'," Asey said blandly when he returned,
"how much easier it is to get three numbers in New
York an' Boston than one in East Pochet. I—"

"What did you find out about it?" Quin demanded.

"Found out that the firm went out of business last
week, the buildin's bein' torn down. Fact is, it's torn down
now. An'—"

"But it was there Friday!" Deal said plaintively. "I
walked home from work, and it was there!"

"That's New York for you," Asey said. "Hand is
pract'cally quicker'n the eye. Well, that's that. Just have

to take your story as is for the time bein'. Got a silencer, Quin?"

"I have one at home," he said. "You can phone and check up on that. But I never had one on that gun."

"You picked it up on the dune this morning?"

Quin nodded. "Yes."

"Knew it was yours?"

"Uh-huh. No doubt about it. Crack on the handle, half a dozen notches on it that Deal had cut when I hit bull's eyes on the harbor target. I knew it was my old gun. Of course I thought she—well, that pawn shop story was hard to swallow, always. And—uh—well, under the circumstances, you sort of find yourself suspecting anybody or anything. I just tucked the gun in my pocket, and after the fire, stuck it into my case. I was going to throw it into the harbor when I got the chance."

"Just where'd you find it?"

"About seventy-five feet from where Frost was. There was a string on it that I took off. Apparently some one twirled it round their head like a hammer by the string, and then let it fly. It was in a clump of beach grass and dusty miller. I'd gone over the place Sunday, but missed it. That—that ought to help, oughtn't it? I mean, I—but then, I never would have been fool enough to use my own gun, let alone something which would have involved Deal. I—I guess—well, what about it, Asey?"

"Frankly," Asey said, "it'd be a lot nicer if Mr. Reinbecker hadn't gone two other places. It's kind of vague'n queer'n fishy anyway. You an' Deal ain't seen the gun since last fall, you say, an' here it turns up. Did you know it right off, Deal?"

"Of course I did," she said wearily. "I thought that somehow, Quin had got his gun back again, and—oh, Lord, Asey, I'm glad you stopped us from—it's all clear now, but it was so awful to think that Quin might have —have had something to do with this. And of course, he thought—but d'you believe us, Asey? Or will Quin be arrested? Or will I? I was the one who had the gun last."

"I believe it," Asey said. "Hanson, how about you?"

Hanson hesitated. "I guess I believe 'em," he said, "but they ain't got no proof. I suppose, though, if they could track down that hock shop man—"

"They already started it," Asey said. "I called your boss an' told him to get goin'. They're sendin' a man over on the aft'noon plane. Hanson, there's some row or other goin' on yonder by the bridge. You'd better run up in my car an' see what the trouble is. R'porters, prob'ly."

Hanson came back in a few minutes, and beside him in the car was a woman.

"Oh, God!" Quin said. "Sob sister! Asey, can't you do something?"

"Where's your eyes?" Asey asked. "That's Lorena Baxter. Well, we're here for a week, now. She's prob'ly all wound up."

Lorena got out of the car almost before Hanson stopped it and marched up the terrace to where we were sitting.

"I called to you, Asey," she announced, "when you was up town with Mrs. Colton.—How do, Mrs. Colton?

Ain't this terrible? But I guess you didn't hear me. When you was up town, I mean. Asey, I got something real important to tell you. In fact, I got two important things to tell you. I guess it'll change your mind about this whole thing! I never thought they was important, at first, but I got to thinkin', to-day, an' the more I thought, the more it seemed to me they *was*. Important, I mean."

Asey pulled up a chair. "Sit down," he said with a trace of resignation in his voice, "an' tell us. Only, we ain't got an awful lot of time, Lorena. You know how 'tis."

Lorena nodded.

"I guess I do know," she said. "I guess *so*. Well, it's like this. Saturday night, I didn't go to sleep till late, because of course, I knew all about what was goin' on up town, an' I never forgot the time that Bingo Cook come home drunk one fourth of July an' went to sleep right on my front door step! And that man thought he was home in bed, an' took off all his clothes—an' the next mornin', when I went down stairs, there he was, naked as the day he was born! An' snorin' on my front door step! That," Lorena added with a touch of malice, "was before the days of mosquito control, an' I'm happy to say he was in bed three weeks with all his bites.

"Anyway, I stayed up till three Saturday night, an' then I went to bed, but I was wakeful. Around four-thirty, I heard a car go by, an' it slowed up in front of my house. I got up an' looked out of the window, an' there was a woman—a woman, mind you, dressed in white, an' she had the top of her engine up, an' was pokin' inside with a screwdriver or something. Had a flash light, she did, an' I could see her jabbin' at somethin'. Just as I started to go downstairs to see if I couldn't call Jimmy B. to fix her car for her, she got in an' drove away. An'—she come from the beach road, Asey! After I got back to bed, I started in to think, an' I begun to wonder if she wasn't that woman I'd heard up at the phone office that was makin' a date with Caleb Frost for Saturday night."

CHAPTER TWELVE

THERE was no particular necessity for Asey to inquire who the woman was and at what time she'd telephoned Caleb. Lorena had the stage, and she was entirely aware of the fact. For the thousandth time I mentally bewailed the cool fortune lost when Lorena decided that running a Gifte Shoppe was her life work; it wouldn't have taken one whit of preparation for her to have forced standing room signs on a vaudeville circuit. The only difficulty would have been the means to remove her from the boards once she got fairly under way.

"I was paying my bill," Lorena went on, deliberately setting out to paint a picture of the scene before she got to the point, "around eight o'clock. Just a little after, I think, because the papers was in. There was a woman in that booth near the door, an' I heard her say, 'I'll meet you at one, Caleb,' an' then she rung off. She didn't come out of the booth, then, though. She stayed in there, looking at the phone book, so I had to leave without seeing who it was. I asked Mary at the switchboard—but you know how close-mouthed she is, for all that she listens in to every call herself! All she said was, that it was a stranger makin' a local call, an' I said, 'Mary,'—"

"What makes you think it was to Frost?" Asey asked. "Did she mention his name?"

Lorena sniffed. "She didn't have to, did she? Mary said it was a local call, an' the only other Caleb in town is Caleb Rich, an' he's ninety-two! No one'd be meetin' *him* anywhere at one o'clock at night! Besides, her car swung off the beach road. I'd heard it comin' all the way. She'd been to Sandbar. Same woman. An' besides that, the only car parked outside the phone office was a coup with a light top, an' the woman outside my house, she was in a coup with a light top, too. So there!"

Asey's habit of hesitating and of weighing pros and cons was beginning to make Lorena bristle, but before she had a chance to express her mind on the subject, Deal intervened.

"Uncle did have a call at dinner," she said. "Gregory answered. He'd know all about it. Why don't you call him out, Asey?"

Gregory seemed to freeze up when Asey asked him about the affair.

"There was a call," he said hesitantly, "but—but it wasn't a woman, Mr. Mayo. She was a man."

He was lying so earnestly that he didn't appear to realize his slip until the shout of laughter died down. Then I thought he was going to weep.

"I mean," he said, "I mean, he was a man. She— that is, he was—"

"I know," Asey said. "A man. Did you know who

she was, Greg'ry, or wasn't he in the habit of spoilin' Frost's dinners to answer her calls?"

"I—really, sir," Gregory said, "I mean, Mr. Frost told me I must never mention that call. He said, Saturday night, 'If that woman ever calls again, you tell her I'm in Africa hunting lions, and if she comes near me, I'll throw her to them! I won't speak to her again. And don't you mention that call, Gregory, either!' That's what he said, sir, and since it was—well, practically his last order, as you might say, I tried to—"

"I understand," Asey said. "I know how you feel. But it's come up that this lady might have some connection with all this, you see, an' it—well, if she was the one who killed Mr. Frost, you wouldn't want her to slip out of our fingers just b'cause you'd promised you wouldn't speak about her. Now—Tom, give Greg'ry your chair. That's it. Now, tell us all about her. D'you know who she is?"

Gregory, sitting like a ramrod, shook his head.

"I don't know her name, sir, and that's a fact. But she's called Mr. Frost often in the last three years. Since Mr. Frost's retirement from the firm, that is. I've often thought she might have something to do about his writing."

"His writing?" Asey asked. "You mean—"

"I think," Ford said, "he means the writing Cale did that we all knew about. The books on ships and antiques, isn't that it, Gregory?"

He nodded. "Yes, Mr. Ames. You see, Mr. Frost used to leave the house every day about nine, and though he usually came home for lunch, lots of days he'd stay away till dinner time." There was a touch of pride in Gregory's voice as he added, "It was his writing."

"Where'd he go?" Asey asked.

"I don't know, sir. He had a place down town somewhere. In an office building. He never told us, because he said some day we'd think it necessary to bother him, and he'd rather come home and find the house burned down than to be interrupted during its burning."

"If he was Cheyne," Deal began.

"Yup," Asey said, "if he was Cheyne, an' writin' Cheyne at fifty words a second, besides doin' these other books as himself, I guess he'd had to have had some one help him. Yup, it fits in. Shouldn't wonder if the lady in white didn't turn out to be his lady secr'tary. Huh. We'll look into what we can look into. Don't s'pose you seen the plates on the car, did you, Lorena?"

"I didn't notice them," she answered sadly. "I didn't. But I don't think they was out of state ones, because I always notice those, an' if it's a nice lookin' car, I always stick one of my gifte shoppe cards," she gave every syllable its full value, "in the door or under the windshield wiper, or somewhere. I think it's a nice business touch."

"I beg pardon," Gregory got up, "but, Mrs. Colton, Mathilde wants to know about the dinner. What time— and the groceries—"

"Early dinner," Jane said, grinning at Asey as I started to become housekeeper again, "and I'll see about provender. Mrs. Colton, you stay put!"

It was very restful to watch her take Gregory in

hand, and I also admired the way in which Asey gave Lorena over to Hanson's care to take back to the bridge. I don't think it dawned on her that she was, generally speaking, being shunted, until after the shunting occurred.

"Pretty smooth master of ceremonies," Quin said admiringly. "But what now, Asey?"

"Now I'll go an' see if I can't find anythin' in Frost's study or in his papers or things that'll tell us anythin' about the lady. Oh, Tom. Run ask Greg'ry what her voice sounded like. Better still, ask Mathilde if she ever heard it. I never seen a woman yet that couldn't tell you all about another woman from just hearin' her voice over the phone; just like the kind of perfume she uses or don't use, tells—Quin, is that a—"

Quin hastily put his notebook away in his pocket.

"Yes, sir," he said. "It's put away, sir. But if you *will* cast pearls, you must expect—anyway, some day, Rutherford Grandgent, the detective who's different, will utter those same sentiments about women and voices over the telephone. He will, that is, if you manage to lift me out of this affair by the nape of my neck. Come to think of it, maybe Grandgent will utter it anyway. Trials take a long time, and boy, what a sensation a posthumous Rutherford Grandgent would make! Mystery Scribe Pens Most Puzzling Case While Waiting Execution—oh, Deal, don't! I—I was just trying to be funny!"

"It's what I call," Deal's voice broke, "sort of—of grim humor! If you must be funny, for heaven's sake stay off the subject of mysteries and murders! And let

me tell you—if Asey Mayo manages to get you and me
out of this mess, you'll never write another mystery story
as long as you live!"

"What?" Quin took off his glasses and stared at her.
"You—oh, come! Why, Rutherford's going to detect with
renewed vigor and goodness me, with what startling accu-
racy! How d'you expect me to support you in the manner
to which you've been accustomed unless I continue to
k—" he caught Asey's warning glance and changed the
probable "Kill people off" to "kindle the public with
sparks from my pen?"

Deal never had a chance to tell him how, because
Tom returned, laughing like a hyena.

"Mathilde," he reported, "says she was gooey."

"What?" I demanded. "Tom, you got her accent
wrong! Gooey, indeed!"

"No," Tom said with a weak bellow. "She said the
lady was gooey like maply frosting! As an afterthought,
she even said 'May-plish.' Just what is 'May-plish'?"

"It's something some one invented under the delusion
that it tasted like maple," I said. "The oleomargarine of
the maple flavoring—but you know, come to think of it,
I *can* picture the woman, can't you, Deal?"

"Picture her? I can paint her portrait and write her
life history," Deal said. "About forty-um. Forty-two or
three. Blonde hair. What Eleanor Martin calls 'was-
blonde.' A leetle mite on the plumpish side. About—"

"About a size thirty-nine, short," I interrupted, my
department store experience leaping to the fore, "but she
pretends it's thirty-eight and splits the seams and then ex-

pects the store to change the dress. I know the type. You should hear Mary Carter hold forth on 'em."

"Very red nails," Deal went on dreamily. "But dirty, usually. Wisps of hair sticking out around her neck. Her shoulder straps show, and her stocking seams are crooked—"

"My God," Ford said, "leave the woman a speck of character and respectability, won't you? Probably she's just—"

"Just a misunderstood woman," Deal said. "That, Ford, completes the picture of her. That's the way she appears to all men, because of her gooey voice and a few plaintive lines at the right moment. Just a misunderstood woman—I wonder if she's got a Southern accent?"

"Deal," Ford said, "I never suspected you could be—"

"So cru-el? Ford, my lad, you've never lived in a succession of female dormitories. At least, I trust not. But if be-yootiful gents like you could ever hear the aftermath of—Pen, what color are her eyes?"

"Blue, of course," I said. "China blue to Ford, watery blue to you and me. And she's a marvelous skin, Deal—"

"Why shouldn't she have?" Deal asked indignantly. "Doesn't she all but sing it to sleep in cotton wool every night of her life? Cleansing cream, lubricating oil, oh, the works!"

Asey covered his ears.

"I hope to God," he said devoutly, "that you two never take an awful active dislike to me! If you can do all that on the word 'gooey'—wheee! You could start a war with one sentence! Mrs. Colton, I want you to come upstairs with me, please, an' see—"

"Why d'you always take her?" Quin demanded. "Why does Pen get the breaks? Why don't you—"

"I take some one," Asey said, " 'cause I don't want to poke around people's things alone. An' I take her— just you guess!"

"The condemned men," Quin retorted in a sing-song, "ate a hearty breakfast of steak and pistachio ice cream, and asked for flapjacks also."

Asey chuckled as he and I went upstairs.

"I wonder," he said, "how much of this foolin' is coverin' up feelin's, an' how much is sheer desp'ration. I know one thing, though. These kids'll be flip to the bitter end, if it comes to that. Wonder why we ain't heard from the Richards boys?"

"Probably," I said, "Ned's answer will take some time. Bud—somehow I anticipate Bud's dropping in almost any moment."

It turned out later that that was the only prophecy I ever made in all my life which actually was fulfilled.

We went first into Lizzie's room, where Malvina Atkins had moved all of Cale's clothes and luggage after Lizzie had been put to bed in his room.

"The check book should show something, shouldn't it?" I asked. "After all, if this woman was in his employ, she'd have to be paid."

"It would," Asey said, "but it's brand new. See? Wheee—what a balance! Looks like the War debts. Know who Frost's lawyer is?"

"Your friend Stephen Crump," I told him. "And Steve's away visiting his brother's family. I'm sure of that, because he dropped in to buy some things to take to the children—furry animals and all that sort of stuff. But you could phone his office and have them get to Caleb's check stubs, couldn't you?"

"We can try," Asey said, "but I bet that Frost never caught himself givin' out checks to this woman. Not," he added with a grin, "if she's the pred'tory animal you seem to think. I bet he paid her in nice cash. By the way, what's your guess about her name?"

I thought for a moment. "Maisie—Daisy—Lucy—no, none of them fit. Cora. Yes, Cora almost does it. Wait till I call Deal."

Deal ran upstairs, listened to my question, and waved her hand airily.

"Name? I've thought of that. Cora. Oh, without doubt, it's Cora. And listen. She uses the Bible to press flowers with. What did you guess?"

"She guessed it too," Asey said, "an' don't either of you try to tell me there ain't no such thing as mental telepathy, 'cause I just seen it. An' let me tell you this. If we do find this woman, an' if she turns out to be a Cora, I—well, you know that ship model I got over home in Wellfleet, Deal? The one you always liked? Well, it's yours!"

"I'd rather," Deal said, "have the ship in the bottle you made yourself. And what'll you give Pen?"

"That's goin' to be a s'prise. All right, the ship in

the bottle, an' one s'prise. An' don't you two chortle. I'm
perfectly safe!"

We went through Caleb Frost's things as thoroughly
as they could be gone through, but they gave us no clew
to any possible secretary or woman in white or anything
else. Just before the gong rang for dinner, Asey called up
Stephen Crump's office manager.

"The long arm of coincidence," he said when he came
back to the table, "is goin' to get a kink in it. Seems
there'd been a mistake in Frost's income tax, an' he'd
told Steve to see to it, an' they had everything like check
stubs an' bills an' everythin' else there at the office.
Hartley'd spent the day workin' over 'em. Says he knows
those stubs backside to an' upside down, an' there ain't no
women payees 'cept Deal an' Mrs. Richards an' Mathilde.
So check stubs won't work. Hm. Well, after dinner, we'll
go see Mary Swazey, up to the phone office. Maybe we'll
get a line on the lady from her."

The night was unusually warm and I found myself
yawning as Asey and I drove along the Stone Crusher
Road where the Swazeys lived.

"Tired to death?" Asey asked as I yawned for the
tenth time. "Golly, I say you shouldn't be worked like a
pack horse, an' then you have to work like two, bargin'
'round with me."

"I'm not really tired," I said. "Half of it's the air,
and the other half plain confusion. Asey, what do you
make of this mess? Zeruah's got to be let off, and then
they can't do anything but arrest Quin—look, have you
thought at all about Ford? It seems incredible to think

of him, but after all, he did know Cale so well! And there
he was, the agent for Cheyne! And meeting Caleb—it
does seem as though he should have figured that out.
And—well, you know what I mean!"

"I know," Asey said, "an' I been broodin' about him.
But—if he was Cheyne's agent, he'll of been makin' a pile
of money out of Cheyne. No reason for him to want to
do away with his gold egg layin' goose, even if he knew
who Cheyne really was. An' then, the girls say he was
snorin'. That's certainly more alibi than any one else's got
—an' where's a motive?"

"What motive," I returned, "has Quin Gunner got?
Except that Jennie Mayo says she saw him and Cale having slight arguments last year on one or two occasions?
Truly, Asey, Cale and Quin always did get along. He told
Lizzie that getting engaged to Quin was the only sane
thing Deal had ever done—though whether or not he had
the Gunner money in mind when he said that, I don't
know."

We drew up in front of the Swazeys' little boxlike
Cape house, and Asey sniffed audibly as he helped me out.

"Honeysuckle an' wild—"

"And salt marsh!" I said. "And mostly salt marsh."

"Marsh nothin'," Asey answered as we went up the
brick walk to the side door. "Ma'sh. This workin' for the
carriage trade's played hob with your Cape accent. Good
evenin', Sol. Mary in?"

Sol Swazey nodded.

"Mind if we come in an' see her?"

Sol nodded again and led us into the dining room.

"Nice day, to-day," Asey observed. "How's quohaug-gin'?"

Sol nodded, shook his head and departed.

"Chatty soul," Asey remarked. "Y'know, Lorena Baxter nearly hooked Sol after Liza died four-five years ago. Case of a pos'tive force meetin' a neg'tive body. Sol'd need a surg'cal op'ration to get a joke inside him. Still, they's a sense of humor in the family. His father was the one that got so sick of town gossipin' an' town gossips that he bought a dog for five hundred dollars up in Boston, brought it home, an' then cut its tail off."

"Why?" I demanded.

"Oh, he done it painless. Y'see, he figgered it'd give the town somethin' to gossip about that was true, an' he thought it might stop 'em havin' to make up things. Worked fine. I—evenin', Mary."

Mary, who gets to Boston perhaps once a year, usually manages to look as smart as Deal. She smiled at Asey and shook hands with me.

"I know why you're here," she said. "Lorena's just gone."

"Lorena?" Asey said. "Huh. Well, her intentions was prob'ly good, but I wish she'd stayed home. Sometimes I wonder if folks with good intentions don't do more harm than nice vi'lent enemies with nothin' but bad ones. If she spreads that story 'round, an' the woman— say, remember anythin' 'bout that woman, Mary?"

"Not much, Asey. She was sort of plump and blonde. And—"

"Deal's ship," I said happily, "is practically in. Go on, Mary, don't mind me. What about her voice?"

"An' if you say 'gooey,'" Asey sounded disgusted, "I—I don't know what I'll do!"

"That's funny you should say that," Mary said. "I mean, Lorena and I were, that is, she was trying to make me remember, and both of us decided she was—well, that she had a cooing voice. But—gooey's more like it."

"Eyes," Asey was downright resigned, "blue. Finger-nails, painted red, an' they was dirty. Age, about forty-two?"

"Why, you have too seen her!" Mary said. "But her nails weren't dirty. They were beautifully pointed, and manicured and everything. She had a lovely skin, too. I'd know her in a minute if I ever saw her again, but—why, you've got as good a description of her as I could ever give you, really. And she did call Caleb Frost, Asey. At least, she called Sandbar. Then she called Wellfleet, I think. I don't remember who, but I know I had a ter-rible time making change. Every one was paying phone bills that night with five-dollar bills, and I had to send the Millis boy over to Smith's to make change."

Asey rose.

"Mary," he said, "you may not know it, but you've just been present at the end of a miracle. Come along, Mrs. Colton. I hate to see that ship go, but you an' Deal earned your r'wards. We'll pop on to Wellfleet an' see what can be seen. You get the idea she might be goin' to stay there, Mary?"

Mary wrinkled her forehead. "I can't remember,

Asey, if she was the one who asked about Lyddy Howes's place or not. There were mobs milling in and out all evening long. You might try Lyddy's, though. It's possible she did go there, but I seem somehow to have the impression that she was on her way to Boston."

Sol appeared to open the door for us, nodded again at our comments on his hedge, and then we set out on our way to Wellfleet.

Asey, who has an infinite scorn for main roads, wove the roadster expertly along narrow sandy lanes, bordered with scrub pines and scrub oaks.

"Can't go so fast," he said with a note of regret, "but it saves about four miles, an' b'sides, I like these paths. S'pose it won't be long before they tar 'em, an' then they'll be covered with tar paper shacks an' hot dog stands—"

"Progress," I said. "Civilization."

"Yup," Asey said. "I know. Personally, I never was a one to find much fault with the feudal system. Only, like Bill Porter says, you'd want to be sure you was in the castle doin' the feudin', an' not the one that was bein' feuded. I don't care much for this new socialism, I don't. I enjoy my fellow men, an' I get a lot of fun out of 'em, but I don't love 'em. Only feller I know of that's got an honest love for human'ty is a first-class can'bal—honest, I can't get over that this woman should turn out like you an' Deal was—tell me, d'you know her?"

"Certainly not," I said. "And we weren't absolutely right. Remember, Mary said her nails were clean. It was luck, Asey. Just luck. But really, if I ever lay eyes on the

woman, I shall probably feel toward her the way a
sculptor feels toward a statue he's created. Pygmalion—"
I stopped short, wondering whether or not Asey required
any explanation. But he surprised me, as he's done on
more than one occasion.

"Bill Porter," he said, "took me to see that play an'
explained all about the feller. But don't you forget, Mrs.
Colton, Pygmalion kind of got stung—hold tight!"

I obeyed him automatically as he swung the car off
the road and jammed on the brakes—so hard that I
bumped my head against the windshield, and the roadster
all but bucked like a horse.

I'd been paying no attention at all to where we were
going, but I found that we were almost at the intersection
of another wooded lane.

Parked squarely across the opening was a car—we'd
missed crashing into it only by a matter of inches, for the
thick underbrush had hidden its tail light. It was a coupe,
I saw, as Asey turned on the powerful swinging search-
light on the running board. A coupe with a light top—

I climbed out of the car and hurried after Asey.

Bending over the bonnet of the car was a woman—
obviously *our* woman. She was prodding futilely at the
spark plugs with a hairpin.

CHAPTER THIRTEEN

I'VE never been able to figure out whether she had actually been too engrossed with her tinkering to have heard us coming, or whether she deliberately ignored us in order to make her breakdown seem a little more poignant. At all events, she continued to jab viciously with the hairpin.

"Have you," Asey finally inquired, "a pers'nal grievance against them plugs, or is somethin' wrong with 'em?"

The woman straightened up, turned around and faced us.

"Oh!" She clutched dramatically at the neck of her dress. "Oh, how you frightened me—where did you come from? Oh—a car! But I didn't hear you at all! I was so busy, trying to get mine going!"

While she spoke, she favored me with the briefest of brief glances. I suppose I didn't really merit more. The voluminous light cape of Lizzie's which I wore was both dowdy and disreputable, and my hair had very definitely been blown out of its usual state of sleekness.

Asey was the one who took her eye and continued to hold it.

Clearly—very clearly, in fact, she approved of his corduroys and flannel shirt and slightly rakish hat. I judged also that she had no fault to find with his lean face and its network of lines. As for his eyes—she looked up into them and cooed.

"How simp-ly wonderful," she said ecstatically, "to have a man to—of course, *you* can tell me what's wrong! Men do know so much more about automobiles than us poor ignorant women! Won't you—of course you will! I just know you'll see if you can find out the trouble for me!"

Without comment, Asey accepted the flashlight she proffered and began a rapid examination of the car's entrails.

"Simp-ly wonderful," the woman cooed softly to me —but it was still a sufficiently loud cooing to reach Asey's ears, "that you and your husband should come along! I simply didn't know what to do, but I know your husband'll know how to fix everything for me. Men are so capable, aren't they?"

"They are," I said dryly, watching Asey's shoulders shake, "but really, you—er—honor me. This gentleman is not my husband. But I'm sure he can fix your car if any one can."

"Oh!" Having satisfied herself as to Asey's status, the woman became coy. "Oh, well, I'm sure I'm very sorry, but of course, when you see two people—oh dear me! I guess I've gone and put my foot right into it, haven't I?"

"Not attall," Asey said cheerfully. "I guess I can stand it if Mrs. Colton can. Y'know, I don't think I'm goin' to be able to fix your car. Seems to be beyond me. Guess the best thing to do is to take you up town with us an' send for a mechanic. He'll know a lot more about what to do than I will."

I opened my eyes wide at that bare-faced lie, but I had sense enough not to comment on it. Asey had without doubt made his own plans.

"How simp-ly sweet of you to take all that trouble!" she said. "Mr.—Mr.—I don't know *your* name, do I? *My* name is Cora Slade, and I come from Boston. I—"

Asey and I looked at each other and shouted.

"Cora!" he said. "My God A'mighty! Cora, huh? Co— well, well, I used to have a cousin named Cora, too. Sort of—of a coincidence, ain't it? You a—huh! You a stranger around here?"

"Well," Cora hesitated, "yes—and no. That is, I'm not exactly a stranger. I've a *very* dear friend who lives in East Pochet, and the truth of the matter is, I came down here to see him, among other things. Perhaps you may know him. He's Caleb Frost, of Sandbar. I'd intended to run over to see him this evening, but dear me, I don't believe I'll ever get there now, with this horrid car just acting like a perfect fiend!"

"You," Asey said blankly, "was settin' out to see Mr. Frost? Caleb Frost of Sandbar? Uh—you been stayin' around here?"

"About a mile away," Cora rattled on cheerily, apparently unaware of the amazement Asey and I were registering. "I've a little tent in the woods—I just *love* being out of doors in the open, don't you? Tell me, do you know Mr. Frost? Don't you think he's a charming man? I think he's a dear."

While Asey was swallowing over that, I goaded myself into making some sort of answer.

"Excellent," I said hurriedly. "Uh—excellent. Oh—very. Er—you've been out here in the woods for several days?"

"Since Saturday," she said. "Of course it was so horrid and rainy Sunday that I just stayed right inside my little tent. It was just as cozy as it could be, but my, I guess I *was* glad to see the sun this morning! And I've had such a terrible time with the car. I was going to see Cale—Mr. Frost, that is, this morning, but that car simply wouldn't start. I just got it going a little while ago, and now the old thing went and stopped again, and I can't do a thing with it!"

"I should think," Asey's voice showed that he too was trying to figure out how the woman could have escaped hearing about Caleb's death and all the rest of the Sandbar happenings, "I should think it would be kind of lonesome, camping out in the woods like that. But you got a radio, ain't you?"

"You dear man!" Cora reacted rather the way I expected her to. "You dear, dear man, to think of me being lonesome! But when I camp, I just cut myself loose from civilization entirely. I just go right back to nature. I don't even have a radio!"

I wondered rather acidly if flowered chiffon dresses

and spike heels and picture hats were a part of getting back to nature.

"Do it," Asey commented with a touch of irony, "up brown, don't you? Well, s'pose you come along, an' we'll drive back to town in my car. Then we can—well, sort of get things settled. Maybe it might be a good idea to go back to your camp an' get a coat for you, 'cause the top of my car's down—"

"You dear, thoughtful man!" Cora didn't seem to grasp the fact that Asey was testing out the truth of her statements about her little camp. "And—yes, my car's locked—and what a simp-ly wonderful car you have! My, it must cost a lot of money to own a car like that, doesn't it, Mr.—you haven't told me your name yet, and you know—"

"Just get in the middle, Mrs. Colton," Asey interrupted nervously. "You're used to—that's it! Now, which way is your camp?"

The directions Cora gave were scarcely lucid to me, but Asey appeared to follow them without effort.

"I know," he said. "You'll be about a mile beyond Syl's house. No chance of turnin' this car here, so you'll just have to be backed till I get to an open space."

After about half a mile of backing, he found a place to turn, and then we rolled off on another series of wood roads.

"You must come here a lot," I said, "to know these back lanes so well."

"Mr. Frost showed them to me," Cora explained with pride. "The next left, and then right. That's it. Yes, indeedy, dear Cale—I mean, Mr. Frost showed them to me."

She ran on and on about Caleb—it was all horrible to me, and I felt desperately uncomfortable. I could see, however, why Asey might choose to keep the news of Caleb's murder from her until he had found out what connection she might have had with him.

"And there—there's my little haven!" Cora finished brightly. "Isn't that too enchanting?"

I suppose there are those to whom the sight of a dingy canvas tent *is* enchanting, but I am afraid that my enthusiasm was forced. Just the same, Cora compelled Asey and me to get out and inspect the tent and its fittings; they'd all come, apparently, from the tiny trailer parked to one side.

Deal would have howled with joy at the inside of that tent, for on a folding table in one corner were at least fifty jars of the complexion creams and muscle oils which she had so truthfully predicted. Cora's cosmetic department, in fact, was far more complete than her culinary department in the rear corner. That consisted of a tiny canned heat stove, several tins of beans, a bottle of concentrated coffee and a package of breakfast food named "Tootsy-wheetsy." I read that label twice and then went outside.

"Been over to Sandbar since you been here?" Asey asked casually as we started away.

"No," Cora said, "I haven't. That's why I was so anxious to get there to-day. Mr. Frost would be hurt to pieces to know I was in the neighborhood and hadn't dropped over to see him—why, here's a car!"

More by the agonized sound of the engine than anything else, I recognized the truck that drew up to let us pass as the one in which Syl had driven up to the boat house on Sunday morning. Behind the wheel was Syl's Amazonian wife, Jennie Mayo.

"Hi, Asey," she called out. "You been takin' the short cut to my house? Say, you found out yet who killed Caleb Frost? I wish you'd hurry. I can't get Syl home an' there's a heap of work for him to do—not to speak of the houses he ought to be rentin'! You hurry it up all you can, won't you? So long."

Cora clutched my arm. "What—what did she say?" she asked in a scared voice. "Did—has anything happened to Caleb?"

"Well," Asey sighed. "Well, yes."

He stopped the car, pulled out his pipe, lighted it, and then briefly told her of what had happened Saturday night. I knew from his crisp sentences that he was no end annoyed that Jennie had upset his plans.

Cora sat absolutely still during the recital. Unlike Lizzie, she indulged in no hysterics—luckily, because there really wasn't room in the front seat of the roadster. As Asey went on, however, I could feel every muscle in her body grow taut.

She said nothing for several minutes after he finished, and then I realized that she was crying very quietly.

"I'm sorry," Asey said, "that you had to be told about it all like this. But I knew, before you told me, that you knew Frost, an' there was some things I wanted to find out from you before you learned what had happened to him. So—"

"Who—who are you, anyway?" Cora asked brokenly. "What have you got to do with it all? Are you a—a policeman?"

"I'm just kind of a pro-tem detective," Asey told her. "My name's Mayo—"

"Asey Mayo!" She sat bolt upright in the seat. "Oh, Mr. Mayo, I've heard all about you! Oh, how fortunate! How fortunate for me that you—that *you* were the one to find me and tell me! I can tell you everything, and I know you'll understand. I know from the thoughtful things you've done so far that you'll help me, see that people don't misunderstand!"

She was, I thought, already launching on the rôle of misunderstood female, but I knew that it was all rolling off Asey like the proverbial water off a duck's back.

"I'm glad," he said gravely, "that you're takin' all this the right way. But tell me, why did you go to Sandbar Sat'day night?"

"Why, I never did—"

"I'm 'fraid," Asey said, "that you ain't quite tellin' what you might term the truth. You see, we know you went there. We know you called Frost a little after eight an' made a date with him that night. An' we know that you didn't come back till after four in the mornin'. In fact," Asey was at his dryest, "we know quite a lot about you. An' what we don't know, we sort of guessed, as you might say. So—what's the story on Sat'day night?"

"You found out all that?" Cora said admiringly.
"How simp-ly clever of you! But you tell me first: am I
wanted by the police?"

"Yup," Asey said. "Now—about Sat'day—"

"Will—will reporters interview me?" Cora had
stopped sobbing and was beginning to tuck in stray wisps
of hair, to smooth out her collar—all those various little
feminine touches which indicate that a woman is re-
covering from an emotional debauch.

"Shouldn't wonder," Asey said, "if they did. But, if
you're countin' on them, remember we ain't goin' to stir
from this spot till you've answered all my questions an'
answered 'em with the truth. Awful sort of p'ticular
about the truth, I am."

At that Cora began to answer questions like an expert
witness.

She had worked as a secretary for Caleb Frost for
three years and had of course known that he was Varney
Cheyne. She'd promised, however, never to divulge the
fact, and I don't think she would have if Asey hadn't
made it clear that we knew already. I remember thinking
that Caleb was rather clever in picking out a secretary
of her type; as long as he'd paid her a little attention, she
would have remained entirely loyal.

"Tell me," Asey said. "How'd you know that Frost
changed his plans about goin' abroad?"

"It just so happened," Cora confessed, "that *I* was
going abroad on the same boat, but dear Caleb didn't
know that. I was going to surprise him! Then, Friday, I
called him at his hotel apartment and found out that he

was coming down here. I thought he intended to write another book, so of course I canceled my sailing right away and left New York right off. He *couldn't* work without me. I called him up Saturday night, but he must have had a lot of company around, because he was very short. I understood, though, and came over to the bar anyway, around twelve-thirty or so. I left my car on the mainland —my, I've done that so many times before! Oh, yes, I often came down here and met him at night, when he had manuscript for me. Ah," she sighed, "those—ah, dear Caleb!"

"Um," Asey said, and asked about Richard Thorne. Cora knew a lot about Thorne.

Frost, it seemed, had had Dick traced from the time he had left Boston, and had kept tabs on him until the past year. Then Dick disappeared from his job as gang foreman on Boulder Dam and no trace of him could be found. The firm of private detectives Caleb employed were positive that he had died or been killed. Asey asked who they were and sniffed when Cora told him.

"It's a wonder," he said, "they ever traced him at all. So Frost knew all about Thorne; I s'pose he begun to write that book after he thought Thorne was dead, didn't he?"

Cora nodded. "Caleb felt *so* terribly about Thorne," she said. "But he said there was no way he could ever have helped out. He gave Thorne plenty of money when he left Boston; don't you think that was a fine thing to do, when he thought Thorne was guilty, to save him from being arrested?"

"It would d'pend largely," Asey told her, "on your point of view. Well, that sort of clears that up. No letters ever come from Thorne that you know of?"

"Never. Caleb would have told me of them. Besides, Caleb thought, for the last year, that Thorne was dead. He told me he'd wanted to write a story around all that for ever so long, but he never did until he was sure Thorne was dead."

"That," Asey commented, "was also gen'rous of him. Huh. So Thorne read the story an' seen the light, an' Frost got Thorne's letter an' seen another. Well, at least we're sure why Frost an' Thorne come here, an' why you was here. D'you happen to know what Frost was goin' to do if Thorne ever turned up?"

"Oh, he had that all fixed," Cora said. "He would just give him some more money and send him away. They never did find out who stole those bonds, you see, so that—"

"I get it," Asey said. "He could get Thorne to be amiable an' make him take some cash an' beat it. Now, a few more d'tails about you an' Sat'day night."

Cora had parked her car somewhere near Bingo's shack, I judged from what she said, and then she had walked along the outer beach to the bench where Asey and Deal and I had been that morning before the fire broke out. The bench was their usual meeting place. Around three o'clock, she had decided that Frost couldn't get out.

"Sometimes," she explained, "he couldn't, without making explanations, and he was very careful with me, for as he said, if people found out about me, they might find out that he was Cheyne, and he wanted that kept a secret forever. So I just decided he couldn't manage to get out without some one seeing me, and went back to the car."

"So you was there from before one till three," Asey said, "an' then you had trouble with your car. I—"

"How did you find that out?" Cora demanded. "Why, I think your detecting is simp-ly wonderful!"

"Uh-huh," Asey said. "You meet any men that night, Miss Slade?"

"Mrs.," she corrected him. "Really, that is, I'm Mrs. Slade, though I call myself Miss. My husband ran away and I divorced him."

Very faintly I heard Asey's murmur: "Hit—or run!"

"But there *were* some men on the beach that night," she went on. "I went up toward them, thinking it—well, I went toward them, but they were drunk! It was awful! Anyway, then I came back to my little camp, and you know the rest."

"An' durin' that interval of one to three," Asey said, "Frost an' Thorne was killed—"

"It's simply horrible," Cora said. "Horrible! I'm sure that Thorne must have killed Caleb—oh, there was that woman I saw, too."

"That what?" I demanded.

"Why, there was a woman who came out of the door on the east terrace around—oh, shortly after I came. She walked out to the dunes, and then walked back around the house and disappeared. She may have gone in another door, but I didn't see her. Oh, Mr. Mayo, maybe it was she who did it all! But you'll see to it that people understand about me, won't you? Of course, I was very fond of Caleb—and—well, Caleb gave me presents. But he was just my employer, always."

Asey started the car.

"I don't s'pose," he said, "that you ever think of takin' a gun with you on these—uh—back to nature jaunts of yours?"

"A gun? Oh, Mr. Mayo! Why, I'd be scared to death! I'm just an old fraid cat about guns. Why, just the sound of them sets me off!"

"Ain't you ever 'fraid," Asey asked, "that some one might try to rob you or somethin'?"

"You dear, thoughtful man!" Cora said. "That's just what Caleb used to say always, too. He always thought I should carry a gun with me when I came down here, but my gracious! I told him I'd be more afraid of any old gun than I ever would be about any burglars! Besides, I think if you have faith, nothing will ever happen to you at all. When I first got my little car, people used to ask me if I wasn't afraid—driving, you know. But I always said, if you don't expect to have accidents, you never, never will! I suppose I'd better knock on wood just the same though, don't you?"

Asey looked at me.

"You an' Deal," he said, "are a couple of prophets. Miss Slade, you know anythin' of a girl named Jane Buckland?"

Cora had never even heard the name mentioned.

"Okay. What about Quin Gunner an' Durford Ames?"

"Why, Ford Ames was a dear friend of Caleb's, and Quin Gunner—why, Caleb admired his work tremendously. He thought Mr. Gunner was very clever. That's praise, coming from Varney Cheyne himself!"

"Don't know of any fights he ever had with either of 'em?"

"Not a one," Cora said. "Very few people ever had any fights with Caleb, Mr. Mayo. He was a dear, good man, and if *some* people were stupid enough to disagree with him, why, it was just because they were stupid. Caleb always said that Ford Ames and Quin Gunner were very brilliant young men. He liked them both."

I pondered on "dear good" Caleb as we sped along toward Sandbar. At the very first, it had seemed to me that Caleb had let his secretary know too much about his affairs, but I realized now how very shrewdly he had picked her. Cora was completely under his thumb, even if, as I could readily see, she might occasionally have proved difficult. I could thoroughly understand, for example, Caleb's comment to Gregory when she called Saturday night.

"Oh!" Cora said, as though some one had suddenly stabbed her. "Oh, the beach road! How many dear, dear memories! And the bridge—why, what a crowd of people! All—why, what's happened?"

There were none of the tourists we'd seen earlier in the day among those who milled about the bridge. They were natives, all of them.

Hanson emerged from the throng and hopped on the running board.

"What a time!" he said. "What a time since you left! Boat house burned down to the ground, gas tins exploded —no, no damage done except that Syl lost his eyebrows and some of his mustache. But listen, Asey—Syl salvaged a couple of boxes before the fire got really going. And what d'you suppose was in them? A watch and a wallet —Thorne's—and two .22's!"

CHAPTER FOURTEEN

"ONE fire," I said grimly as we drove down to the charred remains of the boat house, "one fire is an accident, but—two fires! Asey, that's—"

"Pract'cly a coincidence," he agreed. "Yup."

"Who owns those guns?" I went on. "Whom do they belong to? And don't you suppose—why, of course! Some one must have fired the boat house to destroy them. Why else? That must be the—"

I ran on merrily, feeling that at last I was contributing my share to the whole business.

But of course I was wrong.

Syl, looking almost naked without his eyebrows and scraggly little mustache, sheepishly confessed that he thought he was responsible for the fire. He'd knocked his pipe out against the side of the building, and there'd been shavings there which he'd forgotten all about. And Deal, furthermore, had identified the guns as those she'd been unable to locate in the house.

"She thinks," Syl went on, "that one of the boys must of left 'em down here last fall. They was both way down at the bottom of the box. An' as for them things of

Thorne's, they was tucked in under an ole paint can near the top. See—here they are."

He produced a common every day dollar time piece and a wallet which contained only a few dollars and a card on which was scrawled in pencil, "R. Smith—Boulder City."

"Huh," Asey said. "Prob'ly after Thorne was carried in here, whoever it was that done the carryin' took 'em out of Thorne's pockets an' just thrust 'em in there. First off 'twould seem like he'd been robbed, an' nobody'd think p'ticularly of huntin' so near. Well, we'll go up to the house. Oh, Hanson. This is Miss Slade, who seems to of been a contributin' factor, as you might say—"

"I'm simply thrilled to meet—is it Captain Hanson?" For several minutes Cora had been craning her neck to get a good look at him. "I really do think—"

"We'll run along," Asey broke in, "an' I'll be seein' you later, Hanson. Okay."

Deal, Quin, Ford, Tom, Jane and the doctor were all in the living room, clustered about the fireplace.

"Come have some coffee and food," Jane said. "This fire-fighting—honestly, I never saw a place where there was so much solid exercise. Dune hunting, fire—oh—I—I didn't see that you had a—a guest!"

Asey led Cora up to the group.

"This," he announced, "is—Deal, are you sure you're payin' attention? This is Miss Cora—Miss Cora Slade, your uncle's sec'retary."

"Cora!" Deal's cup and saucer dropped on the hearth and smashed lustily. "Cora!"

"Cora!" Jane said. "No—not—not Cora!"

"Cora!" Ford leaned back in his wheel chair. "Deal, since when have you taken up astrology? It was astrology, wasn't it? Cora—oh me, oh my!"

"I'm sure I don't see," Cora said huffily, "just what all of you—I mean, what *is* it that makes my name so humorous?"

Quin rose to the occasion.

"Miss Slade," he said, "you must forgive our bad manners. You see, Miss Richards here has—er—recently consulted an astrologist. She told Deal, and Deal's just told us, that to-day was the day on which she'd meet a very good looking blonde woman named Cora. So you see—well, it was rather a surprise," he concluded lamely. Inspiration had apparently run dry.

"Aren't astrologists," Cora said, promptly rising to the "good looking" bait, "aren't they simply wonderful? Why, I've a friend in Boston who wouldn't think of— why, she wouldn't even buy a new hat without consulting Madame Rita! What else did she say, Deal? Of course, I should say Miss Richards, but really," she giggled, "dear Caleb's said *so* much about you that I really feel I know you! Now, you must tell me all about it!"

"You tell her all about it," Asey chimed in. "All. Uh. Everythin'. Ought to be quite a long story, I shouldn't wonder," he added meaningly. "Well, Miss Slade, Mrs. Colton an' I'll just leave you here. Good comp'ny, I'm sure."

Deal made a face at Asey as he and I left the room,

crossed through the burned main living room and went up to Caleb's study.

"That," he said, "ought to hold that crowd for some time, an' I guess they ought to hold friend Cora, too. Wheee—maple frostin'! What kind of perfume is it she wears, Mrs. Colton? It's goin' to abide with me till death do us part."

"Abide with you, forsooth!" I said. "I sat next to her!—Look, Asey, where's this all getting us? What's to be done? We follow things up, and we don't seem to get anywhere! Everything leads us more and more—well—"

"More haywire," Asey suggested. "Just plain plum haywire. All comes back to the old truth that if you start with nothin', it don't make no dif'rence how much addin' an' subtractin' an' multiplyin' an' dividin' you do. In the end you still got nothin'. It ain't that this is so plum puzzlin'. You can't call somethin' puzzlin' when there ain't nothin' to puzzle with. Strippin' this down to its bare d'tails, Frost went out Sat'day night to meet Thorne, to give him money to go two other places. B'fore he met Thorne—I'm almost sure of this, now, he met some one else, who upped an' put a .22 through his eye, an' then tossed the gun away; n'en he went through Frost's pockets, took out the odds an' ends, an' tossed them away, too. N'en he met Thorne."

"But why should he have killed Thorne?" I asked. "What possible reason? What possible motive?"

"That," Asey said, "is what's botherin' me a bit more'n anythin' else. Only thing I can think of is, Thorne may of seen what happened. But it don't jell. Like ole Martha Watts used to say of her son John's wife. 'She's as smart a girl as ever stepped up to a flour barril, but nothin' on earth'll make her beach plum jelly jell.'"

"Where d'you think Thorne was killed?"

"Down by that heap of glass an' rubbish by the boat house. That's the only place, beyond that rise, where you wouldn't be seen from the house. Once the murderer stepped out of that line of dunes, he was in pretty clear view, an' there was a moon. I think he got his bottle from that pile, an' then hove the bottle out into the harbor. Near enough, there, to do that easy. Then he took Thorne into the boat house an' left him. Thorne was a big man. Be pretty hard to carry him any greater distance, p'ticularly on this sand. An' the fact that the boat house was opened with Frost's keys makes me certain sure that the same feller killed both men, an' killed Frost first. But then you go right round in a circle again. If Thorne was killed b'cause he seen what happened to Frost, why wasn't he killed up there by the dune, too? Why was there all that dallyin' from that dune down to the boat house? I don't get it."

Neither did I. "But," I made a valiant stab, "suppose that Thorne wasn't a witness to the murder. Suppose he just happened on this person—"

Asey jumped up from his chair. "Say—I—yup, that's one way I hadn't thought out. S'pose Thorne sees some one scurryin' back to the house or back to the bridge. He'll think it's Caleb Frost, won't he? An'—yup, that'll do it, all right!"

Doubtless it would, but I had no idea of what Asey was driving at, and said as much.

"Thorne," Asey said, "would go up to this some one an' say—aw, it's simple. Thorne'll say, 'Evenin', Caleb.' Then this some one'll turn around, an' Thorne'll see it ain't Caleb. Then, dollars to doughnuts, the some one, seein' Thorne with his beard an' dung'rees, this some one'll say, 'Who are you an' what are you doin' here at this time of night?' An' so on an' so forth. An' Thorne— well, what'd he say to him? Chances is he'd say what he said to Syl, an' what he said to Nellie an' Pete Carstairs. 'I'm Varney Cheyne.' See it now?"

"I see," I said. "That is, that's all logical enough, but why would that compel the murderer to kill him? I mean, suppose I walked up to some one and said I was—oh, any writer you care to name. What is there in that to make them kill me?"

"B'cause it seems to me," Asey said, "that Frost was killed not b'cause he was Frost, but b'cause he was Varney Cheyne. That's the only note that Frost an' Thorne jibe on. Yup."

"Asey," I said wearily, "I'm stupid, but I admit it without hesitation. Just elucidate."

"Well, s'pose you'd killed Caleb Frost, thinkin' he was Varney Cheyne," Asey said with great patience. "Then s'pose a feller marches up and announces that he's Cheyne. Wouldn't you reach for the nearest bottle? I think you would. P'ticularly since, after all, you really couldn't be honest certain sure that Frost, whom you'd already killed, *was* Cheyne. Yup, I been thinkin' round that all day, but I hadn't maundered that far."

"But that eliminates almost everybody," I said, "except Ford and Tom and Cora."

"B'cause," Asey said, "you don't admit to bein' a R'publican ain't no reason why you mightn't be. In—"

"In other words, you think that the others may really have known about the Cheyne business? Oh, Asey, this is too much for this feeble—"

The doctor entered the room without knocking, walked very deliberately to a chair, sat down and covered his eyes with one hand. With the other hand he made sweeping, expressive gestures.

"I am speechless," he said at last. "Utterly speechless. I have, in the course of an extensive if not always lucrative practice, met a number of women whom without hesitation I might term deluded. I have encountered hundreds—practically thousands, of females burdened with sundry neuroses and psychoses. It comes as a blow to my pride to discover that what I had hitherto considered a reasonably adequate knowledge is nothing but first grade—bah, kindergarten! That's what! Asey, where did you pick her up? Something ought to be done about eugenics in this country. I mean, she's the Pekingese of two legged mammals—actually, I'm speechless!"

"I take it," Asey said, "you r'fer to Cora. By the way, Mrs. Colton, can you find room here for her? Okay. You been chattin' to Cora, doc?"

"I," the doctor retorted, "have not been chatting to Cora. She's been chatting to us. Ford excused himself, but the rest are manfully sticking it out. I wouldn't be one to guarantee how much longer they're going to stick it out, though. We've heard about astrology, Clark Gable, the dearest little tea rooms—Asey, it's a wonder to me that Frost's ghost doesn't rise and smite her! Undeniably her only excuse for existence is that she must have been a wizard on the typewriter. That, and her digestive system. Beautiful skin. Well, I feel better. I'm going in to see Lizzie. I tell you, a good simple neurotic will be sheer relaxation—oh." He stopped on his way to the door. "Something under this chair here. Tassel off a shoe lace. Better take it now, Pen, or you'll forget all about it."

Automatically I caught the little piece of brown leather as he tossed it to me before he left.

"It's not mine," I said. "Probably Deal's. I'll give it to her, because they don't come with new laces. I worked in the shoes for a week and I know all about such things."

Asey looked at it.

"Funny," he said. "That—nope, that's not Deal's. That's Jane's. I remember noticin' to-day that she'd lost one of the tassels off her brogues. She'd got some of the chemical on her shoes durin' the fire, an' I helped her wipe it off."

"Can't be Jane's," I told him. "She's never been in this room at all, as far as I know. Don't see how she could have—"

I broke off as a knock sounded on the door and Jane came in.

She sat down in the chair the doctor had just vacated and proceeded to remove two handkerchiefs from her mouth.

"Oh," she said weakly, "oh, I'm limp! I'm sorry to butt in, but I simply couldn't stand up before Cora another minute. Asey, are you intending to keep her here much longer? Because every man has his price. I mean, his limitations. It's not going to be very long before even little Tom Politeness gives up. Deal and Quin are jibbering right now."

Asey held up the little tassel. "Yours?"

Jane looked at it. "Yes. Where'd you find it? I thought I must have lost it in Boston Saturday. I noticed it was gone when I went to bed Saturday night."

"You lost it in here," Asey said, with something of a purr in his voice, "while you was talkin' to Caleb Frost Saturday. 'Bout twelve-fifteen or so, wasn't it?"

Jane picked a cigarette out of a box at her elbow and lighted it before she replied.

"I suppose," she observed with a twinkle in her eyes, "that the canary always wonders how the cat does it. But believe it or not, Asey, I've been burning to tell you everything since Sunday morning."

"Would it be too much to ask," Asey replied with a grin, "why you didn't?"

"Well," Jane blew out a cloud of smoke, "there seemed no place in the conversation where it fitted in neatly. I mean, I couldn't have stopped short while Quin was stalking around with that gun this afternoon, could I, and said, 'By the way, d'you know I saw Caleb Frost Saturday night and had a lovely little set to with him?'

Or in the midst of the fire? No, every time I got up my
courage to break the news, you snatched Pen up and
dashed off in your low backed car. So I—"

The doctor came in, frowned at Jane and sat down.

"If you, Asey," he said, "would like to hear a practically virgin theory on this affair, go in and listen to
Lizzie Richards. I don't know where she picked it up,
but she's certainly definite! Rambling, of course, but
many a time I've heard the truth bandied about during
just such ramblings. Did I ever tell you, Pen, what the
head of the Anti-Saloon League said under ether?"

"You mean Sabina Fisher?" I asked.

"Yes. The one from North Pochet. She's dead now,
poor soul, so I can tell it with a clear conscience. But
d'you know, she kept muttering in the most horrified
tones. Took me some time to figure it out. And then I
howled so I had to have Davis carry on. By George, it
makes me weak to think of it even now!"

"Don't keep us in suspense," I said. "What was it?"

" 'For Christ's sake,' " the doctor said weakly, " 'for
Christ's sake, are you giving me beer for a chaser?' "

Asey came back. "Thanks a lot, doc," he said. "I
was just comin' to that. I hardly thought, Sunday mornin', she meant Deal when she yelped about 'that girl,'
just before she started cuttin' up. Okay."

"I'll go back and see to her," the doctor said. "Poor
Malvina! The rest of you may think you're being abused,
but Malvina's the woman who's taking the real beating.
And—oh, yes. About Sabina. A cousin of hers told me
confidentially after she died that she'd spent three years

in a drunkards' home before she took to anti-salooning."

"I like him," Jane said after he left. "Funny how some doctors leave you yearning for a coffin, and others, like him, just brighten your day—don't scowl, Asey. I'll tell you everything, but it's a terribly long story. Did Mrs. Richards hear me? Was that what she was rambling about?"

"Don't think she heard you," Asey said. "She was ramblin' about the other end. Soon's you left, Frost come burstin' into her room an' said you was to leave Sunday mornin', or he'd throw you out in pieces an' lumps. Let's hear about it."

"Very well." Jane leaned back in her chair and crossed her legs. "It begins two years ago. In the spring. My father had money, but the crash got him. He salvaged what he could and went up to his old family place in Maine. I was visiting Dot Marcy in Actonville when a telegram came saying that dad had been in an automobile accident and was dying. In Hanker's Corners, about fifty miles away. Dot has a roadster like yours, Asey, so I took it and set out. I knew the roads and I was sure I could get there in time with that car, even though it was raining cats and dogs and little fishes. I took a short cut about ten miles away from the corners, and ordinarily I'd have got to Dad in about seven or eight minutes. But I didn't, and that's where Caleb Frost comes in."

She lighted another cigarette and held a match to mine.

"You see, the short cut was under construction. Full

of mud holes and crushed stone and puddles, and the rain was getting worse. With my own little car I might have had a chance of getting through, but with Dot's big heavy brute of a thing, I got stuck. I worked for fifteen minutes trying to get it clear of that sink hole, but I couldn't do it. So I started to walk. Just as I set out, I saw headlights coming, so of course I got out in the middle of the road and waved. It never occurred to me that whoever it was wouldn't give me a lift."

"An', he didn't?" Asey asked gently.

"He didn't. The driver stopped the car about ten feet from my roadster and put a spot light on me. I told him about Dad and asked if he'd take me on. And the gentleman laughed and said he was too old a bird to be taken in by that particular snare, and then he went on. And—"

"And left you?" I said. "He left you?"

"And left me there, sort of groveling in the mud, with the tears streaming down my cheeks."

Neither Asey nor I said anything; I don't think we could have.

"I—well, I'd sense enough to look for his number," Jane went on, "but his plates were smeared. I never saw that man's face, though of course he had a good look at me. But I knew his voice, and I knew his laugh, and I swore then that if I ever met him again, I'd try in some small way to make him suffer the way he made me suffer. You see, I had to walk all the way to the Corners. It took me an hour, because it—well, it wasn't easy walking. Dad had died half an hour before I got there. And the instant I heard Caleb Frost's voice Saturday night, I knew he was that man."

"There are those," Asey said, "who would say that if you was the one who shot him, you had ev'ry right. I sort of agree with 'em."

Jane shrugged. "I didn't kill him, Asey, though I— well, that whole incident sort of stuck with me. It's the sort of thing you think about when you wake up at night, or when you're broke or hungry or sick. I didn't know there were people like that, before then. It was something you couldn't laugh off—"

"I shouldn't think," I said, "that you could!"

"No. I couldn't explain it, either. He was a total stranger to me, and I was a total stranger to him. There couldn't have been any personal—well, I finally decided that the only explanation of the thing was that the man might have perhaps been held up once on one of those fake accident robberies. But it was such a god-forsaken road, and even in my most disheveled condition, I don't think I look or act or talk like a lady bandit!"

"An' did Frost admit to bein' the gent, Jane?"

Jane shook her head. "No. He denied it just as emphatically as ever he could. It was the first time I'd ever met him, Asey, though I'd known Deal for years. He told me I was crazy, and insinuated that my coming to his study wasn't exactly the well-bred and ladylike thing to do. Oh, he was really superb! Before he got through with me, I felt like a cross between Hester Prynne and Sadie Thompson. In fact, he didn't really get mad till I muttered something about 'Wasn't the damned rain ever going to stop.' Anyway, I saw I wasn't getting any place and never would, so I left, more than ever convinced he was the man. Deal told me yesterday, after a little cagey questioning, that he'd been held up about two years ago in New York state and had his car snatched, and his money. Apparently I came on the heels of that. Well, that's the story of my interview with Frost Saturday night, Asey. I'd every intention of sending myself a telegram Sunday saying that I was urgently wanted in Siam."

"An' when did you go out, Sat'day night?" Asey asked.

Jane smiled. "How'd you know? It was just after that conversation with Caleb. I had to cool off. I went out the east terrace door," clearly it had been Jane whom Cora had seen, "and walked out to the dune. On the way back, I remembered that I hadn't snapped the lock. Trust me not to remember about latch locks. So I went around to the west terrace and popped in a window I knew was open and near the stairs. But I was back a few minutes after one, because Deal came into my room and we gabbed. Ford was snoring so that neither of us could sleep—why, Asey, the thought's just hit me with tremendous force, but if Deal and I were gabbling from a bit after one till—oh, easily two, that's—"

"Mutually excludin' alibi," Asey said. "Or would be, if you could prove it."

"But the doctor said," Jane screwed up her forehead, "that both men were killed around one-thirty. Oh, I see. You think Deal and I might have got together on the time. We haven't. As a matter of fact, her watch had stopped, and mine's rarely right. Well, I'm pleased and delighted and generally cheered to get this off my chest. I'm not guilty and I'm not a bit afraid you'll land on me. God knows I've seen plenty of innocent people get theirs in the last two years, but I still retain a quaint childish notion that evil doers get punished, and the spotless get rewards—the meek shall inherit the earth, and all that sort of thing. Besides, I've been scrutinizing you, Asey, and I don't think you're going to do any landing till you're sure. And I also have a sneaking notion that you've got some one in the back of your mind whom the rest of us haven't even thought of. I—listen—did you hear a plane then?"

"Thought I heard one a few minutes ago, too," Asey told her. "Couple fellers over Chatham way, they fly down from New York in their own planes. Seems like there wasn't a pasture left where the cows ain't been frightened to death an' left all disc'ntented from havin' planes make 'mergency landin's all round 'em. They found one of Syl's best Jerseys eight miles from his field an' tryin' to swim a crick, the day after Bill Porter's crazy brother smashed up. Offhand, I'd say—"

Somewhere on the roof above us sounded a sickening thud and a splintering crash that mixed themselves up with a tearing of shingles.

"Offhand," Asey continued cheerfully, "I'd say we'd been took for a herd of cows."

CHAPTER FIFTEEN

BY the time we had collected ourselves sufficiently to get down to the front door, Bud Richards appeared on the threshold.

A nervous grin flickered over his cherubic face, and he dangled a leather helmet with elaborate unconcern. Bud is a year older than Deal, but at that moment he looked like a six year old waiting for a spanking—and hoping, cheerfully, that it wouldn't happen after all.

"Absolutely not a bit of harm done," he announced with what was intended to be a casual gesture. "Absolutely not a bit. Just scraped a few shingles off the east wing, that's all. Uh—oh, hi, Asey! Ned cabled me to drop down and report to you for duty. I didn't get your wire till after I got his. Yours got sent to the wrong town or something."

"Mrs. Colton," Asey said dryly, "said she thought you might drop in, but I hadn't thought you might drop quite so lit'rally."

"How are you, Pen?" Bud reached out for one of the leftover sandwiches on the table. "Hi, every one—I say, don't be like this! I tell you, there's not a thing the matter except a few shingles—isn't it awful about poor old Caleb? How's mother?"

"Your mother," the doctor said coldly, "*was* asleep. She—"

"Gee," Bud said. "I—I bet I waked her up, didn't I? Oh, gee, that's tough. I'll just run up and tell her it's all right. Only a few shingles—"

"No you don't, sonny boy!" Deal grabbed his arm before he could start up the stairs. "No, you don't! Whose plane was it?"

"Oh." Bud cleared his throat. "Just Sammy Wharton's. His old autogiro. He flew me up to Boston, and I popped down alone—honestly, Pen, there's no need to look so scared! It was just a few old shingles that—"

"If you say another word about shingles," I interrupted him grimly, "I shall take one of them to you! So you—when did you learn to fly?"

"In college. I've got a license, but uncle never would —look, Deal. Sammy himself said he didn't care what I did to that bus. He's got two new—you see, I was aiming for the cement turntable by the garage. Sammy put her down there last summer all right, but I'd lost my glasses—"

"Bud!" Deal stamped her foot. "And you're near-sighted as a fool! You utter ass, you might have landed out in the ocean! Quin, will you convey this idiot to the garage and take him over your knee? I never heard of anything so—"

"Listen, Sis," Bud said earnestly. "I got here, didn't I? And only those few shing—I mean, only a couple of planks smashed up. Plane's all right, or will be with a little—I mean—I'm going up and see mother."

Deal sighed and turned to Asey. "I don't know," she said, "whether you lock a plane, or what, but will you fix that craft so that that crazy kid doesn't get away in it? Of course the whole trouble is that Caleb made him go into the firm when he wanted to join Sammy's flying business. I suppose this is the way he's chosen to announce his independence!"

"Cheer up," Asey said. "You ought to be thankful he didn't want to be a human fly. He'd be half way up the Empire State, prob'ly, by this time. Mrs. Colton, where're you goin'?"

"Bed," I told him with all the firmness I could manage. "Bed! Two fires, one plane landing over my head—I've had enough for one day! Tell Bud he'll have to sleep here on the couch or wedge himself in with Quin and Tom. Deal, you'll go in with Jane and give Miss Slade your room. Sheets in the linen closet—no, they're up on my window seat." I'd almost forgotten the pile I had been expected to mark. "I'll show you. Miss Slade, you won't mind staying with us to-night?"

"I'd be simp-ly delighted," she said. "This dear, dear house, where dear Caleb—"

"Come," Deal said hurriedly. "I've got a lot of stuff to move, Pen. Oh, that's right, Jane. You'd better help. No, Quin. You and Tom just stay and entertain Miss Slade until we're ready. And you'd best tell Ford what the noise was all about. He's yelping."

Deal cleaned out her room for Cora by the simple

process of tossing all her possessions onto a sheet and dumping the sheet in Jane's closet. I investigated their further efforts in Cora's behalf just in time to squelch the beginning of an excellent pie bed.

"Don't ask me how I know you were up to mischief," I said. "I haven't traveled around with Asey Mayo for two days for nothing. Hurry and unmake it, because I'm practically asleep on my feet."

"What about Cora?" Deal asked. "Was she here Saturday night? Was she really uncle's secretary? Does Asey think she's got something to do with all this?"

I shook my head. "I don't know. At this point I'm certain of my name, but if you questioned me closely, I could have doubts just as easy as falling off a log."

Jane smiled as she plumped the pillows.

"I feel that way, too. It sort of gets you, doesn't it, Pen? Underneath, I mean. I've even found myself looking at you and wondering if you weren't mixed up in it somewhere. I've sort of lost all sense of perspective. But don't you think what I said before Bud dropped in was true?"

"That Asey had something up his sleeve? I wish I could think that he had, but what on earth is there he could have ferreted out that the rest of us don't know about? Oh, I just don't understand anything! If only there were something more we'd found out, or something less! It's all like those horrible brain teasers my father used to make me solve when I was little—if you had so many gallons of something, and only a quart pail and a ten gallon tub, how could you give some one two gills? You know what I mean!"

Jane perched on the foot board. "State your answer in yen," she said. "And—"

"And what is the value of the yen," Deal broke in, "if gold is—"

"The value of the yen is how many eggs," Jane began. "Oh, don't, you wretch! And I had those pillows all looking ladylike! But you're right, Pen. I always thought the farmers were such fools not to have a complete set of measures. It'd have made everything so much simpler all around. But I put my faith in Massachusetts. Asey'll pour till he gets the damn thing right. And *I* think he's got his mind on some one we haven't even thought of!"

Deal turned white.

"Janey, you don't mean Bud? He's a darn good pilot, really. That smash was just because he didn't have his glasses –but it does look as though he were trying to show that he couldn't land without a racket! Jane, you don't think Asey thinks he flew down here Saturday?"

"Of course I don't, you goose! It never entered my head! We'd have heard—"

"Not if he went up around five thousand and cut his motor. When he and Sam were down last summer, they popped in one evening and surprised us to pieces. We'd never heard a sound. And Sam used to land that plane up on the hard sand beyond the dune where Caleb was! And Caleb and Bud haven't been on speaking terms since Christmas! Jane, you've got me jittering!"

"It's utter nonsense," I said. "You sound like Quin, ad-libbing around chapter ten. Run down and tell Cora everything's ready, and find something for her to sleep in. And put all this foolishness out of your mind. Then you go to bed and go to sleep!"

"But who," Deal demanded, "has got a motive in this affair if we, the family, haven't? I—"

"Run along and get Cora," I ordered, "and stop it!"

Just the same, I found myself wondering, and thinking of motives and the Richards family as I dropped off to sleep.

If Asey's conjectures were true, if Frost had been killed before Richard Thorne was killed, then the most important thing *was* the motive for killing Frost. And Deal was right in saying that the Richards family had the soundest motives. They had. But I believed Jane's story. If she had been with Deal, then Deal had nothing to do with the whole thing.

Lizzie was out of the question entirely. She couldn't have carried Dick Thorne an inch toward the boat house, let alone a hundred yards or so. But Bud was a different matter. Bud was always doing crazy, reckless things. Whereas Deal could be sullen or frigidly angry, Bud's temper was actively violent. It took him a long time to get mad, but when he did, he stayed mad.

Still, none of the Richards family had known that Caleb was Varney Cheyne, and Asey seemed to think that was important. Cora *had* known.

And on the other hand, it was possible that the Richards family had known, too.

"Pour the two gallon jug into the half pint tin," I
muttered sleepily to myself, "and then empty the five
quart—ugh! And I came here for rest and peace and
quiet, and a vacation!"

It was like the first day at Upjohn's, when I'd tried
to make out a triplicate sales slip.

I got up early Tuesday morning to help Mathilde and
Gregory. They'd been going about their work stoically
enough, but plainly they needed a managing hand. Jane's
was managing, but carefree.

Asey came out into the kitchen while I sat with the
order book before me, busily scratching down details
about tomato juice and angostura bitters and six quarts of
clams.

"Glutton for punishment, you are," he commented.
"But you looked worse Sunday than you do now. I feel
kind of chipper myself. Been down to Wellfleet an' got
some clean clothes, an'—"

"Asey," I said, "I've never thought—where have you
been sleeping?"

"Syl an' me, we brought in the hammocks from the
terrace to the livin' room. Like old times. I went half
way round Cape Horn last night. List all ready? S'pose
we drive up an' get the things now, an' then you'll be
that much ahead of the game."

"What," I asked him as we sped along the beach
road, "what d'you make of Cora? D'you think she's told
the truth? Of course, it doesn't seem to me that she's
capable of lying."

"As a matter of fact," Asey didn't reply until we

slowed down in front of the grocery store, "as—huh, ain't open, the lazy things. Well, we'll just set an' wait. Yup, as a matter of fact, Mrs. Colton, little Cora's a dum good liar. I—"

"Asey, what's she lied about? Have you found out something about her? Where? When? Tell me everything!"

"There ain't a lot to tell," Asey said. "But when you happen on a person like her, it's always sens'ble to think twice. Usually turns out to be the better part of valor to give 'em the ben'fit of the doubt. It ain't pos'ble for any one to be as much of a fluttery nitwit as she let on to be. That is, it's pos'ble. She took in the doc, an' she took me in for a while. But wouldn't Caleb Frost want a little mite more sense in a secr'tary? Somethin' more'n the abil'ty to pound a typewriter quick an' ac'rate? I think so. An' I know for sure that she's lied about one thing, an' she's sort of elided the truth in a couple of others. Also, there's plenty she ain't cond'scended to let us in—oh, here we are! Mornin', George. Want me to get the stuff, Mrs. Colton, or will you come in?"

I followed him and George into the store. After the usual exchange of pleasantries, local news and weather items, Asey brought out the list.

"George," he said, "you got any good butter?"

I smiled, because I'd known that Asey would begin just like that. It's a Cape habit to ask for "good" eggs or "good" butter, as though a few superfine samples were stocked among otherwise definitely spurious merchandise.

Item by item, we marched through the lengthy list.

"There," Asey said, "I guess that's about all there is except for 'save hatched hearse.' Got any of that, George?"

"Let me see," I said, taking the list. "Oh, that's Gregory's. At least, that's his writing. 'Save'—I have it. He means salve. Apparently burned himself again. And— Asey, that's no 'hatched hearse.' That's baked beans! He says they help his indigestion, and I don't doubt it one bit. Six cans, George."

"Canned beans!" Asey said in disgust. "D'sgraceful, that's what. Somehow I can stand for canned radio music an' canned movie voices, but canned beans is nothin' but sacr'lege."

"Just the same," George said, "there's more folks buys canned beans these days than ever before. Why, I had a woman in here yest'day mornin', I guess it was, an' she bought a dozen cans, just for herself. Stranger, she was, but Bill said he'd seen her before. She told me she never ate anything else when she camped out. She didn't look the beany sort, either, if you know what I mean."

I looked at Asey. Clearly he too was remembering the tins of beans in Cora's tent.

"Say," he said, "did she buy some Tootsy-wheetsy, too, George?"

"She didn't," George said, "because I won't stock it. I don't put any faith in that stuff at all. She asked for it, though. Friend of yours, Asey? Blonde and sort of gushy, she was."

"I wouldn't call her a friend," Asey said, "but I know the lady. What time was she in here?"

"Oh, round ten or so. Place was crowded an' everybody was all upset about Frost. Say, Asey, who done that, anyway?"

Asey shrugged.

"I just heard over the radio," George went on, "that they'd let Zeruah off an' you had some one else—say, it wasn't that blonde, was it?"

"That," Asey said, picking up as many of our bundles as he could stagger under, "that r'mains to be seen."

"They said," George announced as we labored out to the roadster, "that they're goin' to arrest some one before to-morrow. That is, they said you said you was. That so?"

"That," Asey said, "is what they think. They thought so last night for twenty minutes over the phone, an' they said so some more this mornin'. I ain't given out no encouragin' sentiments, God knows. Thanks, George. Oh, an' have your boy bring some oil down to·the bar before noon. We ain't got five gallons left."

"Then Cora," I said excitedly as we started back home, "Cora must have come up town yesterday even if she told us she didn't! And so of course she knew all about Caleb! But why did she stay around if she knew?"

"Dunno," Asey said, "I dunno."

"And she lied to us about it. Asey, what else did you catch her up on?"

"Matter of a gun," he said. " 'Member she told us she was an ole scardey cat about guns? Well, the butt of an automatic was stickin' out under her pillow. I sent Syl back last night to get it an' prowl around. It was a .45.

Not the sort of toy cap pistol most women'd tote around if they toted guns reg'lar. A nice hefty weapon, it was. Nothin' I'd keep under my ear if I was an ole fraidy about guns an' their nasty horrid noises. But that ain't more'n half of it."

"What's the other half, Mister Bones?" I demanded.

"Well, Syl drove back the car. Only trouble with it was a couple of loose c'nections. Rumble seat an' the side compartments was all locked, but I worked around till I got 'em open—"

"Blow torch?" I asked interestedly, "or mental suggestion? How simp-ly won-derful, Asey! Did you pierce them with a stare or was it astrology?"

"I shipped out of 'Frisco once," he said, grinning, "on a boat where the cook was an ex-second story man from St. Looey. I had to teach him how to cook, an' he was so grateful he taught me all he knew, too. Anyway, pendin' the lock pickin', as you might say, I found out that the car was registered in Frost's name. So just for fun, I decided to see if I could find out anythin'. Seems as if little Cora had fifty thousand in cash tucked away in a bag inside that car."

I was so startled that I dropped the eggs.

"What? No wonder—no wonder you said you felt chipper this morning, Asey! What d'you make of it? That Cora—d'you think she killed him for the money? Maybe—why, of course! He probably had that money— Caleb had it, I mean, for Thorne. And if he was killed before he met Thorne, then Cora killed him and took the—"

"I don't figure it out quite like that," Asey said. "My idea is, Cora come back from New York like she said, but she come to pick up the money for Thorne an' to bring it down here for Caleb to give him. I think that's why she come to the bar. She had the hush money for Thorne. Her orders was to wait on the bench, prob'ly, till Caleb came. But Caleb didn't come. Huh, it'd have had to be that way, if she run from Tim an' Bingo an' the other fellers. Seems to me the care of fifty thousand'd be the only restrainin' factor—but there you are."

"Then you don't think," I was disappointed and showed it, "that she killed him for the money?"

"I did first," Asey said, "but then I begun to brood about it. Whyn't she use the .45? Why'd she stick around? If it was the money she was after, whyn't she take it an' run? An', if she knew Frost was Cheyne, an' if she knew Frost was so crazy to keep it a secret—why, she had a hundred times fifty thousand waitin' for her in nice r'fined blackmail. Nope. Frost was worth more to Cora alive than he ever would be dead. Now, I want Cora to come clean on this, but I ain't got any chance just by askin' her. I got to bully her or bluff her. Tell you what. You get the others to be real gay an' cheerful at breakfast, so's she's feelin' all s'rene, an' then I'll see what I can do."

"I can't see why you should be so sure that Cora's innocent," I said. "I—why, she *must* be guilty! After all, if the woman packs a big .45, a .22 would be child's play!"

"Uh-huh. But Cora's a girl," Asey said, "who knows

what side her bread's buttered on. You an' Deal was
partly right in makin' her out brainless. She ain't endowed
with what you might call a mammoth int'lect. But Cora's
shrewd. She's got all the fem'nine shrewdness in the
world packed right into that blonde head. My guess on
her is that Frost realized that, but he got more shrewdness
than he bargained for. Take the way she's played up. She
may not have known who we was or why, when we come
on her last night, but she sensed what we was after. She
don't know how much or how little we know, but she's
acted right up to snuff so far."

"Asey," I said, "she's charmed you."

"Charmed me nothin'! I'm just pointin' out that she's
99.44% fem'nine! You take Jane, or Deal—or even you.
None of you could make yourselves play the part Cora's
playin'. You got too many brains. You can trip up folks
that try to fight with their brains easier than you can
them that fights by instinct. Takes sharp wits an' a good
mem'ry to lie your way out of anythin'. But once you get
goin', you can hardly help makin' a slip sooner or later.
But Cora's not tried a lot of lyin'. She's just kept back
the truth. She's actin' in'cent an' misunderstood, an' she's
doin' a crackerjack job. If you or Jane or Deal tell me a
lie, I'd know it. But I can't tell where Cora's lyin' leaves
off an' where she begins. Ho-hum. I'm glad I'm a bach'-
lor. Anyway, you get the others goin'," he concluded as
we drove up before the house, "an' I'll see if a little
Yankee bluff won't do it."

Getting the others to provide the gayety and mirth

Asey desired as an accompaniment to his bluff proved far more difficult than I had anticipated.

Tom was as polite as ever, but glum. Ford complained that his ankle was worse, and indeed, he didn't look at all well. Quin confessed that he had been up half the night trying to make sense of the whole affair, and the dark hollows under his eyes testified to his truthfulness as well as his zeal. Bud was curiously subdued; the tenseness of the atmosphere had begun to creep under his skin. Even Jane and Deal, who rarely needed half a chance to pour forth their miscellaneous nonsense, devoted themselves to black coffee and enormous quantities of toast without uttering half a dozen words.

Cora, strangely enough, was the only one who seemed entirely at ease. Asey listened to her babbling and flicked one eyelid at me.

"Let her," he whispered when he got the chance, "p'rvide her own music if she wants."

"No fairs," Jane protested, "whispering in people's ears. Out with it, Asey."

"I was just wonderin'," he said mildly, "what's come over you an' Deal. Kind of quiet, ain't you?"

"Well," Jane said, "she and I aren't in entire accord this morning. We had to share a bed last night, and it seems, Asey, that Deal kicks even in her sleep. Half the night she pretended I was a piece of chewing gum on her shoe, and the rest of the night she decided I was something at the end of her niblick in a sand trap. We've had words over it."

Deal sniffed. "I'd rather have been kicked to a pulp,

myself," she said coldly, "than to have some one murmur Spanish at me, in tantalizing little bursts. I shouldn't have minded, Janey, if I could have understood it all. But what bits I got were highly interesting. And the remarks addressed to—"

"Look," Jane turned pink, "no hitting below the belt! If you're going to be like that, did you ever tell Quin about that lad from Yale who—"

Gravely, Deal extended her hand.

"Pax," she said. "It was Russian you spoke and I don't know a word of it. Persian. Sanskrit. In fact, you really don't talk in your sleep at all."

"Handsome is as handsome does," Jane said. "I shall never mention your kicking in public again. Oh, Asey— are you going to make a speech? And Hanson—he's got handcuffs! Asey, you don't mean that you've—"

"I mean," Asey said in his most purring voice, "that we got a lot done last night. Quite a lot. But there's no need for all of you to get upset. You see, Mrs. Frost is wanted—"

"Mrs. Frost?" I said weakly. "Mrs. Frost?"

Cora jumped up from the table and threw her arms around Asey's neck.

"Oh, Mr. Mayo, how did you find out? How did you?"

I sat there and gaped with the rest. One thing was certain. Asey's Yankee bluff had achieved results.

CHAPTER SIXTEEN

"HOW did you know," Cora went on as Asey firmly disentangled her, "how did you know I was Caleb's wife? How did you find out?"

Asey smiled briefly at me.

"Now," he said briskly, "what about the money in your car, an' the gun under your pillow, an' all your tryin' to make us b'lieve you didn't know nothin' about Frost's death at all?"

Cora looked at him and her face fell.

"You didn't know!" she said accusingly. "You— why, Mr. Mayo, how simp-ly wonderful you are! You just guessed it, didn't you?"

I began to understand what Asey had meant when he said that Cora, while she might not grasp what people were driving at, automatically sensed a situation.

"Yup," Asey said. "I guessed, but it wasn't such hard guessin'. Now—what you found now, Syl?"

Syl, looking a little haggard, presented him with a key ring.

"Found it over in back of the seat of her car," he said, nodding toward Cora. "I think they're Sandbar dupl'cates. Any rate, they open the g'rage an' the kitchen door."

"Are they?" Asey asked Cora.

She nodded. "But I can't see what—Caleb gave them to me a long while ago! I don't see why you should all look so simply aghast at them! After all, I guess I've a right to have keys to this house if I want, haven't I?"

There was no answer to that, except that if Cora had duplicates and had been on Sandbar Saturday night, it was highly possible that her keys, and not the ones Syl had previously found, might have opened the boat house that night. And if Asey's theories were true, the person who had opened that door was the murderer.

"Haven't I?" Cora repeated.

"Guess so," Asey said. "That's all, Hanson, unless Mrs. Frost ain't goin' to tell us what we want to be told. How 'bout it?"

Cora looked at the shining handcuffs and hesitated only the merest fraction of a second.

"Why, Mr. Mayo," she said, "of *course* I'll tell you anything you want. I haven't refused to answer any questions you've asked me so far, have I? Only, must there be so many people around? I'm just—"

"I know," Asey said. "You're just an old fraidy cat about crowds. We'll go out on the terrace. Mind if Mrs. Colton comes?"

Cora smiled and hooked her arm in mine.

"'Course not," she said brightly. "'Course not! We'll go right out, won't we, Pen? You don't mind if I call you Pen, do you? You've been so kind to me—"

As we passed out of the room, I caught a portion of the lurid language escaping almost soundlessly from Deal's lips. The rest, apparently, were beyond speech.

Asey pulled up three wicker chairs, adjusted an awning and lighted his pipe.

"Now," he said, "let's d'spense with play actin' for the time bein', Mrs. Frost. Why'd you lie to me about guns?"

"Because," Cora said promptly, "I'd recognized you. I was afraid."

"An' I s'pose b'cause you recognized me was likewise the reason for your lyin' about not knowin' what'd happened out here?"

Cora hesitated. "I was afraid," she said, "because of you. Caleb had a picture of you and he often talked about you. Often times when he was dictating, he'd stop and say, 'I wonder what Asey Mayo would have done.'"

"An' then," Asey remarked with a grin, "I'll bet he went an' did the op'site. Uh-huh. Go on."

"And then, I was afraid about that money," Cora said. "I didn't know what to do with it. And I wanted— oh—I wanted so badly to come here and find out what really had gone on, but how could I? I've always told Caleb that if anything ever happened to him, my position would be unbearable." She took out a tiny chiffon handkerchief and touched her eyes with it.

"That money was for Thorne, wasn't it?" Asey asked.

"Yes. That's really why I came back from New York. I didn't know what to do, when Caleb didn't come as he'd planned. I had the keys, and I wanted to come in the house and find out, but I didn't dare. It was awful, sitting there and not knowing what had gone on! And then, yesterday in the village, when I found out! Oh, Mr. Mayo, it was terrible! I thought—it was all I could think, that Thorne had killed Caleb. I wanted to tell some one about it, but that would have meant exposing Caleb, and all that Thorne story. And the papers didn't seem to have found out that he wasn't—oh, it's too, too terrible!"

"Where was you bound when we happened on you?"

"I was coming here," Cora said. "Oh, I wasn't going to say anything about being Caleb's wife. It was no time for that. I was just going to come and say I was a friend of his, just to try to find out what had gone on."

I didn't want to in the least, but I found myself feeling sorry for the woman. It had dawned on me that her "dear Caleb's" and all the rest of what had seemed rather tawdry sentiment, were undeniably sincere. She cared for Caleb Frost, certainly as no one else ever had, anyway.

"And—you won't believe this," Cora went on, "but I can prove I had nothing to do with killing Caleb, as you think. There—no, there's no use to say anything about it. I can't prove it really, I suppose. I don't even know the— I couldn't find—ah, well," she concluded dramatically, "do with me as you will!"

"I don't want," Asey said, "to do much of anythin' with you but get the truth of this as far as I can. But if you got an alibi, I think it's kind of silly of you to keep it back."

Cora shook her head. "I know what's going to happen. I know all there is against me. You think, because you found that gun, that I can shoot, and that I'm not afraid of guns the way I said, and that I killed Caleb. But that was *his* gun. I was bringing it to him. I had it with me Saturday night. But I'm still just as scared of it as I can be. I never fired it, or any other gun, in all my life. You think I shot Caleb and went away with the money. I didn't. I just waited there on the beach. On the way back to my car, I met those drunks and I was frightened to death, with all that money and that awful gun. I—"

"Was one of them," Asey interrupted, "your alibi?"

"No. No. No, I can't do anything about that. You can arrest me if you want to, Mr. Mayo, but I had nothing to do with this."

Asey chewed at his pipe stem and watched the gulls swooping over the harbor.

"I sort of think," he said at last, "that I'm kind of inclined to think that you hadn't, an' Lord knows I got reasons enough to want—what's up, Bud?"

"Look, Asey,." he said nervously, "about those guns down in the boat house. I left 'em there last fall. Awf'ly sorry. I mean, it came near getting Sis into trouble. Look. She says, and Quin thinks, that you think that I might have flown down here Saturday night. She and Quin think you think that I might have, well," he swallowed, "that is, they think—"

"I get your drift," Asey said. "But don't go through all them 'thinks' again, Bud, or you'll choke to death. Get to the point."

"Well, d'you think I came down here Saturday night

in the plane and killed Caleb?" Bud blurted it out so fast
that the sentence turned into one word.

Asey leaned back in his chair and laughed.

"It's no laughing matter," Bud said seriously. "Quin
said that those shingles getting torn off, and all, last
night, might make you think I was trying to show you
that I couldn't have landed here without being heard. I
could, you know. I have. And Caleb and I hadn't spoken
for six months. He hated me, and I—well," he looked
at Cora and hastily changed his mind, "I didn't like him
much, either."

"Caleb didn't hate you," Cora said. "You always
said such nice things about the Cheyne books."

"I'm glad." Bud sounded as though he meant it.
"Deal and I both feel rotten that we were both so darn
unpleasant the last times we saw him. But, Asey, I'm a
good shot, and—"

"Will you stop this?" Asey demanded. "Or are you
tryin' to shield Deal, too?"

"Well—you haven't checked up on me, Asey!"

"Who says I ain't?" Asey asked cheerfully. "When
I find a man drilled by some one who's an expert shot,
don't you think I check the expert shots in the fam'ly
before I do anythin' else? I checked on Ned before I
wired him, an' I called Mike Rodman about you before I
wired you an' told him to send me all the dope—"

"How'd you know I was with Mike?" Bud asked.

"Didn't you make me give you the name of a feller
I knew that was such a good guide last fall, an' didn't
Mike write me an' ask about two young squirts—yup,

you an' Sam?— You go tell Quin to save himself for writin' books. He's got murders from an autogiro on his brain. Say, where'd that tel'gram of mine go? Sanford?"

"Danvers," Bud said. "That's what made me think you hadn't—"

"An' I spelled it out six times," Asey said. "Nope, you run along, Bud. You an' Ned was my first p'rcau-tion'ry measures, you was. I ain't heard you talk about Caleb Frost in gunny holes half your lives for nothin'."

Bud grinned and left, but Gregory appeared so quickly that I knew he'd been waiting by the terrace door for the chance.

"I'm sorry to bother," he said, speaking to Asey, but eying Cora with undisguised curiosity, "but—the salve, sir?"

"On the hall table," I said, "with your cigarettes and Mathilde's chewing gum and the baked beans. At least, I think that's where Asey left 'em, didn't you?"

"Yup. I opened the package by mistake. Quin wanted cig'rettes, an' I thought yours was the others."

"We found all of them," Gregory said, "but not the salve."

I sighed. "Then it fell out, or didn't get put in. Ask Miss Deal to get you something. Is it a burn?"

"Mathilde cut her hand, Mrs. Colton."

"Then run up," I said, "and get Mrs. Richards's nurse to fix it for you. I'm beginning to think that we have a variety of the Loch Ness monster around here which exists solely on salve."

Gregory smiled. It was clear that he thought I'd forgotten about it completely.

"Well," Asey said, "back to you, Mrs. Frost. Don't you want me to—what's eatin' you, Tom?"

"I'm sorry." Tom edged back toward the door when he heard the slightly irritated tone of Asey's voice. "I thought you were through, when I saw Gregory out here. Just something I wanted to tell you about. It'll wait. But can I have next chance at you?"

"Yup," Asey said. "Now, Mrs. Frost, what's your opinion of all this?"

She leaned forward and pointed to the door through which Tom had passed.

"You don't mean him?" Asey asked.

"I do. I don't know much about him, but Caleb did. He was the man who hung around the post office boxes and trailed Caleb all the time. He—"

"How'd you know him? How'd you know what he looked like? From Frost's description?" Asey asked curiously.

"No. Caleb took a picture of him one day with one of those cameras that newspaper men take candid camera pictures with. I don't know—"

"Leica with a tel'photo lens," Asey said. "Huh. He *did* think of that, like I thought he would. Go on."

"Then he had the picture enlarged and showed it to me, so that if ever he came to the office, I'd be all prepared for him. I didn't know his name until I came here—neither did Caleb. But I recognized him right off. He's good looking," she added as an afterthought.

"Rather like those new tooth paste ads, don't you think, Pen?"

"Now that you mention it," I said with a touch of irony which missed its mark entirely, "he does. Mrs. Frost, if you're going to stay here, won't you take charge of things?"

For the first time since I'd laid eyes on her, Cora was completely at a loss.

"I wouldn't know—it wouldn't seem—oh, no!" she said hurriedly. "This is Mrs. Richards's house. I shouldn't dream—really, Pen, I haven't any idea of doing anything like that! Oh, my goodness me, no. Is that all, Mr. Mayo?"

"For right now," Asey said, "'less you'd care to break down an' tell us about your alibi."

Cora rose. "No, I can't do that. But I truly do think that Tom Willing—so many times he nearly found out who Caleb was, and just missed by the skin of his teeth. The same way with Ford Ames. Caleb and I laughed and laughed every time we thought of how he and Ford stood by that post office box, waiting for Varney Cheyne to appear."

"You're sure," Asey asked, "that Ford didn't know?"

"I'm positive," she said. "Positive. If any one knew, it was Tom Willing. Is that all?"

"All," Asey said, "this trip, anyways."

"What d'you really think about her?" I asked after she had gone. "And how in the world did you guess she and Caleb were married? I—that's dazed me. Caleb—the perpetual bachelor!"

"But if you was Caleb," Asey said, "an' you didn't want it to be known about your bein' Varney Cheyne, an' if Cora knew, I kind of guess you'd of married Cora, p'ticularly if she suggested it. Seems to me she really liked the feller."

"But think of what Cale said to Gregory after she called Saturday—all that business of lions and Africa!"

"Wa-el," Asey drawled, "you wouldn't hardly say, 'That's my wife, Greg'ry, an' she's bringin' fifty thousand dollars down here t'night to give a man whose life I ruined, because I never liked him, an' everybody else did, an' they didn't like me!' Would you? You'd just sort of scatter red herrin', an' I gather that was the way things stood. No, I guessed about the marriage business when I found the car registration made out in Frost's name. He wouldn't of done that just for any ole secr'tary, even if they was what you might term pally. Now—come along, Tom, an' tell us your troubles."

"I don't know where to begin," Tom said, "even though I've rehearsed this for hours. You see, while Quin's been wondering how to drag more people into this, I've wondered how to get a few of us out. Look, you've talked with Jane, haven't you? You know she was out Saturday night?"

Asey nodded. "Yup. But how did you?"

"I saw her go," Tom said, "and I heard her come in. You see, I was on the point of starting up to Frost's room to interview him on the Cheyne proposition, when I saw Jane go up. Later I was in the bathroom downstairs, and I saw her start out to the dunes. I—well, I wanted to follow her out, but I'd only just met her, and I was in pyjamas and my mouth was full of tooth paste—I'd forgotten to clean my teeth and that's why I was up."

"I suppose you've been told," I said, "that you resemble the tooth paste ads?"

Tom grinned. "I ought to. Friend of mine took those pictures and I posed for some of 'em. Anyway, I'd given up the thought of seeing Frost that night. When I came back to the bedroom, Quin was sleeping like a baby. I couldn't get to sleep myself though, because I was worried about Jane. After all, this is a lonely place. Then I heard her open the window and come in."

"How'd you know who it was?" Asey asked.

"Heard her heels clicking. I went to sleep, then. But it was just a few minutes after one, Asey. And she and Deal were talking to-day; it seems they sat and gabbled after Jane got in. Wouldn't that alibi Jane, if those two men were killed around one-thirty or so?"

"You're sure of the time?" Asey asked.

"Positive. Anyway, I know Quin didn't stir all night —wouldn't that let him out? And the two girls?"

Asey wanted to know why Tom hadn't told us that before.

"Because, Asey," Tom said, "I didn't want to tell you about Jane's going out till after she'd told you herself. It would have seemed too much like trying to accuse her in a backhand way. And I couldn't say anything about Quin without beginning with Jane. It all sort of leaves me without a leg to stand on, but I don't think—

well, I'm not guilty, and there's no need for me to worry. That's all I had to say."

He smiled at me, nodded to Asey and left.

"Hm," Asey said. "I b'lieved Jane an' Deal an' Quin, but it's nice to get 'em straightened out proper. Does it occur to you, Mrs. Colton, that Tom might have been the gent Deal referred to when she was kiddin' Jane about her Spanish oration?"

"It does," I answered, "and it did then. Jane looked at him before she began to blush. Lord, to think of romance blooming in the middle of a thing like this! Asey, where are we getting?"

"Well," Asey said, "we can take Tom's word an' 'lim'nate Jane in spite of that car business, an' Deal in spite of her fights an' threats, an' Quin in spite of that gun. That helps. We also got rid of Bingo an' Zeruah an' all them. That narrows it some more. We'll cut out Greg'ry and Mathilde on principle. You—after all you done that day, I shouldn't think you'd of had the spirit for any murderin'. The girls say Ford was snorin', an' just for fun last night, I hung outside his door an' found that he did. That fixes him. Somehow, I b'lieve Tom. Somehow—"

"Somehow you believe Cora," I said. "I see it coming. Somehow, I don't. I mean, I've been feeling sorry for her, in a way. She may have achieved an ambition in marrying Caleb, and she may have liked him, but I don't feel she had such a cheerful time. I'll admit her story sounds true in spots, but most of it is just plain fishy, if you ask me. Now go ahead and tell me that truth is stranger than fiction."

"Is sometimes," Asey returned, "like the feller said when he first seen a g'raffe. Just c'nsider this gun of Quin's, Mrs. Colton. I ain't had no word about it yet, but if Deal's story's true, ain't it fishy that it should turn up here? Whoever bought it might of bought it with the intention of killin' Frost, but I don't think they ever knew it was Quin's gun. I don't think they could ever have known in this world that it was, or that Quin'd be here, an' all the rest. It was a fishy thing to happen, an' it still is. Coincidence. Yet it don't seem to me much more of a coincidence than that time in Hong Kong when I looked at an ole sword in a Chink shop an' found it was the one some one'd stole from my uncle 'Lisha down in Wellfleet when I was a boy. Had his name 'graved on it. An'—"

"Telephone," Gregory interrupted breathlessly. "Mr. Crump's back in Boston, sir, and wants you."

Asey's face when he returned some fifteen minutes later, was a study.

"What is it?" I demanded. "Have—don't tell me the gun's been traced to Deal or Quin?"

"Steve Crump," he said, "has just d'spensed a little tid-bit he thought I might like. Cora ain't mentioned at all in Frost's will. He didn't know nothin' about her 'cept her name—"

"How'd he find that out?" I interrupted.

"Seems," Asey filled his pipe with great care and deliberation, "seems like she's mentioned as the beneficiary of Frost's life insurance. One hundred thousand dollars, cold. Maybe—you know, gettin' myself all worked up about that fire in the livin' room yest'day made me wonder if I wasn't sort of dodderin'. Gettin' over-suspicious an' all het up over nothin'. Maybe I swung too far back the other way an' got myself too credulous like. Maybe—"

"Maybe *I* was right about Cora," I said. "I told you it was all fishy. You seem to think she could get more money from Caleb alive than Caleb dead. Well, perhaps. But a hundred and fifty thousand in the hand, counting Thorne's money, isn't anything to be sneezed at. I mean, I'd be willing to take the cash and let the credit go for a hundred and fifty thousand, I think. And all the rumbling of distant drums wouldn't do much to deter me, either!"

"I know that piece of poetry," Asey said. "It's Betsey Porter's fav'rite—huh, I wish Cora wouldn't be so lady-like an' ret'cent about this alibi she says she's got."

"Do you really think she has one?" I demanded. "Oh, Asey, to think she's taken you in! What possible alibi *could* she have? And why on earth, if she had one, shouldn't she promptly produce it? That's—"

"I think she has," Asey said. "I think there's another man connected—"

"Don't tell me you think there was another man on Sandbar Saturday night whom we don't know about!" I said. "Why, Asey, the place must have been a seething mass of humanity! And would Cora carouse on dunes with another man while she waited for Caleb?"

Asey grinned. "Seems to me that the bar was pract'cally a Coney Island durin' a heat wave, Sat'day night," he said. "No reason why—here's Hanson drivin' up—"

I turned around as one of the police cars stopped in front of the house.

"Asey!" I exclaimed. "I know that little man in the front seat! He's a floor walker at Upjohn's. Why—Mr. Winpenny!"

Mr. Winpenny wiped his thin face with an exquisite silk handkerchief. "There," he said to Hanson, "there! I told you I knew her—Mrs. Colton, is this Asey Mayo?"

"It is," I told him, "but—do come up and sit down and cool off! You look utterly exhausted—how d'you happen to be on Cape Cod? What are you doing here?"

"I heard you talk so much about East Pochet," he fanned himself with the brim of his Panama, "that I thought I'd spend two weeks of my—I'm interested in birds, you know. I thought it—but, Mrs. Colton, I've been camping on the bay shore, and I didn't hear a word of all this terrible thing until this morning. Do you know," he leaned forward, and every muscle in his slight body seemed to be fairly twittering with excitement, "do you know that a person who could have given you most valuable information on this affair has been kidnaped?"

Asey and I stared at him as though he were a circus What-is-it, pickled in a glass jar.

"Fire," Asey murmured plaintively, "an' more fire, bashes, shots, silencers, airplanes—yup. All we really lacked in this was a good kidnapin'. Rounds it out, as you might say. Who is this person you speak of, Mr.—uh—Mr. Winpenny?"

Mr. Winpenny leaned back in his chair and began to roll the brim of his hat nervously between his fingers.

"Well," he said rather lamely, "I only—I mean, that's just it. You see, I was—"

He broke off as Cora came out of the house, took one look at him, and shrieked. Absolutely shrieked. As for Mr. Winpenny, he dropped his Panama and all but tripped over it in his effort to dash across the terrace to her.

"Benjamin!" Cora held out both arms. "Benjamin! Oh, it's the will of heaven! Now—oh—"

"Just what," I inquired of Asey while Cora and Mr. Winpenny continued to embrace with mutual enthusiasm, "what do you make of this?"

Asey tipped his Stetson on the back of his head and chuckled.

"Offhand," he observed, "it would seem like Brother Benjamin wasn't drunk Sat'day night."

"What? What d'you mean?"

"I mean," Asey said cheerfully, "I happened to be right. Cora's got her alibi."

CHAPTER SEVENTEEN

FULLY fifteen minutes elapsed before Cora ceased burbling and Mr. Winpenny lost the edge of his enthusiastic glow.

"Now," Asey rubbed his chin and smoothed down the corners of his mouth, "now s'pose we have the story, Mr. Winpenny, from A to Z. Sort of a gen'ral exposay an' grand enlightenin'."

"I thought—I mean, Mr. Mayo, as soon as I heard about this from the papers this morning," Mr. Winpenny began, "I went to her camp. And her things were all mussed up and she was gone, so I came right to you—"

Asey said we had practically gathered that.

"But why," he added. "Oh—I get it! You didn't either of you know the other's full name, huh?"

Mr. Winpenny blushed.

"We really didn't know each other well enough," Cora replied coyly. "Besides, when he asked me my name, I just told him 'Cora.' And he told me his was Benjamin. That's why I couldn't tell you, don't you see? It would have been too silly. You didn't entirely believe me, but

248

if I'd told you about this, you'd have thought everything
I'd said was a lie!"

Asey's lips twitched.

"Yup," he said gravely. "I see. An' I'm inclined to
agree with you that if you'd told me you spent your time
on Sandbar Sat'day night with a stranger named Benjamin, I'd most likely of doubted you real strenuous.
Now, we'll let Mr. Winpenny spin his yarn."

In those precise and formal tones which he employs
to guide Boston matrons around Upjohn's, Mr. Winpenny
spun.

It seemed that, quite unintentionally, I had been the
inspiration for Mr. Winpenny's trip to East Pochet. I'd
been so eloquent about the place that he decided to spend
two of his four weeks' vacation gazing at East Pochet
birds and studying the Cape flora and fauna in general.
He arrived Saturday afternoon and set up his camp on
the bay shore—Asey and I decided it was somewhere in
the vicinity of Nellie Carstairs's house. Then, Saturday
evening, he had rented a boat from Nathan Ricks and
rowed around the inner harbor.

Around eight o'clock he was sufficiently worn out
from his labors to turn back, but it occurred to him that
it was too dark to find Nathan's wharf. Showing more
sense than I should have credited him with, he anchored
his boat off shore somewhere along the beach road, intending to wait till the moon came up, and until he got
second wind, before returning.

He walked to the outside beach, sat down and
listened to the surf and watched the waves. Then, in an

adventurous mood, he walked along the outer beach to the Sandbar bridge. He read the signs which said it was private property—Caleb had peppered the bridge with them, but he also recognized the name Frost. Some one had told him that I was spending the summer at the Frost estate. So, with a sublime disregard for the "No Trespassing" warnings, Mr. Winpenny strode over to Sandbar, and, keeping to the outer beach, strolled along its entire length. He watched the moon come up, and then, tired out from his driving, rowing and striding about, he fell asleep.

"When I woke up," he said, "it was after twelve o'clock. I started back to the boat, but I was very stiff and I couldn't walk very quickly. Just beyond the house, on the outer beach, I saw a woman walking alone, and it rather upset me, because I knew she saw me. I guessed I'd frightened her, for she started to walk in the shadow of the dunes. I thought it was some one from Sandbar, and I really was very bothered. Embarrassed. It occurred to me for the first time that I was really trespassing."

"So he came up to me," Cora said, "and apologized for being there. And I decided that I hadn't better let on that I was really, in one way, trespassing, too! He looked tired, so I asked him if he wouldn't sit down on the bench, and he did."

"Wasn't you afraid," Asey asked, "that Frost might not care for the idea when he come out?"

"He always flashed a light from the terrace," Cora said naïvely. "Anyway, that didn't bother me. I was only bothered when Caleb didn't come. Then Benjamin and I got to talking."

She looked at Mr. Winpenny and they smiled at each other. Neither, however, seemed at all desirous of continuing the "gen'ral exposay."

After several minutes, Asey asked them questions until, item by item, he'd yanked out the rest of the story. I thought irrelevantly of the time a tooth which my dentist had been extracting suddenly broke into bits.

It appeared that Cora had, under the influence of the moon and the rest of the romantic setting, told Benjamin that she was married to some one in the house, but that she was staying by herself in her little camp. I gathered that Caleb's failure to appear, coupled with the sympathetic ears of Mr. Winpenny, led her to comment extensively about her unhappy marriage.

"You see," she explained hurriedly, "I was very fond of Caleb. He was a dear to me. I loved him, in—well, in a way. But he didn't always treat me awfully well. I mean, he gave me everything I asked for, like the car, and clothes, and money, but—oh—you—you understand, don't you?"

Mr. Winpenny had understood, anyway. And by a strange coincidence, it seemed that he too had been unhappily married, and only within the last year had secured a divorce. He advocated one for Cora. Until after three o'clock, they poured out their troubles to each other. Then Mr. Winpenny remembered his boat.

Acting on Cora's advice, he had hurried ahead, returned the boat, and then waited at the crossroads for Cora to drive up.

"I found the man I'd rented the boat from lying on the path outside his house," Mr. Winpenny said. "He was very drunk. So I left a bill in his hand and went along. Cora didn't come for half an hour or so. Then I drove back to her camp with her, because I didn't think she should go into the woods alone at that time of night. When I saw everything was all right, I went back to my own camp."

"So you was with her from one till three, an' afterwards?" Asey asked.

Winpenny nodded. "And—I haven't seen her since. We—we decided before we left that we wouldn't see each other again. Not—not under the circumstances. I've stayed out by myself on the bay side ever since. I—well, I wanted to be alone. This morning I had to come up to town for supplies. I read the papers, and at once I thought of Cora. She hadn't told me she was married to Frost, but I had sort of guessed it. I thought some one might have seen her, and I thought at any rate that she would know something—and when I got to her camp and found it all mussed up, I was so worried that I didn't know what to do. I decided some one must have kidnaped her, probably the murderer or something."

"And I couldn't tell you about him," Cora said, "could I? I didn't know one thing about him except his first name. We'd only talked about ourselves, and what we felt about things, and—and all. Why, I don't even know what he does—but I'm sure," she added hastily, "that it's something splendid."

Splendid was hardly the word I should have used to describe a woman's department floor walking job, and I judged from Winpenny's face that he rather felt the same way. In fact, he looked so miserable that I rose to the occasion as nobly as I could.

"Mr. Winpenny," I said in my most impressive tones, "holds an important executive position at Upjohn's, where I'm a lowly clerk."

"Oh," Cora said. "Oh—Ben!"

Asey looked at them and rose.

"Thank you both," he said, "very kindly. This's cleared up a mite more. Mrs. Colton—uh—"

I followed him into the house, while Cora and Mr. Winpenny sat and stared at each other speechlessly.

"Brother Ben," Asey said, "ain't got a chance. But if you ask me, he won't run, like number one, an' he won't treat her like a retriever, the way Frost done. Just the samey, she done her duty by Frost."

I nodded. "Think of poor Winpenny, sitting out there on the bay shore for three days, brooding over his lost love. Lord, what an idyll! Asey, now what?"

Before he could reply, the phone rang, and he crossed to the hall to answer it. Jane stuck her head in the door from the east terrace.

"Come on out," she said, "and tell us everything. Did Asey go to the phone? Tell us, who's the little man?"

Briefly I summed up the story of Cora and Benjamin.

"So," I said, "Cora and her boy friend are all out of the picture. I—"

"Wait!" Quin said excitedly. "Are you sure? Is Asey sure? Winpenny divorced his wife, didn't he? And Caleb, Cora's husband, is murdered. Now you say they're in love. And if it's true that Cora gets Caleb's insurance money, why—I don't see how Asey can believe them! I tell you, *I*—"

"Half a glance," I said, "should be enough to convince you that Winpenny couldn't tell anything but the truth if he wanted to. He's honest as—Lord, Quin, he even left a bill for the rowboat's rent in Nate Rick's drunken paw! Can you see a floor walker tearing around a sand dune, shooting people and bashing people, and— why, I'd as soon expect one of the show window figures to start in dancing a jig!"

"The trouble with you, Pen," Quin declared, "is that you just reduce things to absurdities! I can see a floor walker in the act of murdering two men just as easily as I can see Cora doing it. Pen, it's *got* to be one or the other of them!"

"Doubtless it would be," I retorted, "if you were writing this story! But it's just as sane to take their word as to take yours. Or mine. Look at me, for all you know—"

Asey came out to the terrace, smiling cheerfully.

"That," he said, "was about that gun. Seems that hock shop went out of business just about two leaps ahead of the police. One of them crooked little affairs that grows bigger an' smellier the more you prod it. Whole

story's your meat, Quin. Alderman, two racketeers, an
ex-beer baron, an' God knows who else, all mixed up—
anyway, one of the clerks broke down an' admitted
buyin' Deal's gun. He'd been what you might call worked
up, I gathered, into an admittin' mood, feelin' that the
more he told, the nicer it'd be for him, an' the sooner.
So—that's that. 'Cept he's c'nveniently forgot who *he*
sold it to. But—there you are!"

Deal got up, kissed Asey gravely on both cheeks and
sat down again. Ford pushed his chair over and shook
her hand, while Quin and Jane executed an impromptu
war dance.

"Thank God," Quin said at last. "No, no more active
rejoicing, Janey. This old body's near worn out. But tell
me, Asey, how'd the gun get here? D'you suppose some
one bought—but they couldn't have known it was mine.
How about it all?"

"Coincidence," Asey said, and told them about the
sword in Hong Kong.

"I didn't really think," Quin said, "that things happened like that!"

"New fields," Asey said, "for you to plow under with
your pen. You want to stop an' think. With so many
things an' so many folks in this world, an' so many kinds
of both, there's 'bundant material for coincidences. I always wonder that more funny p'culiar things don't happen—anyway, that seems to dish everybody up."

"Dish is right. Asey, this would be," Quin stretched
himself out in a deck chair, "the blank despair chapter,
in a book. Do I smell rubber burning, or is Gregory

burning himself again? Thought I smelled it—no matter. Anyway, this would be the blank despair chapter, Asey. You've gone through all the likely suspects and all the unlikely suspects, and all their sisters and their cousins and their aunts, not to speak of boy friends, and you've drawn a blank."

"What," Asey drawled, "would Rutherford Grandgent do? What does the master rec'mend?"

Quin looked hurt. "I—recommend to you? Don't be silly! Anyway, as I was saying, after you've convinced everybody that you're at a dead end, you have to push forward the transcendental detective, who shows up all the common or garden thinking. So all you've got to do, Asey, is to become transcendental. We're sufficiently convinced of the dead endness. Go ahead."

"What about the trans—the master mind b'hind it?" Asey asked. "You be the mind, Quin, an' show me how."

"I'm serious, Asey," Quin said. "Truly I am. I honestly expect you to say 'A—B—C. See?' Besides, it's no good kidding me because I always know the end before I start. I start, and work away from it. Just like a magician pulling rabbits out of thin air. He chats so amusingly about this and that, and makes so many superfluous gestures that are watchable, that you don't look where you should. But, Asey, I expect—why, it's only natural that you've looked all along where you should have!"

"If you mean that," Asey said, "you're a bigger fool than I thought you was. What you take me for?"

"I think," Quin said, "that you're one of the cleverest men I—"

"Cleverness," Asey said, "is knowin' how dumb you are, an' then keepin' it hid. I—"

"And I think," Quin went on, "that you've the finest mind I ever met up with. Like a steel trap. I—"

Asey turned to me. "Come on, Mrs. Colton!" he said. "Hurry! Come on! Quick!"

"Why?" I demanded, getting up hurriedly. "Why—"

"Come on," he said. "We'll go be transy! So long, Quin! I—what's the matter, Jane?"

"Can I trail along with you?" she asked. "I want to."

Asey nodded. "Hustle! Hurry! My goodness, I never even tried to be transy before—hop along!"

He led us out to his roadster, piled us in, and before we knew what was happening, he was tearing along the beach road toward town.

"Is this a bluff," I asked, "or are you really up to something?"

"I wanted to get away from there," he said, "while my hat still fitted. Jane, you know that Tom alibied you?"

"Yes, and that's what I wanted to talk to you about. You're not sure, are you, that while he might have been telling the truth about the rest of us, he was lying about what he did, himself?"

Asey looked at her curiously. "He may have seen you go, an' heard you come in, but with Quin asleep, they ain't no guarantee that he didn't leave by the window you come in, so to speak. Why?"

"Because the man who killed Frost would have had to have been a pretty good shot, wouldn't he?"

"Reason'bly."

"Well, that's the point. I was talking with the others while Tom was talking to you. Quin said something about your knowing that Tom was out of it. I asked what he meant, and he said that Tom's father had killed himself when Tom was eight or nine. Tom had—well, he was in the room. You know how that sort of thing affects people. He has never touched a gun in all his life, or even fired one. Quin says he practically jitters when he sees a firearm, and that a couple of back fires can make him grow white and sick all over."

Asey stopped the car by the side of the road.

"Will you tell me," he demanded, "why in the name of common sense Quin Gunner never told me that?"

"I asked him if he had, and he said no. That you'd undeniably have found it out by yourself. He's really serious about this transcendental stuff, Asey. He really meant what he said. And—well," she smiled at him, "I sort of agree, as you say."

Asey leaned his elbows on the wheel.

"Uh-huh," he said. "I been pretty spectac'lar to date, ain't I? Just like two matches goin' out in the wind. Look, Mrs. Colton, you know me. Will you tell me why I can't stick to my last? I can tinker with cars, an' machines, an' I can fiddle with boats, an'—"

"It *is* your last," I said. "You couldn't keep away from a thing like this if you wanted to. You know it, too."

Asey sighed. "Huh. You're out. Jane's out. Ford's out. Quin's out. So's Cora an' Benjy. So's them servants.

So's Bud an' Deal an' Bingo an' all the rest. An' the doc an' I had a long talk about Mrs. Richards, but even if she's a good shot, she—"

"Isn't it just possible," Jane asked, "that she may have found out about Cora? And she—well, she talked to you about Deal, didn't she?"

"Yup, an' you, too. An' she ain't got no alibis. An' the doc says he thinks a lot of her carryin' on's been faked. Thinks she's cooked up a lot of her sickness, like throwin' them glasses around the other day. Just so's she'd be able to stay in bed an' be out of everythin'. Same theory as a weepin' lady just shoves all the r'spons'bility on some one else's shoulders, an' lets herself in for a lot of attention an' pity. An' here's the doc, coughin' along in his ole buggy. I tried to make him take my ole car, last month, an' he wouldn't. Said it'd embarrass him to drive a car hittin' on all sixteen when he wasn't used to but three, an' b'sides, he said his patients'd never pay any bills even once in a while."

The doctor drew up on the opposite side of the road.

"Morning," he said blithely. "I'd have been out your way sooner, but when I called up, Malvina said Lizzie was improving, and then this thing I laughingly call a car decided to act up. It's the carbureter, Asey—at least, that's my impartial diagnosis. You'll have to come over and patch it up, or feed it sulphur and molasses or something, when you've got this business over with. I—"

"I'm tired," Asey said with grim firmness, "of havin' people think this was a sort of gen'ral holiday, clam bake an' corn roast, designed just for my own special ben'fit!

What d'you think, I'm goin' to pull the murderer out of
my hip pocket an' wave him 'round my head till he turns
into an American flag?"

"Don't be so violent," the doctor said soothingly.
"It's bad for you. Hurts the digestive system and does all
sorts of things to your various and sundry glands. It has
already been announced over the radio that Asey Mayo
will produce the murderer within twenty-four hours."

Asey snorted.

"Well," the doctor said, "you must expect that sort
of thing when you have a reputation, Asey. You just have
to live up to it. Why, when I first started practising, it
just so happened that my first five confinement cases
turned out to be boys; the sixth mother nearly killed me
—and never paid me, because it was a girl. You've made
a name for yourself, and there you are! This glum note
you're striking doesn't run true to form. Usually about
this time, you purr like a cat. Why the growls? I—" he
broke off as another car slowed up. "Okay, Joe, I'll move.
Sorry to block you—"

"Park it," Asey ordered, "an' then crawl in my
rumble. You— I'm sick an' tired of this business! I'm
goin' to drive you all over to the back shore where it's
quiet, an' do a little reviewin' for you. An' I want you
to see if they's any chance on God's green footstool for
me to find the fly in this ointment!"

Out by the back shore he stopped the car and turned
around.

"Now," he said, "you fellers listen to me! Caleb
Frost starts out to meet Thorne, expectin' to c'lect fifty

thousand from Cora on the way. He don't. He gets as far
as the dune where we found him, an' some one puts a
bullet through him. That some one's got to be a pretty
good shot, an' got to be reasn'bly sure Frost is Varney
Cheyne. Now—"

"I've been thinking," the doctor interrupted, "about
Lizzie Richards, Asey. She's no weakling. She's big, but
more of her than you'd suspect is muscle. And these
nerves of hers; think of the time that house they used
to have on the neck road got on fire. She put it out herself, without saying a word, because she said later that
she didn't want to bother the children. They were all
asleep. Yes, Lizzie'll go off the handle on little things,
but on a big thing, she's right there. Keeps her head."

"I ain't forgot Lizzie," Asey said. "I ain't forgot
nothin'. But get back to this business. The feller or lady
kills Frost—I finally got it doped out why he or she
walked down by the boat house. I got that far. There's
a ridge there, an' by walkin' diagonal, you'd never be
seen crossin' by any one, from the house or anywheres
else. Now, let me tell you. In my mind, I've started at
the bridge, an' I've started from the house, an' from each
of 'em, I've walked to that dune. An' then from there I've
crossed to the boat house. I've done it so many times
that I've worn a path right square through what gray
matter I got. An'," he laughed shortly, "an' d'you know
what I do, when I get to the boat house? Know what
your ole transy detective does?"

"What?" Jane asked obediently.

"By gum, I sit down an' take off my shoes an' empty

the sand out of 'em! That shows you how good I am. I—"

He stopped short and a look of abject surprise came over his face.

"I sit down," he said, "an'—by gum!"

He started the car and backed it so quickly out onto the road that Jane, who had been sitting up on top of the seat, catapulted down on top of me. The doctor escaped with a bumped head about which he was intensely annoyed.

"I'm speechless," he yelled to Asey, "with rage! What's the idea? What's got into you, man?"

Without turning around, Asey jammed his foot a little harder on the accelerator and shouted back a happy answer.

"I'm a dum fool, doc. Hold on, 'cause I'm transcendin' in earnest this time! Ole transy Mayo is hot on the trail—an' he's got the trail to be hot over, too!"

CHAPTER EIGHTEEN

ONLY a determined cubist with a ten by twelve canvas could begin to do full justice to that ride back to Sandbar.

In one corner of the picture there would be a telephone pole from which a blur of green for the scrub pines, a patch of blue for the sky, and a daub of yellow for the sand all streamlined crazily together. And somewhere, I am sure, would appear the face of Sir Malcolm Campbell, expressing not only admiration, but a slight twinge of envy as well.

Asey hopped out jauntily when we drove up in front of the house, but I was too dazed to move. So were the doctor and Jane.

"I forgot," Asey paused at the foot of the steps and turned around, "I forgot to tell—my gorry!"

He surveyed the three of us, sat down and laughed till the tears ran down his cheeks.

I didn't blame him.

The doctor was slumped down in the rumble seat, still grimly holding on for dear life. Jane's left arm was hooked into mine, and both of us were clutching the dashboard. The doctor's hat had been blown off just before Jane's béret slatted away. My hair would probably have aroused sincere awe among the wilder natives of Borneo or Sarawak.

"You can laugh," the doctor spluttered at last, "you can laugh all you want to, Asey Mayo, but—"

"Oh m'God," Asey said weakly, "you look like you'd frozen into a Rogers group in modern dress. 'After the Ride.' Say—unbend! You're all right—"

"All right?" the doctor said. "All right! Thanks to a benign providence, and nothing more! I'm speechless. Must you kill three innocent bystanders in order to prove your worth in catching one murderer? Man alive, it's—"

"I know," Asey said. "'Rithmetic's against me. But I got things to do. Mrs. Colton, will you an' Jane please c'lect this mob on the east terrace? I think most of 'em's out there still. Greg'ry an' Mathilde, too. You c'lect 'em, an' keep 'em there till I say otherwise. Doc, you go sit with Lizzie an' Malvina. Oh, an'—"

"Wha—what are you going to do?" Jane said as she helped me out of the car.

Asey grinned. "An' don't you forget Cora an' her Benjy! Run get 'em, Jane. They're strollin' around aimless just beyond the g'rage. Remember what I said. You all stay put till I give you the word. An' don't you say nothin' about this brain wave of mine. It may roll right out to sea again."

"But what *is* all this?" I demanded. "What have you found out? What have you hit on? Why must we herd together? What's—"

"My rep'tation," Asey announced with a gesture, "is at stake. One thing to see where the road should go, an' another thing to cut it. Now is the time for all good men to come to the aid of the party. Vamoose!"

There was something in his tone which forbade further inquiries, so we vamoosed. Jane rushed off to collect Cora and Mr. Winpenny, and even the irrepressible doctor marched up to Lizzie's room without favoring us with another of his speechless tirades, though I felt that he probably had one on the tip of his tongue.

I walked through the charred living room to the terrace and made futile attempts to parry Quin's flood of questions.

"Where have we been?" I said. "Oh, we've been out. Why? For a little fresh air. Whom did we see? The doctor. Why are we back? We had enough fresh air. What does Asey think? Heavens and earth, Quin, Asey's thoughts aren't wrapped in cellophane like easter eggs or children's rompers! But I will say this much. He's transcending."

During the next hour I lost weight trying to listen to Asey's movements about the house. I knew he was wandering about, because I caught occasional glimpses of him as he flitted through the living room. Jane, who was perched on the arm of my chair, could also see him, and I gathered from her far-away expression that she was straining her ears, too.

As far as I could make out, Asey went into every single room upstairs, though I couldn't tell what he did or what he was looking for. Bud Richards had brought out a battered banjo, and from time to time he presented carefully muted noises which he described as "choice renditions of old favorites." Somewhere during the third verse of "The Man on the Flying Trapeze," I saw Syl come in, and watched him nod half a dozen times. Apparently Asey was giving him instructions. And of course in the intervals of comparative silence, some one or other wound a watch. I had never previously noticed that there was an over-supply of watches in the crowd, but from the number of windings I was forced to listen to, I judged that an enterprising burglar could have set up a jewelry store on the strength of one haul.

Half way through "My Mother Was a Lady," Syl appeared at the door and beckoned to Bud.

"What," Quin spoke for all of us when he finally returned, "what's up? What did Asey want?"

"He didn't," Bud said promptly. "He's going off. And he said—"

"What? Where? What for? Why?" Quin flung the questions out as though he were blowing them through a bean shooter.

Bud shrugged elaborately. "I should know? He said to tell Mrs. Colton that her instructions—whatever they were—were canceled, but that 'Nary a one of us was to set foot off the terrace till he got back.' Tom, can you do the tenor to—"

I got up and dove for the west terrace just in time to see the low-slung roadster disappearing over the bridge.

Jane, who had followed me, whistled at the cloud of dust.

"For a reasonably conservative gent," she said, "he has ideas about speed. He may think like a sage, but he drives like a fool. Pen, what's it all about? Why should sand in his shoes work him into a frenzy like this?"

"Sand gets in your shoes," I said. "You could make a song of it, couldn't you? At any rate, it's been singing through my head ever since we started home from the back shore."

Hanson and Syl strolled up to the house, but they only laughed at our questions.

"I don't know," Hanson said, "as much as you do. I've stopped thinking. But Syl was given a question to ask you, Mrs. Colton. It doesn't make sense to me, but it may to you. Ask her, Syl."

Syl looked meaningly at Jane, who smiled and went back indoors.

"I sort of like her," Syl said, gazing after Jane thoughtfully, "even if she does put paint on her face an' don't wear no stockin's. Look, Asey wants to know, what's the fire insurance on this house?"

I sat down and stared at him. "What's that got to do with anything?"

"Dunno. Happen to of heard the amount?"

"Thirty thousand," I told him. "Deal and Quin mentioned it after the living room blaze."

"Gosh," Syl said in honest awe, "dollars? Well, that's what Asey wanted to know."

"Syl," I said pleadingly, "won't you tell me what this is all about?"

Syl said that he would if he could, but he didn't

know. Asey had not enlightened him. "Y'know," he added confidentially, "at times I sort of think Asey's plum cracked."

"What!"

"I do, though. You know that song about smoke gettin' in your eyes? Well, he went off hummin' it, only he was singin' somethin' about sand gettin' in your shoes. Now, can you beat that?"

I couldn't, and I think I was the only one who didn't spend the day with paper and pencil, figuring.

"Just," Jane said disgustedly around tea time, "as though it were a parlor game! Ugh! Pen, I'll play Russian banque with you, but if I figure any more, I'll go mad. Asey's not human, and this whole business is beyond human ken. Possibly that man knows what he's doing, but I'm sure I don't!"

No more did I—or the rest.

As our mental activities became more and more involved and fruitless, a general nervous tension surrounded us—just, as Jane remarked under her breath, as though it had been cut into chunks with a knife and patted over us with a trowel. Once during a lull, Tom scratched a match; Quin and Deal literally bounced off the couch, Ford shot half way across the room in his wheel chair, and Jane called "Stop!" to me, even though she was the one who'd proudly placed a red seven on a black ten.

Bud sat by the radio and switched it energetically from one station to another, finally tuning in on some South American broadcast—a series of squeaking tangoes through which code signals buzzed shrilly. Gregory,

looking like the camel on whose back the last straw was
about to be loaded, crept in from the kitchen and turned
the thing off, finally, with only the grimmest and briefest
of apologies.

Only Cora and Mr. Winpenny appeared really at
ease. They sat before a card table and played jack straws,
and I found myself becoming increasingly annoyed at
the steadiness of their hands. It didn't seem decent,
somehow.

I suppose the truest display of our state of mind
came around nine o'clock, when Deal moaned loudly and
announced in horrified tones that we had run out of
cigarettes, for all that Asey and I had bought three car-
tons at George Hastings's in the morning. Hanson was
hastily summoned, and one of the troopers made a flying
trip to town for more. Yet, after we got them, no one
wanted to smoke.

At eleven o'clock we dispensed with all further pre-
tenses and went to bed.

With considerable forethought I provided myself
with two new packages of cigarettes and the "Vase to
Zygo" volume of the Encyclopaedia Britannica. I couldn't
have read a connected narrative if I'd been offered a prize
for it.

It was after one when I turned out my light, and
even then I had no desire to try to sleep. I settled myself
in the easy chair before the window and stared out over
the starlit dune.

After my eyes became accustomed to the dark, I discovered two figures in the shadow of the terrace. One

was easily distinguishable as Hanson—I caught the silhouette of his peaked cap and tightly fitting breeches. The other man was a stranger to me. He wore civilian clothes and a soft felt hat. Only when the couple moved along toward the wing did I realize that the stranger was Asey, apparently dressed in what Syl invariably refers to as "his city clothes."

In just about two shakes of the proverbial lamb's tail I exchanged my mules and negligee for noiseless rubber soled shoes and a heavy flannel dressing gown. In two more shakes I was downstairs. I bumped into Asey and Hanson on the threshold of the living-room door.

Hanson's right hand was firmly clamped over my mouth before Asey could stop him.

"Let her be," he whispered softly. "Come!"

I followed them around the house to the garage.

"By gum," Asey said as he slid the door to behind us, "I thought the beans was spilled then, for sure. Look, was it your light that's been on all this time? 'Twas, huh? How 'bout the others upstairs? They all asleep?"

Feeling a little guilty, though I couldn't quite tell why, I said that as far as I knew, every one was slumbering soundly.

"But," I added, "what are you up to?"

"Still transcendin'," Asey said with a chuckle. "Want to stay out here, or will you be too chilly?"

"You couldn't remove me if you wanted to," I announced. "Now that I'm here, and things are going on, here I'm going to stay. And I have a pair of excellent lungs."

"All right, threaten us!" Asey rummaged around Quin's car and produced a blanket which he draped over me. "Hanson, you go tell Syl to start in, an' get your men set. The doc—"

"Is he here?" I demanded. "When did he come back?"

"Round ten, with me. He—"

"You came back here at ten? And you never let us know?"

"Yup. He's up with Mrs. Richards an' Malvina an' Bud's there too. Hop along, Hanson, an' if you hear the slightest noise from upstairs, stay put for ten or fifteen minutes. You'd better let Syl do it all. He's quiet as a cat. Your fellers' boots make too much noise. I'll be round when it's ready."

"Asey," I said, "what *is* this? What's going on? What were those pails of water on the terrace for? What's that package Hanson took? What's at the bottom of all this?"

I couldn't see his face in the darkness, but I knew he was undoubtedly grinning from ear to ear.

"This is act three, with only a few minutes to go, Mrs. Colton. Them pails is where I been practicin'—you know. The pourin' the two pint into the six quart, like you was talkin' about. I don't like to pull this stunt, but it's the only way I can think of to get what I want. You just pr'tend the curtain's bein' lowered to d'note a lapse of time, an' p'sess your soul with patience. Think of Job an' Griselda."

I hugged the blanket around me and kept still. If

Asey wasn't going to divulge his plans, he wasn't, but I know that twenty years were added to my life during the following ten or fifteen minutes.

Syl poked his head in at last. "Okay," he said, "you want to begin it?"

"Yup," Asey said. "Blame's all mine then if it don't work. Done the other thing I told you to, Syl? Good. How's for the noise?"

"All s'rene upstairs, an' Ford, if he's the one downstairs, is snorin' soft but reg'lar. Doc's all set. Butler an' his wife's asleep. Mrs. Colton comin'?"

"Yup, guess she'd better. Then she can stay on the terrace an' pretend to be number one man. Nary a sound, Mrs. Colton. Nary a sound at anythin', see?"

"Nary a sound it is," I promised, "but if I burst, on your head, so to speak, be it!"

We edged around to the west terrace, and I stood by the door with Syl and Hanson while Asey went indoors. And it took just about all the self-control I possessed to keep silent when I saw a match struck and applied to what seemed to be a heap of rubbish in the center of the already charred living room.

It came over me suddenly that Syl had spoken nothing but the truth when he'd confided to me earlier that Asey, at times, was just plum cracked. Nothing short of insanity could explain his deliberately setting the house on fire, even though I understood at last why he wanted to know about the insurance. The fire had been a part of his plans since before he left—but it didn't make anything any clearer to me.

Asey returned to the doorway and stood beside us.

In absolute and utter horror, I watched the flames blaze up. Then something hissed and filled the room with dense smoke which began to filter up the stairs and out to us. And no one lifted a finger to do anything about the business at all.

"Now," Asey said to Syl as the smoke got thicker, "now, run in an' speak your piece!"

Syl burst into the house, and with more force and volume than I should have believed him capable of, he shrieked out "Fire—hey—fire!"

He kept on yelling till my hair began to prickle on the back of my neck.

Jane and Deal dashed down, plunged through the smoke and promptly made for the stairs to Lizzie's room.

Asey moved away from the door and prodded Hanson, who in turn prodded two of his troopers. The buckets of water I'd seen on the terrace were brought in just as Ford, with a coat around his shoulders, limped out of his room. Quin and Tom helped him outside as Gregory and Mathilde appeared on the scene, both screaming at the tops of their voices. Finally, Mr. Winpenny appeared with Cora. He, poor man, looked sillier than any one else in a pair of Quin's loudly striped, billowing pyjamas. Jane and Deal and Bud, all coughing and weeping, groped their way out beside me.

"Mother's all right," Bud said reassuringly. "Honest, Sis. There—Syl and those men have got it all out. See? Is it all right, Syl?"

Panting a little, Syl announced that it was all out.

"Can't understand it," he said. "Some one must of left a cig'rette goin'. All that smoke must of been from the water hittin' the r'mains of the chemical we used yest'day. I—"

"But we haven't been in there!" Quin said. "We've been in the other living room all evening! I don't understand— Syl, hasn't Asey got back yet?"

Blankly, I looked around. Asey was nowhere to be seen!

"He ought to be," Syl said. "I had an idea he'd be back by midnight, an' seems—why, here's his car now, ain't it? Yessiree, that's him!"

Asey, apparently, had slipped away, run off to wherever he'd left his car, and was now proceeding to arrive officially.

"What's wrong?" he asked anxiously as he got out of the roadster and came up to the terrace. "What—my gum! Ain't been another fire, has they? What happened, Syl? What's all this smoke?"

Syl shook his head. "Dunno, Asey," he said mournfully. "Minute we put water on, seemed like it smoked. I think it was from that chemical. Don't know how it started, 'less some one dropped a cig'rette, or else maybe them floor boards been smolderin' all the time. I don't get it!"

It occurred to me that romancing at short notice was a characteristic of the Mayo family.

One of the state troopers came out and spoke to Hanson.

"All out, sir," he said. "We dumped sand on it, and it's all right."

I looked into the bucket he carried as he passed by. Without doubt the remains of what had been used to set the fire and to provide the smoke effects were in it under the layer of sand. Asey, it seemed, had thought of everything.

"Well," Quin said, "I don't see—now that the smoke's cleared some, I'm going in to investigate. Coming, Asey?"

Gravely, Asey nodded. "Some home comin," he said. "Say, that r'minds me. Some one want to get me some food? I ain't had a morsel in hours. Maybe some coffee'd go pretty good all round. An—"

"What've you found out?" Jane demanded. "Tell us, Asey, and get it over with!"

"Jane," he said dejectedly, "I ain't found out a thing. Not a single thing. It was too transcendin', I guess. Now, we'll look at this fire an' then we'll have some food. You all better get indoors before you catch cold."

Personally I didn't know whether to believe him or not. And I still couldn't see any earthly reason for the fire.

Mathilde was too upset to be coherent or capable, so Deal and Jane and Cora and I raided the larder and produced a somewhat disconnected picnic supper. The doctor came into the kitchen, looked at the array of food and grinned.

"I've got lots of bicarb," he said brightly, "if any one needs it. Your mother's all right, Deal. She didn't even wake up. So—"

"What are *you* doing here?" Deal asked suspiciously.

"Malvina called me half an hour ago," the doctor lied fluently as he picked up a handful of olives. "She said she didn't like Lizzie's temperature. I'd just got in from Weesit Harbor. Funny thing." He peered into the store room. "That Guinness? Guess I'll have some. Got a roast beef sandwich for me, Mrs. Frost? Thanks. Yes, funny thing. Fellow starting out on his vacation. Man from Hartford. Walked in his sleep and punched his fist square through the window. You never saw such a mess." He chuckled. "His name was Glassfell Cutts. Sort of funny."

"Not for him," Deal said. "Here, take in this tray. Make yourself useful if you're—look, that's roquefort! You'll have to use the bicarb yourself if you keep on. Doctor, is Asey really stumped?"

He shook his head. " 'Fraid so. Too bad, because he had such high hopes."

I almost believed him, but I caught a little flicker of his eyelid as he carried off the trays.

In the living room we found Quin still puzzling audibly over the fire.

"There *was* a blaze," he insisted, "and smoke, and there's not a blessed thing there *to* blaze or smoke! Perhaps you're right, Asey, but I don't see it. It seems to me there must be something *to* all these fires!"

"I don't think so." Asey filled his plate. "First fire in there was when a spark hit the ker'sene from the overturned fire lighter. Boat house was when Syl knocked his pipe out into a pile of shavin's. This—nope, I can't seem to see no reason for it, 'less it was a spark that smoldered. Fires are funny things. I r'member when the No'th Eastham meetin' house burned down—say, turn on the radio soft, Bud. Let's have a little music."

Bud snapped on the radio. "Gee," he said, "somethin's happened. Doesn't light. That's queer. It was all right this evening, because I had it on. How about the vic?"

"No use," Deal said. "It needs a new spring. I wound it up too much or something last fall, and Caleb was going to get an electric—oh, Ford, haven't you got that little electric phonograph you were talking about?"

Ford yawned. "Linda's? Yes. Some one go in and get it. There's a superb collection of small records, too, if Asey'd like 'em. Christopher Robin and Peter Rabbit. But it'll play regular size."

Tom went in and brought out the tiny machine.

"It's got to be plugged in somewhere," he said. "Where's a floor plug?"

"I'll fix it," Asey said. "You get some records. Don't know why I feel like listenin' to music, but I sort of do. Always like music when I'm tired. An'—move your chair, will you, Deal? I got to grovel down here."

"Asey," Quin said as he brought over a pile of records from the big machine, "honestly, have you given up? I—I can't believe that you have!"

Asey took the records and bent over the little phonograph.

"Sort of ashamed to say it," he said—and he sounded as though he meant it, "but I'm stuck. This the jigger—

ain't it cute, huh? Records ain't no bigger'n a postage stamp. Yup, Quin, I'm licked. Ole man Mayo's not what he used to be."

He flicked the lever on the machine and stood up and thrust both hands into the patch pockets of his well tailored tweed suit.

I'd noticed that he had put on a small record and not one of those Quin had given him, but I was totally unprepared for what followed.

CHAPTER NINETEEN

THE tiny disc spun around slowly and then gained momentum; there was a scratch and a squeak, and then came a long drawn out snore. Then there was silence.

"Why," I said, "what kind of record is that?"

"It's a barnyard one," Jane said with a laugh. "That's the pig grunting, or something, isn't it?"

Again there was another snore; then silence. Then another.

Jane's face began to grow white. "It's—it's—" her mouth moved, but the words didn't come.

Then Ford rose from the couch, his eyes blazing.

"I broke that record!" he shouted. "I burned it up! I—" his right hand clutched at his left arm pit and then fell slowly to his side.

"Forgot it, didn't you?" Asey said. "Forgot somethin' else, too, when you hurried out of your room. Too bad, but—"

"Asey!" Quin said. "Asey, have you—"

"Deary me, yes," Asey said briskly. "Just sit still, Ford. I've got you covered. Hanson an' Syl are at the window b'hind you. Yup, Quin. Don't you rec'nize this? This is your ole 'A-B-C. See?'"

It may have been A-B-C to Asey Mayo, but to the rest of us it still resembled Choctaw.

Dr. Cummings drained his glass. "D'you," he asked casually, "want me to take a look at that foot?"

"You'd better, I guess." Asey raised his voice. "Come in, Syl 'n Hanson! Yup, doc, you'd better. Don't mind, do you, Ford?"

Ford, who had slumped back against the couch, shook his head.

"Go on," he said quietly. "I'll be glad to have you, believe it or not."

To the surprise and bewilderment of all of us, the doctor didn't unwind the bandage on Ford's sprained ankle. Instead, he removed the leather slipper from his right foot.

We crowded around the couch as he drew off a crude, stained dressing from the sole of Ford's foot. I took just one quick look and then turned hastily away.

At last my brain began to click. I understood about the disappearing salve, the sand in the shoes, and all the rest of it.

Ford had stolen the salve to put on his foot, which he'd cut when he stopped to empty the sand from his shoes, near the pile of glass and rubbish down by the boat house. Ford had killed Caleb Frost and Dick Thorne; his alibi had been the snoring record. His motive—it finally dawned on me that Ford's relation to Caleb, after all, was exactly the same as that of the Richards family.

Caleb had financed him; he, too, was under Caleb's thumb—

"Wah!" the doctor said. "No wonder you've looked sick and white! Bud, run up to your mother's room, send down Malvina with my bag and stay up there yourself. Syl, wheel in that chair from Ford's room. Deal, put on some water to boil—"

"Wait up," Asey said to Syl. "Bring out his gun an' give it to me. Shoulder holster. An'—no heroics, Ford?"

Ford smiled briefly. "No heroics now, Asey. I feel too beastly rotten. This foot's poisoned. How'd you get it? Connect the salve and the broken glass on that heap?"

"Partly," Asey said. "With other things. I'll wheel you in."

"Now," Quin ordered when Asey returned some fifteen minutes later, "now, tell all, man!"

"In a sec." Asey beckoned to one of Hanson's men, sent him into Ford's room with instructions to stay there, and then passed over a paper to Hanson. "There you are," he said. "I was right. Go tell them ravin' lun'tic r'porters, only for Pete's sakes, wash your face before they take your pictures. You're all grime from that fire. Hustle, an' make your calls before you say anythin' to the paper lads."

"But you," Hanson said uncomfortably, "you've got to—"

"Fiddledeedee," Asey said. "Run along. I'm half starved. You ought to be an of'cer anyways. Beat it!"

He brushed Hanson out much as though he had been a fly, and then began a stanch attack on the food which was still lying untouched on his plate.

"Go on," Quin said impatiently, "what about the salve? Had you guessed all along?"

Asey grinned at me. "I didn't start pourin' into the right pail," he said, "till I got to broodin' about the sand in the feller's shoes. That salve'd bothered me, though. When I hitched the two, it was simple. Sand—glass—cut —salve."

"Oh, Asey," Deal said, "break down and fill in the spaces!"

"I will," Asey said between bites, "but remember that transcendin's hungry business. That's somethin' I always meant to suggest to you about your books, Quin. No one ever eats in 'em. Come to think of it, they never do in any detective stories. Just smoke cig'rettes all the time or else drink cocktails till you'd think the whole caboodle'd be under the table."

"Then that rubbery smell," Quin marked more hieroglyphs in his notebook, "was the record burning in the fireplace in Ford's room? Hm. I _guessed_—"

"Nope," Asey said. "That was the repeatin' jigger you smelled more'n the record. I found out all about them repeatin' jiggers to-day. Y'see, Ford had to snore for a good long time, an' that record wouldn't of lasted much more'n a minute."

That squelched Quin sufficiently for Asey to tell the rest of his story in comparative peace.

The disappearing salve bothered him, just as it had bothered me. But only that morning, out on the back shore, had he connected his mental trail of the murderer with the rubbish heap and its broken glass, and the cut foot and the salve.

Ford admitted that everything happened as Asey had thought. He'd gone up to Frost's room a few minutes after one, soon after Jane came in from the dunes. He found Caleb coming down the corridor and persuaded him to come out for a walk; Asey assumed that Caleb intended to hurry back, wait a while, then go out and attend to his own business with Thorne and Cora.

At all events, Ford had shot Caleb out on the dune, covered him with sand, taken the things from his pocket and then cut down by the boat house, to escape being seen coming back to the house alone. He'd intended to throw the watch and the money in the harbor, but tossed them, instead, in a clump of grass, hoping that it might add a confusing touch. Down by the boat house he'd stopped to empty his shoes of sand. Then Thorne had appeared.

Again Asey had been right. At Ford's startled question, Thorne had said, simply and easily, that he was Varney Cheyne.

"Good God!" Jane said. "And he'd just killed Caleb, thinking he was Cheyne, and then a strange bearded man appeared and said that!"

"Just so. An' 'member, he'd thrown his gun away, too, knowin' it couldn't be traced to him. He says he didn't have any idea it was yours, Quin. Bought it from a bum in a speakeasy. Anyway, Ford picked up a bottle from the rubbish pile, stood up an' lunged. That's when he cut his foot, when he stepped forward with one shoe off.

I'd sort of thought, by the way, that it was some one in the house after Cora told her story; if Frost'd been alone when he left the house, he'd of come right out to her. Anyways, Ford carried Thorne into the boat house. He was keepin' the keys to slip back to the house with, but then he found a dupl'cate master key, so he took it off, an' tossed the ring under the steps. Another confusin' d'tail that worked, 'cause I thought, at first, if the keys was left there, it wasn't some one from the house."

Ford had realized as he walked back that the cut was a serious matter. Remembering that Gregory and Mathilde were always laden with salves, and having none himself, Ford went into the kitchen before he returned to his room and took the two tubes from the shelf where he knew they kept their various and sundry remedies. His foot had seemed all right, Sunday morning, but after dune hunting Sunday night, it began to pain him.

"Y'see," Asey said, "he *had* to hunt, too, after all he'd said about findin' Caleb's murderer. But sand got into his shoes an' ground into that cut, for all his bandage an' salve. That's why he had to twist his ankle next day— sure, that was a fake, though he was pretty realistic about it. He knew he had to keep off that cut foot. So he pretended to sprain the other, 'cause if he'd pretended to hurt the cut one, it'd of been found out."

"But why couldn't he have let it be seen?" Quin demanded. "He could have said he stepped on a tumbler in the bathroom, and—"

"Hah!" Asey threw back his head and laughed. "Hah —all the bathroom glasses here is that unbreakable kind of comp'sition stuff! Nice detective you'd make, feller! He couldn't say that cut'd happened *since* Sunday; wouldn't be no reason for his not speakin' of it. An' if he said it'd happened *before* he went dune searchin', people'd ask why he hadn't spoke of it an' excused himself. An'— it was a glass cut. An' we'd already chatted about that rubbish pile an' the busted glass. He was cornered on it."

"But why did Ford—why—" Deal began.

"Ford was beholden to Caleb Frost, like you an' your mother an' Bud was, only more so. Cale rubbed it in to him just as he rubbed it in to you."

"What a nitwit I—but of course!" Deal said. "Why, Caleb was always making Ford do things! Don't you know he said he was going to the Paulsons's, but Caleb inveigled him—but Ford was always so amiable about everything!"

"He had to be. Frost had to look out for his fam'ly, but there wasn't no reason for him to keep on helpin' Ford, if Ford didn't do what he said. Anyway, it seemed queer to me all along that Ford didn't guess about Cheyne. An' though Ford got a whale of a lot of money from handlin' the Cheyne stuff, the way things was, he could of got all—"

"Then money was the motive, too," Quin said. "I— gee, I feel stupid! Ford's an extravagant chap. His clothes —he has so many, and everything he has costs mints. Was he in debt?"

"Head over heels," Asey said. " 'Nother thing I found out to-day. But who'd of known, the way things stood, if Cheyne *was* dead? Ford could of sent out checks to fancy addresses, signed the name Cheyne used, an' there he'd be. When people wanted more Cheyne stories, he could always say Cheyne'd decided to retire. No one'd known but Mrs. Frost—no, Ford didn't know about her. But he could of got out of it by sayin' he'd sent the checks out as usual. B'fore she'd of spoken, a good many checks would of gone. An' she'd have written Ford about it. He'd of had plenty of warnin' an' plenty of time to cover his tracks, an' plenty of money in the next few months. Pretty hard to trace him."

"That's what worried us," Tom said. "When a man's absolutely unknown—"

"Let Asey go on," Quin said. "What about the phonograph?"

That, at first, had passed right over Asey's head, because Ford had explained it so casually.

And Ford *did* snore; Asey had proved that to his own satisfaction. But after he connected the salve and the rest of it, he began to wonder. Everything pointed to Ford, except that Deal and Jane were sure he was in his room. Then he connected the phonograph and the smell of burning rubber. So he'd driven to the Paulsons's at Newport, and found out that Ford had already given Linda a phonograph for her last birthday.

"They said he'd prob'ly just forgot," Asey said. "But I copied off the name of the place where the machine come from, called New York, an' found he'd bought two complete outfits last year, an' a couple of repeaters that he'd had made to order. Seems he'd been waitin' his chance some time."

"But what about the record *you* played?" Quin said. "If Ford destroyed his—"

"I had that made in Boston," Asey said. "Oh, yes, I was there too. I covered a lot of ter'tory to-day. Yup, I had that made while I was delvin' into Ford's school past. Found out he'd been on a pistol team in school. I thought, maybe, if things was as I thought, I might play that record an' force him to speak up, him thinkin' he was so safe. An' my, what a time I had gettin' that dingus made! I don't snore easy. After tryin' out a dozen folks, I picked up a sandwich man an' brought him into the record place, an' he didn't do without half a hour's rehearsin'. N'en I just stuck the record on to-night. Had it in my pocket."

"And now, Nero," I said, "what about the fire?"

"Oh, I had to set that," Asey said. "You see," he waited for the yells to die down, "Ford had a gun in a shoulder holster, though I never noticed it till this mornin'. It'd sort of 'curred to me after we come back from the back shore that I might just ask to take a peek at that other foot, but with him packin' a gun, I didn't want to, 'cause I remembered how he'd kept his hand draped over his left side. He just told me he'd have shot himself if the problem'd been brought up. I wasn't sure he wouldn't of potted some one else in the bargain. N'en, they was a lot of things I wasn't clear on. That's why I left to clear 'em up, an' why I called out Bud before I left an' give him a gun so's he could keep an eye peeled. Anyways, I had to set that fire."

Jane said plaintively that she didn't understand even then.

"Why," Asey said, "Ford come limpin' out, along with the rest of you, but he limped on his s'posedly bad ankle, an' kept the other foot off the ground. Didn't any of you notice that? Deary me, Quin, it's a wonder to me you ain't on the dole! An' besides, Ford left in too much of a hurry to pack his gun. Then I just stuck on that record an' hoped for the best. I'd found out enough by then so's I could bully it out of him."

"But why'd he spoil everything?" Quin demanded. "If he'd planned and planned, and got all the details thought out, to an untraceable gun and an electric phonograph and a repeater, and if he'd destroyed that and the snoring record—and you say the Paulsons just thought he'd forgotten the other—why, he was all set! No man in his right senses would have given the show away then!"

"But Ford ain't," Asey said gently. "He's sick. That foot looks awful bad to me. The doc's goin' to stay here t'night an' take him to the hosp'tal early to-morrow mornin'. From the way that looks, I think he's goin' to be lucky if he keeps that leg."

The whole thing was thrashed over again and again before we went to bed. I knew that Ford was a double murderer, but just the same, I'm afraid my sympathies were with him. It remained for the next morning to change all that.

Asey breezed in at breakfast time, just as Lizzie, who'd made a most astonishing and complete recovery, was beginning to quiz me about the sheets that were to have been marked, and the laundry that hadn't been sent out, and the grocery bills that were altogether outrageous, and the consistency of the oatmeal. Lizzie likes it elastic. I'd ordered it soft, and Lizzie thought I certainly should have known better. I could see that history was about to repeat itself.

"Where's Deal?" Asey asked, producing a quart bottle in which a full rigged ship reposed. "This's hers. Where's the doc? What's he got to say about Ford's foot?"

"I haven't seen him," I said. "Is—"

"Ain't he shown his face this—didn't the ambulance come? Ain't—"

Asey put the bottle on the table and raced for Ford's bedroom, and I followed just as fast as my legs could carry me.

The bedroom door was locked. It took the combined efforts of Asey, Syl, Quin, Tom, Gregory and three state troopers to break it in.

Lying on the bed was the doctor, neatly bound and gagged. His face was purple with rage, and for once in his life, he was literally speechless.

Slowly and with difficulty, for his tongue was swollen and his lips were bruised from the tight gag, the doctor told us what had happened.

As soon as Asey had left, around three o'clock, and during an interval when the trooper was out of the room, Ford had produced another gun.

"From under the mattress, I think," Cummings said. "Anyway, he told me my orders, and ground that gun into my ribs when Harry came back—Asey, I couldn't do anything but tell Harry to go. Then that rascal took a

can of my own ether—you know, I'd already begun to
have doubts about that foot. I didn't think it was as bad
as he pretended. It was blotched and it seemed swelled,
but I think he'd smeared it with mercurochrome—"

"But those streaks of green and purple!" Quin said.

"Ink," the doctor said, "I'm sure. He'd smeared it
up himself to take us in. He must have guessed the game
was over when you left, Asey, and planned accordingly.
Wasn't there a case of waterproof drawing inks out on
the desk? That's what he used. Anyway, when I came
to, there I was, tied up with my own adhesive tape. Look,
will some Christian soul provide me with a glass of
water, preferably one in which a large quantity of whisky
has been placed? He's got five hours' start—damned clever.
I felt sorry for him last night, but I'd ruin him myself
if I got the chance, the way I feel now!"

"How'd he get away?" Quin demanded.

The trooper named Harry gulped. "A car—gee, I—
he took one of the—"

"Took one of the police cars," Asey said wearily.
"Right outside the door, wasn't it? An' he prob'ly came
through the house an' phoned for the ambulance to stay
away—an' did I or did I not tell you to lock all the cars?"

"You did," Harry said, "but after you got him, and—
well, I went out to get some cigarettes and left the keys
in—gee, I thought he was safe enough! He looked like he
was going to die!"

The officers at the bridge admitted that a state car
had gone by shortly after three. There was a man in it
with a uniform cap, and they'd thought it was one of

the extra troopers who'd been sent down—there were four or five not regularly attached to the local station. The man had even slowed up, said that Asey had caught the fellow he was after, and he was going to Boston for Asey.

Hanson, his men, and Quin, simply went stark staring mad at that point. Police radios, teletypes and regular radio stations were promptly thrown into what must have been a frenzy. When the smoke of battle cleared away, Asey, Syl and I were the only ones left at Sandbar. Mathilde and Gregory, and even Lizzie, with Cora and Mr. Winpenny—all had raced away on searching parties.

"Well, Asey?" I asked. "Well?"

"Fooled," he said, "by a city slicker, that's what. No use sayin' that if Harry'd stayed in there like I said, an' left the cars locked—well, anyway, this place seems awful restful," he settled himself back in one of the terrace deck chairs, "when it's empty. Y'know, I never seen the point to lockin' the barn door after the hoss was gone. That's what these fellers is doin'. Nope, Quin can cable all the steamship lines, an' all the liners, an' all the airports, an' all the transcont'nental planes, an' Hanson can have fellers waitin' with machine guns at ev'ry cross road from Dan to Beersheba—but, nope, I don't think so. Got a gun, Syl? Well, take one from that ars'nal Hanson's left so careless on the livin' room table. 'Pears to me we'd better pick up this hoss before we get laughed at."

"Can I come?" I demanded, as the two strolled out to Asey's roadster.

Asey hesitated. "Um. Seems a pity to leave you out, an' I don't like leavin' you here alone, 'cause—but you ain't exactly bullet proof, Mrs. Colton."

"Neither are you!" I retorted. "I'm coming. Besides, Ford didn't kill the doctor. He might kill you, but I'm sure he wouldn't harm me!"

"Ladies' man," Asey murmured as we got into the roadster, "just like Deal said. Huh!"

Rather slowly, we rolled over Sandbar Bridge and along the beach road past Bingo's shack. About a mile further on, in a clump of scrub pines, Asey stopped the car and turned it around.

Grinning broadly, he got out. "C'mon, Syl," he said. "We'll r'connoiter, we will. I—"

"Asey," I said, "d'you mean to tell me you know where Ford is?"

"I got an awful good idea," Asey replied cheerfully. "Bingo's barn's padlocked, an' Bingo never locked anythin' in his life. Yup, it seems to me that's what I'd of done. Drove the car in there, waited for everybody to scatter, an' then either taken Bingo's boat or gone back to Sandbar an' swiped one of Frost's cars. Now, in about fifteen minutes, Mrs. Colton, I wish you'd drive up to Bingo's, blow the horn and yell out that you want some fish. Lobsters'd be a nice touch. Don't you get out of that car, but you keep the horn goin'. If nothin' happens in five minutes, you drive back here. But, while you're p'rvidin' d'straction, we'll see if we can't sasshay in the rear. Plenty of underbrush for us to wiggle up there through, an' he can't see but what we've gone to town."

Seventeen minutes later, by the clock on the dash, Syl and Asey appeared with Ford.

"Good attempt," Asey said approvingly, "but—"

"But you can't fool the master, eh?" Ford said amiably. "Well, I'd hardly hoped—but I've plenty of time, Asey. You won't *always* be around. How'd you guess?"

"Took a leaf out of Syl's philos'phy," Asey said. "He's the hunter of the fam'ly. I—"

"What're you talkin' about?" Syl demanded as he lashed Ford's wrists together expertly. "I never—"

"Oh yes, you did," Asey said. "Don't you r'member your famous story about the feller that found the lost hoss? 'I thought if I was a hoss, where'd I go? An' I went there, an' he had.' Well, I did, an' you was, Ford—"

At that moment, Bingo poked a white face out of his door and then rather cautiously followed it out with the rest of him.

"Bingo!" I said, "you look as white as the sheets I'm supposed to have marked! I—"

"That r'minds me," Syl said, "when d'you want to go into your house? This aft'noon? You can, 'cause Jennie's got it all ready. I—"

"What house?" I demanded, "what *are* you talking about?"

"Oh," Asey said. "That the s'prise I told you was due for your guessin' Cora, Mrs. Colton. Seemed to me you d'served it—"

"But Asey!"

I protested, though of course I gave in eventually, and that time my benign optimism received no rude shocks.

Still, there are those of my friends who say that after seven days of Sandbar Sinister, almost anything would have appeared peaceful, quiet and carefree.